MEDICINE HAIR

By Mark Wildyr

Published in the United States by STARbooks Press, PO Box 711612, Herndon, VA 20171. Printed in the United States

Cover Design by John Nail (tojonail@bellsouth.net)

Long, dark decades we languish,

mere shadows of

a paler people.

Where are our silent drums,

our sad, broken flutes?

Stanza from the poem "Echoes of the Flute"
by Mark Wildyr

CONTENTS

PROLOGUE

Monday, September 10, 1883, Turtle Crick Farm, Dakota Territory

Puzzled by the rosy hue of the crick water, he shifted his gaze to a western skyline pulsing with spectacular crimsons and striking corals. The horizon appeared ablaze, yet a cool breeze lapped his face. No hint of heat. No taste of smoke. His horses grazed placidly. This was no wildfire. It was another of those remarkable prairie sunsets.

The bizarre events had started a *senight* ago. He'd sensed movement beneath his feet. A few days later, air currents in a normally calm season. Hazy, filtered light. Sun dogs, usually rare and most often observed in cold months, now frequent. Moons the color of moldy cheese one night and as blue as a jay's wing the next.

Despite his education, he heard the singing of his tribal blood and thought of witchcraft. Powerful medicine was at work.

CHAPTER 1

I rose with the dawn from my solitary bed. A 240-acre farm demanded more than I could give now that my cattle operation had grown. I'd always been a farmer with cows. Nowadays, I was leaning toward a cowman with a farm.

Arrow Wind, my buckskin war horse, snorted as I turned him and the black trace mare into the corral. I bypassed the smithy on the way to the fields. My eighty acres of sweet corn were already spinning silk. Wheat and vegetables took up the rest of the tilled land. Wheat, my money crop. Corn and other vegetables for Matthew and me ... and for trading.

Beyond the fields to the west, I held fee title to another 100 acres, most of which were behind a Pennsylvania worm fence, a zigzag affair of stacked poles and brush. My 150 head of Texas Longhorn steers were presently free-ranging, but I would soon bring a few head behind the fence to fatten on ungrazed grass for our own use before Matthew and I hazed the rest to the cattle barn in Yanube City.

In the far distance, my "hired hand" came alert and spotted me. I couldn't have managed without him. Two years back, I'd traded a wandering peddler out of an unlikely-looking blue puppy with black and tan markings. A Blue Heeler, a cross between a wild Australian Dingo and a Kelpie, the critter herded anything and everything ... including me. We'd had more than one tussle before he was convinced I ran the place.

Todoh – Blue in the Lakota tongue – had grown into a magnificent animal, even with a crumpled left ear that refused to stand straight and tall like the right one. The dog was smarter than I was; and if he'd possessed an intelligible tongue and opposable thumbs, I'd be working for him. Both he and the cattle were self-sustaining.

He streaked across a quarter-mile of prairie to lunge at my chest, almost bowling me over. I held Todoh, so he could lick my face before dropping him and ruffling the fur on his neck. After spending five minutes reaffirming our relationship, I gave the dog a piece of jerky and sent him racing back to the cattle. He'd sniff out every steer until he was satisfied they were all accounted for.

As I pumped well water into a pond on the high side of the fields to irrigate the crops, an army patrol came trotting up the south wagon track, a familiar figure at its head. Heart in my throat, I walked up the hill behind the cabin for a better look. Once there, fresh footprints diverted my attention. Moccasins. Not Matthew's ... or Shambling Bear's as he'd be calling himself now. The prints were wrong. Whoever it was had reclaimed his mount and ridden north toward Trickling Water. A nick in the pony's left front shoe niggled at me, but I couldn't call to mind why. If Todoh hadn't been out on the range, I'd have had warning of the intruder. The brute was a good watchman.

3

I turned my gaze back to Lt. Gideon Haleworthy and his patrol. The troopers' easy gait let me know the mission wasn't urgent and allowed my anxiety to ebb. I was halfway fond of Gideon. He'd been courting my sister, Rachel Ann, even though my family lived at Teacher's Mead fifty miles east of his post at Fort Yanube. That, plus Ma's lukewarm acceptance, put a damper on things.

I came down the hill as he dismounted his men on the south side of the crick to water their horses before he rode across the bridge. A new pair of silver bars sparkled in the sun as he threw a long leg over Blackie and dismounted.

"You're looking good, Speckle-Head."

He referred to one of my two physical abnormalities. I'd inherited onyx eyes peppered with bits of gold from Pa. He'd also given me a thick black mane interspersed with strands of Ma's Scandinavian yellow. Like most Indians, I had more than one name. To the whites, I was John Jacobsen Strobaw; my earth name was War Eagle. Touch the Clouds, a Miniconjou chieftain, had labeled me Night Sky Hair, and Gideon now added one of his own. Soon they'd be calling me Many Names.

"You didn't ride seven miles just to let me know you made captain." I stepped forward and clasped his hand in the white man's way.

He removed his hat and inspected the shiny bars. "Look pretty good, don't they? Got them last week. No, I'm patrolling up the crick and just stopped to see how you're getting along and ask after Matthew."

Was the army still keeping an eye on Matthew Brandt? A Teton Sioux and Yanube mix, he'd taken off on one of his jaunts last month when word reached us Sitting Bull had returned to the Standing Rock Agency. To the white man's thinking, the Hunkpapa medicine man was trouble ... danger. And Matthew craved adventure just as much and just as helplessly as I craved him. It was coming up on four years since we'd pledged ourselves before Touch the Clouds – who sat on the council at the Cheyenne River Reservation – and his friend, Buffalo Leg. They'd both helped free Matthew from military custody after a jealous Cheyenne claimed my lover was Red Star, a fugitive follower of Crazy Horse.

"Congratulations on the promotion. Does that mean you'll be getting new orders?"

The new captain shook his head. "So far as I know, I'm stuck out here in this backwater for the rest of my career."

"To answer your question, I'm getting along fine, and Matthew hasn't come back from ... wherever."

"How do you put up with it?"

The hair on my neck rose. Did he suspect the nature of our relationship? My eyes stole to the leafy branches of what I called the Otter Tree. Back in the summer of '79, my spiritual grandfather had been hanged from the cottonwood while his companion, James Morrow, perished in their burning cabin, victims of just such a union as Matthew's and mine.

4

"Put up with what?"

"An unreliable hired hand."

I drew an easier breath. "He only goes fiddle-footing once or twice a year. Stays a month or two. He'll be back in time to help with the harvest and to herd our steers to Yanube City. Besides, he's no hired hand. He's got some of his own silver invested in this place."

Gideon smiled, easing my mind a smidgeon. "You noticed what's been going on lately?"

"Hard to miss if you mean weird sunsets and strange moons. You got any ideas about them?"

Gideon nodded his good-looking Yankee head. "Heard about it over the grapevine." That was his way of saying the telegraph. "You ever heard of an Indonesian island called Krakatoa?"

When I said I hadn't, he explained that the peculiar events we were experiencing resulted from a series of powerful volcanic eruptions half a world away. The final, cataclysmic explosion last August blew away two-thirds of the island and was heard for three thousand miles. Tsunamis rocked ships as far distant as South Africa. Tidal flows hit the English Channel. Massive columns of ash and pumice rose miles into the heavens and scattered to cloak the planet and darken the atmosphere. Lavender suns, green and blue moons, and incredibly brilliant sunsets amazed and frightened people around the world.

After finishing his explanation, Gideon gave a lopsided grin. "I get a real kick outa telling you something you don't already know. You read everything you can get your hands on, but the telegraph is a whole lot faster than a book. Why do you read so damned much, anyway?"

I rubbed an itchy place on my chin. "You never know when a little knowledge is going to come in handy."

"That's all well and good, but I don't see how knowing about an Indonesian island blowing itself to pieces is going to come in handy."

Seemingly unaware he'd demeaned the value of his own news, Gideon tipped his new captain's hat and returned to his men. After watering Blackie, his big cavalry horse, he mounted the troop and rode up the crick.

Gideon was a West Point man, so he did his share of reading. He probably considered that natural. But somehow it was a matter of wonder when an Indian shared his intellectual curiosity.

CHAPTER 2

Gideon hadn't tarried long, which made me wonder if he'd said everything he had come to say. Had he really made a fourteen mile roundabout ride just to give me news of an Asian catastrophe? No, more likely he was actually leading a routine patrol. I laid aside such thoughts and went to work. After putting the finishing touches to a watering bucket in the forge, I went out to tend the fields.

A little later, I was headed to the house for a glass of milk and a bit of jerky when Todoh set up a yammer. A line of six horsemen rode through his territory directly toward the house, and he didn't appreciate the intrusion. Still, he had sense enough not to press his objection too strenuously.

From this distance, the riders looked to be tribesmen. A lot of fringed buckskin and a feather or two. Coming from the stretch of badlands up on Trickling Water Crick, probably. Their slow pace indicated I had nothing to worry about, but I moseyed over to the porch where my Henry rifle – with fifteen cartridges in the sleeve and one in the breech – was propped beside the cabin door. After taking a sip of water from the earthen jug customarily resting in the shade of the overhang, I leaned against the porch to wait, arms folded over my chest.

A few minutes later, five ponies rounded the base of the hill, making straight for the yard. The sixth rider was likely atop the mound to act as lookout. The man in front lifted his arm in the open-handed greeting.

We had exchanged *hah-ues* before I recognized Crow Hop, Buffalo Leg's son. I smiled and stepped forward to give him an Indian handshake after he dismounted. A year or two older than my twenty and four, he was taking on some of his father's heft. A pleasing man of aquiline features, he started making polite talk while I gestured for his companions to take water from the keg. They were all fit men of Crow Hop's age or younger, but for one. He had probably seen his thirtieth summer. His erect carriage and piercing eyes caught my attention. He held his tongue through the getting reacquainted talk. Finally, it was his turn.

"I am Firm Foot," he said. "I have been to this place before when I was but a boy called New Star. This was back when the whites were fighting the war between themselves and militias ruled the land. The Yanube who lived here did us a great kindness."

"That would have been my grandfather, Otter." He had been gone long enough, so it was safe to call his name aloud. And these men would understand my term of respect.

"Just so. My father is Spotted Panther and my grandfather was Grass Dancer. Otter sheltered us and gave us provisions as we passed through and came to our aid when the militia caught up with us."

7

"That was his nature," I said. "He helped when he could. Sometimes at his risk."

"We heard what they did to him," Firm Foot said.

I couldn't help glancing at the cottonwood. "I saw six horses in the distance. Yet there are only five of you."

Crow Hop motioned with his chin to the hill. "One of us keeps an eye out for a patrol."

My eyebrows shot up. "You are renegades?"

Firm Foot shook his head. "Nay, not as you mean it. But the army declares any who leave the reservations renegade. When we leave, they call it 'breaking out' and figure we're digging up hatchets to make war. I'm surprised they haven't put you on an agency."

"I have too much white blood for them to make the effort. Besides, my *tiospaye* is gone. Murdered over thirty years ago by American soldiers. Dragoons they called themselves back then. I'm a farmer, and that's what they want us to be, isn't it?"

Firm Foot looked down his nose. "They'll not make a dirt scratcher of me. I am a warrior. The militia turned me into one the day they shot down Grass Dancer and my sister on Trickling Water north of here."

Crow Hop nodded. "White men are good at turning us into warriors. Not so good at turning us into farmers."

"I have nothing except coffee and tea and water to drink, but you're welcome to that. I can probably find enough bread and cheese and jerky for a meal."

Firm Foot accepted my offer. Fifteen minutes later, we all gathered on the porch, most of my guests sitting on the planking to eat and sip and converse. After more talk, it became clear they were on the hunt for provisions because allotments at the agency were slow to arrive and often short. I offered one of my steers. Even though this was why they had come, they remained seated. Lord, don't let this turn into one of those long, protracted things where it takes forever before a blood gets around to talking turkey. Nature intervened to speed things along.

One of the younger braves grunted and lifted his chin. Most of us were under the cover of the porch and had to stand in the yard to see he was pointing to a sun enveloped in a wispy purple hue.

"Witchcraft!" someone muttered.

Crow Hop nodded agreement. "A bad omen. Something's gonna happen."

I spoke without thinking. "It already has."

They all turned in my direction. Then Crow Hop walked over and removed the hat from my head. "Tell us what you know about these things, Night Sky Hair."

Others of the group muttered when they took in the strange peppering of yellow in my black mop. Now that I'd stuck half a foot into the affair, I regretted it. The reservation schools hadn't been very successful if I understood correctly, so most of these men probably had little formal education.

"I know why the sun is playing tricks on us and the moon is changing and sunsets look like prairie fires," I said.

"*Pho!*" Firm Foot exclaimed. "Tell us."

"Far beyond Turtle Island, so far that it is on the other side of Mother Earth, there is an island the foreigners there call Krakatoa. During the last moon, a volcano on the island blew up. You understand what a volcano is?"

The young brave who'd spotted the sun changing colors nodded. "It's like the Land of Vapors where hot water shoots into the air and smelly mud comes up out of holes." He referred to the Yellowstone Country by one of its Crow names.

"Yes, like that, except it springs from a mountain and is many, many times more powerful. It blew up – what they call an eruption – and threw most of the island into the sea. The explosion spewed a thousand times more dirt into the air than the Yellowstone geysers. And it changed everything."

"How so?" Crow Hop wanted to know.

"It threw so much ash and pumice and smoke into the air that Father Sky waved it away to keep from choking and sent it all around the earth. And that cloaked the sun and covered the moon and infected the sunsets. We will see these things for a long time."

"How do you know this?" Firm Foot asked in a rising voice.

"Medicine," Crow Hop said. "Can't you see from his hair that he has medicine? My father told me this man's Spirit Dream foretells great joy and dancing and a bloody slaughter. A battle we will not win."

"And the murder of a great man," I said. "One of our own."

Firm Foot regarded me for a moment before stepping forward to finger my hair. With a somber face, he announced that from this point on, I would be known as "Medicine Hair."

"You misunderstand," I said. "I learned all of this from the whites who have singing wires that circle the world. You know that Mother Earth is round, don't you? Like a ball."

Most of them nodded, but some put a lie to the gesture with widened eyes.

Crow Hop and Firm Foot put their heads together for a moment, and then Spotted Panther's son walked up to face me. "I do not trust anyone who claims to be a medicine man. Better that he should demonstrate it and let me discover him as such. I now understand why my world has changed, and it is you who have given me this knowledge. It is as I said. You are Medicine Hair to me now."

I did not argue with my friends. After all, their perception of me didn't rule my life. I got aboard Arrow to go pick out a steer for them. Otherwise, Todoh would have taken them on when they tried to claim one of his charges. He still put up a fuss when a man dropped a loop over the animal

I chose. Then moved by impulsive generosity, I gave over a second steer to them. I had to coax Todoh into jumping up in the saddle and holding him in my arms as they rode away. Else he would have chased after them to reclaim his lost animals.

After the riders passed out of sight, I turned Arrow and pulled to a halt. A man astride a long-maned pinto stood silently twenty yards away. The sixth rider. I'd forgotten him. The hair on my neck rose, and the significance of that imperfect horseshoe track I'd found on the backside of the hill struck me. I eyed my empty saddle holster. My Henry still rested on the porch. I was unarmed but for a knife.

"I see you, War Eagle." The man's deep voice still disturbed me in my stones.

"And I see you, Raven Strongbow." This was the army scout who had denounced Matthew and then disappeared. "We thought you were dead."

Todoh growled at my tone. I released him, and he went on alert as soon as his paws hit the ground.

"Nay. Not dead."

"So you ran off."

He rode closer and put a half-smile on his handsome features. He looked little different from the last time I'd seen him four years ago. "It seemed the thing to do when your three messengers came for me," he said.

"Crow Johnson and the other two scouts?"

"They always followed his lead. They made it plain it was worth my life to remain in the barracks."

"So you proved you were a coward and ran away."

His expression did not change at my slur. "So I was prudent and left. I knew I would see you again one day. Just as I knew Red Star wouldn't remain faithful. That he'd throw you over for a woman or a boy. Where is he, by the way?"

"I know nothing of Red Star, but Shambling Bear will be home soon. Our bond is strong. We pledged ourselves before a council, so we're married, Raven. Go away and leave us alone."

"How often does he desert you to go to his other family?"

My back puckered. I reached for the rifle that wasn't there.

He noticed and smiled again. "Don't worry, I wish you no harm. But I still want you, Eagle. I'm haunted by the memory of fucking you, feeling you respond to me."

I kicked Arrow's sides and sent him straight at the man. But Raven moved his pony aside, and I rushed past, making straight for the cabin. When I arrived, my Henry was no longer on the porch. He hadn't stolen it, merely moved it inside the door. His way of letting me know he'd violated my home ... just as he'd violated me four years ago.

I snatched the weapon and rushed to the top of the hill behind the cabin, but he was already out of sight, following the trail laid down by his companions. I collapsed in the dirt and leaned against my rifle as tortured memories swamped me.

Raven had been a new scout at Fort Yanube when I first laid eyes on him. I already loved Matthew, although we were still fumbling our way to a relationship that was strange to both of us. Nonetheless, my interest had quickened when I saw the handsome Cheyenne, and he noticed my attention.

One night, while I was here at Turtle Crick Farm — Matthew had stayed behind at the Mead — Raven came for a visit and remained overnight in the barn loft with me. This was before our cabin was rebuilt after Otter's and James's murderers burned it. I woke in the middle of the night with him inside me. Half asleep and believing it was Matthew, I responded. Only belatedly did I remember Matthew was fifty miles distant and jerked free of Raven. He'd declared his love and his determination to win me. I spurned him.

Acting on some dark perversion of that love, he'd tried unsuccessfully to bushwhack Matthew. Then he told the military my lover was Red Star, a follower of Crazy Horse who had escaped from Fort Robinson after his chieftain was killed. Touch the Clouds and Buffalo Leg had used my speckled hair to help Matthew escape the charges. So maybe it did hold some medicine, after all.

When we'd returned from Fort Robinson, free men, we believed Raven was dead. That belief held steady until today. I dreaded telling Matthew of my rapist's reappearance. Raven Strongbow's presence had nothing to do with a volcanic eruption on the far side of the world, but it seemed just as cataclysmic to me. Something deep in my heart said I should chase after Raven and shoot him dead.

Instead, I went to the loft and sent a white homing pigeon to the Mead. Pa needed to know Raven lived. Then, still moved by the unexpected sight of the handsome warrior and missing Matthew terribly, I lay back in the hay and masturbated.

CHAPTER 3

I was bound for the barn to see to the horses the next morning when my nearest neighbor, Andre Tiller, rode up. After exchanging greetings and information on the condition of our crops, Andre swung around in the saddle and looked to where Todoh watched over my cattle.

"You missing any beef?"

I stepped off the porch. "Donated two steers to some men from Pine Ridge yesterday. The agency's slow paying their allotment, and they needed food for their families."

"They musta figured you volunteered one of mine, too. I had ten, now I got nine."

"Sorry. Didn't think they'd bother yours."

"It's not a crippling loss, but I'm gonna feel it."

Andre was a well-formed, good-looking man, but he hadn't seen fit to find a new mother for Libby. Libby was his thirteen-year-old daughter. He'd raised her alone since renegades killed his wife and two boys not long after Libby was born. Back before I discovered my love for Matthew, we'd given each other relief a few times, pleasant experiences I recalled fondly.

Andre didn't have a bridge at his place and used ours to cross Turtle Crick in his buckboard, so I knew he was going to church more often now. The resurgence of his Christian conscience was likely more for his daughter than for him. Still, if he was looking to find a wife, the Main Street Methodist Church was as good a place as any to look.

"The six braves who stopped here yesterday headed for the break country up on Trickling Water in case you want to recover your steer. They're not hostile," I said.

"Not to you, maybe. But I think I'll just call it a loss and be done with it." He straightened in the saddle. "I was heading for town, but now don't know if I should. Might not be smart to leave Libby alone with … strangers in the neighborhood."

"Send her over here if you want. Or out with Todoh. Probably safer with him than with either of us."

He laughed. "Happier, too. No, I'll put off the trip until tomorrow and take Libby with me."

Andre paused a moment longer to discuss atmospheric conditions and listen to my recitation of Gideon's explanation of the cause. Then he headed back to his place a mile west of me, passing through Todoh's territory on the way. The dog raised his voice, but it was a friendly one. He knew this man had something to do with the girl who played with him from time to time.

# # # # #

13

Thoughts of Raven Strongbow would not leave my mind either at the forge or in the fields the next morning. I know of only one way to handle such problems, and that is to face them. The sun was beginning its descent when I boarded Arrow and headed ten miles north to Tricking Water Crick. I paced it upstream to the stretch of badlands where Firm Foot and his companions had likely spent last night. If they had butchered the steers, they might still be in some side canyon jerking the meat. I had no firm plan in mind for confronting Raven when I entered the breaks, a poor way to tackle any enterprise.

The trail was easy to follow into the broken country people called a break. If Firm Foot and Crow Hop were as cautious as they seemed, they'd make for the shelter of one of the draws or small canyons that gave the place its name. Within two hundred yards, the trail I followed was laid down by only two horses. The others and the cattle had peeled off one by one. Soon the tracks vanished altogether. The Indians had obfuscated the trail after that, so it would be difficult to find them.

Unwilling to spend hours searching the coulees and small gorges littering the place, I settled for calling out to the hunters and soon heard an answer. Even with their assistance, the group was not easy to find. Sounds echoed off the clay walls and reverberated on all sides. Eventually, I found Crow Hop at the entrance to a big gully and followed him into the deep hollow. One of the other men went out and blurred my tracks.

The gloom in the steep-sided gulch was deeper than the gathering dusk outside, but a small campfire made seeing easy enough. All six were present, once the man returned from erasing my trail. The group was eating sparingly of their meat. A good sign the beef was truly meant for their families on the reservation. I could see racks of drying beef, which made for easier transfer. I joined them in the eating of one of my steers ... or perhaps Andre's, which provided an excuse for my presence.

"I gave you two of my steers, but I followed the tracks of three. My neighbor is missing one of his."

"Times are hard back on the agency," Firm Foot said. "Allotments promised by the white men are short or sometimes don't come at all. Your neighbor is a white man and has but himself and his little girl to feed. There are many of us. It seemed fair he should share."

They had apparently scouted out Andre's place. I nodded. "He has accepted his loss. But another one would be a hardship for him."

"He does not intend to raise an alarm?"

"Not since I talked to him about it."

Crow Hop spoke up in Lakota. "More of your medicine. I do not know many white men who would not go squalling to the army over the loss of a beef."

"He is a fair man. It would be better if you do not bother him further."

"He has your protection?" Firm Foot asked.

"Aye. Such as it is. Some of you may remember a man called Dull Lance from your youth. He attacked the farm and killed my neighbor's wife and two sons. Mr. Tiller has paid a blood price for occupying the land he farms."

Raven moved closer. "And this is why you ride to the breaks? To speak to us on behalf of a white farmer?"

"That ... and to tell you to stay away from me, Raven."

"*Pho!*" Firm Foot exclaimed. "Do we have bad blood here?"

I turned to Crow Hop. "This is the man who betrayed Matthew ... Shambling Bear ... to the army. He is the reason Bear was hauled in a jail wagon to Fort Robinson four winters back and thrown into their prison. He is the reason both of us were put behind bars and beaten. And he ran away after he spoke his betrayal rather than face us like a man."

By the light of the fire, Raven's complexion looked like last night's moon ... moldy. "This *winkte* threw himself at me. And when I took him, he pretended to be offended."

I stood, fists clenched. "It was no pretense. You took me while I slept. When I woke, I put an end to it."

"Yes, but not before you snuggled your hind side against me for some more of what I was giving you."

I wasn't sure who was on the defensive now. "I thought it was my betrothed. I belonged to another, and you knew it, Raven."

My face flamed. In Otter's time, such an admission would have caused little concern. But these were young men a generation or so removed from the time when deviants were accepted and sometimes honored. Crow Hop and most of the men were Lakota, but Firm Foot and one or two of the other men had spoken Dakota. That fire held no truck with two-spirits.

"Oh ho," Firm Foot said. "There's a tale to be told here."

"It is already told. That is the total of it," I said.

Crow Hop sat on the ground beside me. "Nay, the best part is yet to come." The others took seats around the fire before he continued. "When this man came to my father's tipi after following Bear to Nebraska, Buffalo Leg took one look at his hair and knew he was someone. And that speckled head freed Shambling Bear from the army's jail." He laughed. "But first it got this one thrown in the jailhouse along with the other one."

The group was quiet as Crow Hop told of my hair bewitching – his word – the two Indians with no-good reputations who were the army's witnesses against Bear. When the camp commandant brought the prisoner outside the guardhouse so everyone could witness the identification, Touch the Clouds snatched off my hat and shoved me forward, so the two malcontents could see me. Crow Hop claimed they were instantly befuddled. They named me as the fugitive, Red Star. Enraged, the commandant threw both Bear and me into jail while he sorted things out.

What Crow Hop undoubtedly knew but wasn't saying, was that Buffalo Leg and Touch the Clouds had spent the previous night drinking with the two witnesses, one a drunkard and the other as avaricious as a white man. My two friends spoke repeatedly of Red Star's hair – black as night with stars sprinkled in it. And thus deceived, the two turncoats made their identification of me.

After seeking to beat admissions out of both of us, the guardhouse sergeant went too far and tried to kill us. After that, the army released Matthew and me.

"But Medicine hair is a warrior as well as a shaman," Crow Hop finished his tale. "Even though wounded through the side, he killed the renegade sergeant who ambushed them on the road home and saved himself and his lover." Crow Hop nodded into the night. "And what he claims is true. He and Shambling Bear declared their intentions before Touch the Clouds and my father. He is Bear's win-tay wife."

A round of exclamations and whispers swept the group. The Cheyenne sat still and erect, as though he were not a part of it.

"What say you, Raven?" Firm Foot asked.

"He admitted me to his bed and then thought better of it. Perhaps he lured me there with his medicine in order to trap me." He shrugged, as if tired of it all. "Whatever the cause, I am freed of his magic now. He has nothing to fear from me."

"I do not fear for myself, but for Bear. You tried to shoot him from ambush before you betrayed him to the army."

The camp was absolutely silent but for the crackling of the fire and the snort of horses grazing in the distance. Firm Foot stroked his chin and studied the flames. Finally, he roused and spoke in Lakota.

"This man has provided sustenance for our families. He has demonstrated the power of his magic. Crow Hop gives the witness of his own eyes to its strength in thwarting the army's aim. Not many of us have walked away from the white man's justice when the army is bent on doing something. I see no dishonor in what he has said or done."

Raven jerked ramrod straight and rose to his knees. "Are you saying I am not honorable?"

Firm Foot stared across the flames. "I see truth in Medicine Hair's words. You will stay away from this man and his home. So long as you ride with us, no harm will come to him or his."

Raven scrambled to his feet. "I will not suffer this treatment from you. I will leave."

"Why?" Crow Hop asked. "So you can do him harm or because you are offended?"

"For my own reasons."

Firm Foot spoke up and delivered his judgment. "Raven, we broke out of the agency to find food for our families. Take your share of the meat and go. We'll not set eyes on you again until we return to our families."

Banishment, the ultimate sentence, unless some member of an aggrieved family saw fit to extract vengeance. I had no interest in that. If he left, that was all I wanted.

#

I returned to the cabin in darkness. Edgy, I took a good look around by the feeble light of a blue jay moon but found no trace of Raven. I took care of Arrow and cleaned up before turning into my blankets.

Was it too much to hope the Cheyenne was humiliated and had returned to the agency to lick his wounds? It was more likely he would nurse his mortification closer to Turtle Crick Farm. Would he seek to harm Andre and his daughter since I had put them under my protection? I came near to rising from my bed and riding over to give caution, but decided it would take Raven time to nurse his hurt into action.

It was past the point of midnight when Todoh set up a racket. Raven was proving me both right and wrong. He was still around, but it was not the Tillers he had in his sights. It was my cattle and my dog.

Dressed only in the short cotton breechclout I slept in, I stepped into moccasins and swept up my Henry before bursting through the door. The new moon was blue again, casting little discernible light. I peered west, but saw nothing as Todoh continued to yammer away. I rushed to the barn and twisted my fingers into Arrow's mane to swing aboard his back without pausing for saddle or halter. He responded to the pressure of my knees and made his way west past the plowed fields. On the other side of where I judged the worm fence ended, a flash of light preceded the boom of a gun.

I slowed to a walk and listened. I could see little beyond Arrow's nose. I had never before lived through so dark a night. Lack of sight heightened my other senses. Oleander and manure scented the night air. A breeze raised a chill on my naked flesh. After a pause, Todoh started barking again. At least, the Cheyenne hadn't hit my dog.

Realizing Raven could see no better than I could, I halted and took up my rifle to be ready if he tried for the dog again. He did. I aimed a little lower than the flash of his rifle and sent three quick shots in his direction. Then I dug in my heels and sent Arrow forward, so he couldn't advantage my muzzle flashes, as I had done his.

I rode blind. The night was quiet now. Todoh had stopped barking. The only sound came from water in the crick, which told me I had arrived at the spot where the waterway widened and rushed down a shelf of rock. That was beyond the end of my penned pasture, so I turned my pony north, hoping the dark, amorphous shapes that stirred in the gloom were steers. Soon I heard a growl to my right. The dog. The animal was a herder, so he could likely track.

"Easy, boy," I whispered. "Find him. Sic!"

I sensed rather than saw him move past me in the darkness. Arrow apparently saw better in faint light than I did and followed the dog. When he halted. I slipped from his back and examined the small patch of ground I could see. The dog panted somewhere ahead of me. My rifle at the ready, I crept forward. Within a few steps, I made out a form on the ground. Not a man, too large. It was the long-maned pinto Raven rode. I'd shot his horse from under him. Had I hit the Cheyenne, too?

Todoh appeared and sat at my side. I patted his head.

"Good boy. Now find him for me."

Without a sound, the dog rose and headed east. East toward the farmhouse. That made sense. Raven was without a mount, and the nearest horse was the black trace mare in my barn. I scrambled aboard Arrow and headed straight for the cabin as fast as the lightless night allowed. It took longer to get back to the barn than I had hoped. I desperately tried to calculate if Raven had had time to walk or run to the barn. The darkness would hamper him, as well, but I'd spent time locating his downed pony. It would be a close thing.

As I rode into the yard, a glow came through the barn door I'd left ajar. But I hadn't lit candle or lantern. He was here. Just as I reached the outhouse, the mare tore out of the barn, Raven astride her back. I startled him as much as he surprised me. I started to take after him until I caught a glimpse of burning hay in the horse crib. Forced to abandon the chase, I ran inside and grabbed a rake. The flames, still confined to the stall, were reaching for the rafters. I used the tines to pull the burning hay into the center of the earthen floor where it quickly burned itself out.

I splashed water from the ponies' trough on the smoldering wall, but the fire hadn't had time to ignite the timbers. After everything was under control, I scaled the ladder to the loft. There was no evidence of burning rafters, but I lit a lantern for a better look around. If any spark or flame remained, it could ignite the hay and render the building into ashes.

By the time I was satisfied the fire was truly snuffed, it was pointless to give chase. So I went inside the cabin, pulled on some clothes, and had a light meal of jerky and sweet milk. Then I clamped my hat on my head and climbed the hill behind the cabin to sit with my Henry and await the dawn. As the slow hours passed, I fought an urge to go check the cabin or the barn or the cattle. A man with assets was disadvantaged against someone bent on mischief who had none. My home, my fields, my cattle were all vulnerable to a renegade who valued none of them.

I started awake with my head resting on the arm that held my rifle upright. I'd dozed. Had the rising dawn roused me, or was it something else? Able to see a bit now, I silently rose and scouted out the area. Nothing was out of place. Todoh was silent, so the cattle must be all right, unless Raven had managed to get to the animal. Not likely. The dog would hear the Cheyenne long before he got close enough to use his knife. And no booming gun had awakened me.

Even so, I saddled Arrow and rode out to check on things when I recalled seeing a bow and quiver hanging from the Cheyenne's gear. Of course, now the weapon was on the saddle of his slain mount unless he'd recovered it during the night.

In the distance, Todoh rose and went on alert, but he soon recognized me and ducked his head, his tail wagging feebly. Something was wrong. The big carcass he'd been guarding told me what that was. Raven had managed to slit the throat of a half-grown side of beef before Todoh took him on last night. Now the dog acted as if it were his fault. I spent extra time playing with him to restore his pride before salvaging what beef I could. The morning was half done, and I was covered in blood by the time the steer was butchered and stored safely in my cellar cool room. I decided to offer Andre some of the fresh meat in partial payment for the loss of his steer.

Andre and Libby. Were they safe? Had the snake harmed either of them? I cleaned up as best I could in the crick and rode in sopping clothing to Tiller Farm, bearing some of the green beef with me. Andre was already in his fields, and I caught sight of Libby working nearby. They were safe.

Alarm painted Andre's features as I explained what had happened. He knew of Raven's perfidy in denouncing Matthew. We argued a few minutes over reporting the presence of the deserter. In the end, he rode for the fort, leaving unsaid the fact a white man's alarm would carry more weight than mine. Libby came with me back to the farm until her father returned.

We rode the range checking for other steers Raven might have killed or injured but found nothing. Todoh jumped up into the saddle with Libby, who was mounted on Otter's war horse, White Patch. Matthew and I had gifted her with the pinto after Otter's death. She had suffered a loss the night of the murders, too. James had all but adopted the girl. He'd left the farm to me but bequeathed Liberty Belle Tiller all the funds from the sale of his Virginia plantation after the southern rebellion, so she'd be wealthy when she came of age.

After we returned to the farmhouse, Libby went into the fields and worked right alongside me. Strong and industrious for one of her years, she seldom frolicked like a child. Todoh was her only playmate.

When Andre returned midday with Gideon at the head of a squad of troops, I wondered if I had thought this thing through properly. If there was a single tracker with Gideon, he would know immediately there had been a number of riders in the yard yesterday. While I wanted help in hunting Raven, I had no wish to call down trouble on the other five Indians. And reporting their presence might do just that. Sometimes the army sounded an alarm when braves left the reservation; at other times, no one in the military seemed to care.

I reported coming face to face with Raven Strongbow while out checking on my cattle and gave a modified version of our verbal exchange. I spent most of the time on what had happened later that night and this morning. Gideon took a description of my black mare since that was what Raven now rode. I directed them to the tracks that went past the east side of the cabin before heading northwest for the breaks up on Trickling

Water. As I watched Gideon lead his troopers north, I prayed Crow Hop and the others had moved on by now.

I weeded and watered and rode out to check my cattle. Todoh abandoned his task of chasing carrion birds to walk along beside Arrow as I made my rounds. The persistent buzzards flocked both Raven's dead horse —stripped of both saddle and weapons sometime during the night — and the butchered remains of the dead steer. Nothing seemed amiss, so I returned to the house. As I dismounted and led Arrow into the barn, I came to a halt. The black mare stood in her stall looking as if she'd never left. I pulled my Henry from its saddle scabbard and searched every inch of the farm, even the necessary.

Then I smartened up and read the tracks. No one had dismounted from the horse, so I traced her hoof prints backwards. Half a mile to the northeast of the farmhouse, I found the tracks of two ponies. Raven had obtained another mount somewhere and released the mare, so she would make her way home. Why? It made no sense. Ponies represented wealth. Some tribesmen still pursued the age old and honorable practice of stealing them. So why return her to me? A peace offering?

I went back to the barn and started wiping down the two horses before feeding them. That's when I saw what I had missed before — a small, undecorated wooden flute tied to her mane. Raven was sending a message all right, but it wasn't one of peace. A flute represented love to most braves. But in this case, it was twisted into something else.

CHAPTER 4

I worked my fields with frequent pauses to check the horizon. Given the distraction the reappearance of Raven had caused, perhaps I should think about getting a second dog to keep watch around the house. I knew from reading his journal – now burnt to ashes to protect its secrets – that Billy Strobaw, the man I had believed to be my grandpa, and Cut Hand, my true grandsire, once had five such beasts at Teacher's Mead: four trained to protect a certain area, and a fifth to keep watch over the house. Cut Hand and most of my *tiospaye*, my band, had been murdered by the army before I was born. Billy had taken my father, then just a child known as Dog Fox, into his household and was the fount of all that I was. A college graduate from New York, Billy had fled prejudices against Tories following the War of Revolution and came to the Dakota country. He'd taught Otter everything he knew. Otter, the constant companion of the last two decades of his life, had made certain my brother and sisters and I had as good an education as he could give us.

As I paused for a repast of jerky and a can of yellow peaches in sweet syrup along toward high sun, Todoh set up a yammering that drew me to the top of the hill. Gideon's returning patrol was close enough to excite his interest. My heart thudded. One trooper led a horse with a man slumped over the saddle. Hope died. The wounded man wore a uniform. It wasn't Raven.

When the patrol rode into the yard, I insisted Gideon lay out the wounded man, a two-striper, on the porch while I went inside for Otter's Pandora's box of medicines. The corporal's shoulder wound had likely broken a clavicle, so all I attempted was to clean the bullet hole with boiled stone root and apply a few chewed plantain leaves to both the entrance and exit points before sealing the puncture with honey. Then I bound his shoulder in clean white rags and gave him a sip of laudanum for pain. That would hold him until the fort's sawbones – yet some seven miles distant – assumed his care.

As I had worked over the wounded man, Gideon told me that upon the patrol's arrival at the breaks, they'd spotted a party of Indians ahead of them apparently searching for something. He was intent only on palavering with them, but one of the renegades shot at the patrol from ambush, bringing down the soldier. The troops returned fire on the Indians, although Gideon was unable to state if any had been struck. Leaving a man with the wounded corporal, he gave chase, but the fleeing party took refuge in a small canyon. Following a sporadic, desultory exchange of fire, shooting stopped. It was only after a period of time that Gideon became suspicious and rushed what he had assumed to be a box canyon only to find the renegades had taken a difficult but manageable riding trail out the other end. Unwilling to set his men up for a trap should the Indians remain in ambush at the top, Gideon elected to return to the fort and get help for his wounded. The telegraph would alert others of the raiding party.

I put a leash on my anger and explained as calmly as I could there had been neither a raiding party nor renegades but simply a group of men foraging for their families.

"Then why did they open fire on us? Why is Corporal Williams lying here on your porch?"

"You said someone shot from ambush. Did the party ahead of you open fire?"

Gideon hesitated. "No, they ran when we attacked them."

"Who did you originally set out to find, Captain?" I asked.

"The deserter, Raven Strongbow."

"I can hazard a guess as to who shot your man." I explained my meeting with the party yesterday and my donation of two head of cattle. I told him of later finding the Indians butchering and jerking the beef for easier transport. I told it all honestly and plainly except when he asked if I knew any of the men besides Raven. Unsure of their treatment at the hands of the army, I denied knowing them.

After Gideon left with his troopers for the fort, I mounted Arrow to check out the ambush site for myself. Suspecting Firm Foot and Crow Hop may have been forced to abandon their store of jerked meat, I took the black along as a pack horse.

The tracks I followed told the tale plainly. I found where Corporal Williams had fallen and discovered a spot atop a coulee and where Raven had lain in wait. Had the Cheyenne known the soldiers were coming or had he been stalking his own companions? He likely knew about the patrol. Raven would have seen me on the range with Todoh when he released the mare to return to the barn. It's possible he'd spotted the troopers in the distance as he made his escape and set up his ambush. The question was ... where had Raven gotten his new mount?

I shook my head. This was a man who hid a vengeful mind behind a cloak of uncommon masculine beauty. To look upon Raven Strongbow was to like and trust him. But as Matthew and I had learned, he did not suffer slights and rejection easily. Doubtless his unnecessary ambush of the patrol was for the sole purpose of bringing down the wrath of the soldiers on his companions. Revenge for his expulsion from the hunting party.

I followed Raven's trail into the canyon where his companions had taken refuge during the battle with the cavalry and up the difficult trail they'd used to escape the breaks. Once Raven broke out onto the prairie, he abandoned his former companion's trail and rode northwest. I diverted my attention to the foraging party but found no traces of blood in the dirt, which gave rise to the hope Crow Hop and his friends had escaped without loss. Then I realized there were signs of four horses, not five. A little later, tracks indicated two of the party had circled and headed back to the breaks. A puzzle.

I returned to the broken country and located the small canyon were the Indians had started jerking the meat. Most of the curing meat had been abandoned even though the two riders who'd returned from the prairie had reentered the coulee ahead of me. They hadn't been intent on recovering beef; they merely conducted a hurried search of the area. I recalled Gideon had said they seemed to be hunting for something when he came upon them.

Now I knew where Raven had gotten his mount. He'd taken one of his own party by stealth and stolen his pony. That explained why there were only four horses in Crow Hop's party and why two of them had returned to the breaks. They were looking for their missing companion. The tracks were too confused to read more of a story than that.

I loaded the abandoned jerky on the mare to take back to my cool room, all the while fighting the urge abandon it and track down Raven. Yet the meat needed to be saved in case Crow Hop or Firm Foot returned for it, so I headed home. Near the mouth of the breaks, where the south bank of Trickling Water rose and the crick widened into a shallow pool, I reined in. Something had caught my attention. A noise. There it was again.

I dismounted, pulled my rifle from its scabbard, and peered over the edge of the embankment. A tribesman knelt on hands and knees trying to drink water from his palm. His head was caked with dried blood. He was shaky, almost falling into the pool as he tried to slake his thirst. When I called out to him, he twisted over on his backside and tried to scramble away.

I held up my palm to show it was empty. "*Yata.* Peace, brother. You need help."

As I made my way down the embankment, I recognized the youngest member of Crow Hop's party, the man who'd called our attention to the lavender sun as we sat on my porch eating and talking. I didn't remember his name.

"I'm John ... War Eagle," I said.

He reached out to me and blinked rapidly. "*Hin Phejuta?*"

"Yes, I am Medicine Hair. Let me help you."

I dragged him out of the crick bed. He was so weak he was unable to mount alone, so I boosted him onto my saddle and crawled up behind him.

Zintikala Waniyetu ... or Winter Bird in the white man's language ... was a comely man my younger sister Hannah's age. Once we arrived back at the farm, Winter Bird made things clear while I tended his wound. Yesterday, he'd ridden to the crick to see if he could hand a few small trout in the stream onto the shore. He'd thought nothing of it when Raven appeared on the trail above. After the Cheyenne joined him, Raven had struck Bird on the back of his head and left him for dead. The young

Lakota remembered nothing until regaining consciousness sometime this afternoon.

When his head was treated and bandaged, I put Bird to bed in my sleeping room and went to move the jerky into my cellar. I checked on the wounded man after tending to the horses. He was sleeping soundly, which brought a bit of unease. Otter had always claimed concussions required wakefulness ... at least for a period of time. Nonetheless, I didn't have the heart to disturb him.

Abandoning my chores, I sat on the porch to think. A man without a horse and provisions in this country – particularly a tribesman – was a dead man. I checked on Bird one more time before boarding Arrow and heading for town to haggle over a gray riding pony and a pack horse. After purchasing tack gear at the livery stable, I went to the gunsmith's for an older model rifle and some ammunition. On the way back home, I stopped at the fort and waited patiently until a private hunted down Captain Haleworthy for me.

When Gideon stood before me, I explained what I had found, even to confessing one of the party was lying wounded in my cabin. It took a great deal of serious talking to disabuse him of the notion of taking Winter Bird into custody.

The resolution of the thing was agreed when he decided to ride with me to Turtle Crick Farm and talk to the wounded Indian for himself. That served my purpose, as well, because I wanted Raven labeled not only as a deserter, but also as a dangerous man.

Bird woke with a start when I shook his shoulder. Puzzlement became alarm when he saw an army officer at my side. I calmed his fears and explained in Lakota that he should tell the captain what had happened. After the young Lakota collected his wits, he explained everything, including the fact that rations hadn't been distributed at the agency for the last two moons. He and his companions had started out as a hunting party, but as there was little game, their trek took them farther and farther from home. Finally, he spoke the words I wanted to hear, saying Raven had attacked him, left him for dead, and stolen his horse, a roan gelding with Winter Bird's handprint painted in white on his right hindquarters. I was relieved when Gideon did not press for the identity of his companions. Getting a man's name into army records, even for the most innocent of reasons, sometimes brought unwanted attention.

As we stood on the porch and watched Gideon take his leave, Bird asked how I knew he wouldn't return with a patrol and haul him off to jail.

"Would he need soldiers to do that?"

Bird looked at his trembling hand. "Nay. I couldn't fight off a brace of ducklings right now." The young man turned to stare past my right earlobe. "How did you get the army to walk away and leave me in peace?"

His glance wandered to my hair. "You truly are Medicine Hair. A shaman."

"No, Winter Bird. I am just a farmer who happens to have some white blood in him."

When I led him to the barn to show him the horses and the tack gear and the rifle, Bird was overcome.

"When you are strong enough, you will take the jerky the others left behind and return home with provisions for your people." I paused before asking if he'd ever run into a warrior named Shambling Bear.

His eyes brightened. "*Pho!* I have met him several times. He is a good man. Handsome. All the girls want him."

Speaking around the lump in my throat, I said in the manner of a joke that he must take a great many of them.

"Nay. They say he is married and is satisfied with just one wife. Strange because he is much man. I am sure his loins could service many wives."

I don't believe he caught my sigh of relief.

CHAPTER 5

Winter bird required three days to regain his strength. Stressful days for both of us. He kept a close eye on the southern horizon, anxious over raising a column of cavalry on its way to arrest him. We did, indeed, see troopers, but they remained south of Turtle Crick. I assured him it was merely a routine patrol.

My distress came at night. My house had but one sleeping room, and we shared the bed. The first night he was still addled from the blow on his head, but on the next I stared through the moonlight at the rise and fall of his bare brown belly while he slept. How easy it would have been to take him in hand. But he wasn't my mate, so I resolutely turned away from him.

I made certain he knew of Raven's perfidy in betraying Matthew ... Shambling Bear ... to the white soldiers and asked him to warn my lover that Raven lived should he chance upon Matthew on the way home. Bird had issues of his own with the Cheyenne, but tribesmen of my acquaintance detested treachery and deceitfulness almost as much as they eschewed cowardice. Bird was a vocal young Oglala who would repeat the story to anyone who would listen. My aim was to deny Raven a home among our kinsmen. Banishment would do one of two things: send him to another part of Turtle Island or bring him to me on a mission of vengeance. In either case, this matter would be brought to a conclusion.

Bird's gratitude was touching as he mounted his new pony and took the reins of the pack horse laden with jerky from my cool room. He asked me to remove my hat and leaned from the saddle to touch my locks. I sighed. More tales would fly around campfires about Medicine Hair. No doubt others might come to consider me a medicine man ... a shaman. This was not something I desired, but what could be the harm? On top of this, I worried over whether I'd made the right decision in asking him to reveal that Raven lived should he chance upon Matthew. While my Other Heart needed to be aware of the danger, he was apt to go on the hunt for the Cheyenne snake absent my restraining influence.

Todoh barked Winter Bird a goodbye as he skirted the edge of the dog's territory. The young warrior's departure that Sunday both heightened my loneliness and brought relief. Relief because it removed temptation of the flesh. Loneliness for obvious reasons. I applied myself to farm work until mid-afternoon when Andre and Libby halted on their way back from church. Horseback, they had forded the crick on their way to town but chose to use my bridge upon their return as a way of being neighborly.

Libby went straight to the pigeon cote in the loft of the outhouse to visit the birds housed there. In her absence, I warned her father about Raven.

"And I may have called you to his attention without that intent when Firm Foot asked if you were under my protection," I finished the telling.

"So he may harass us in order to put a bee in your bonnet. I take it Captain Haleworthy didn't catch up to the fellow."

I told him how Raven had provoked a gunfight between the Indian hunting party and the troopers and made his escape.

"I'll keep an eye out. Libby's been after me to get a dog for the place. Maybe I'll deliver on her wish."

At that moment, my hayloft doors flew open and Libby called down to us. "Mr. John, you must not be taking very good care of the pigeons. There's a gray up here with a message on it." She was well aware the gray pigeons considered Turtle Crick as home. The white ones were bound to Teacher's Mead.

"Thank you, Libby. I promise to do a better job. Will you bring down the message, please?"

A minute later, she handed over a small scrap of paper. I read it quickly.

"It's a reply to my message to Pa that Raven has reappeared. He urges caution."

My neighbors declined a meal and left for home after Andre accepted my offer of herding his remaining nine steers to my range where they would be under Todoh's care and protection.

As I hoed weeds from rows of crops the next morning, Todoh set up a great noise. The dog had several voices, and this was a sustained yip of joy. I walked out of the head high corn stalks and saw a man kneeling and patting the dog's head. Todoh would have none of that and almost shoved him over backwards trying to crawl into his arms. My heart took flight. Matthew was home. His flea bitten gray gelding stood at the end of his reins. Our horses had an uneasy relationship with the blue.

Matthew rose, spotted me, and lifted a hand in greeting. I waved but willed myself to allow him to come to me. He swung a long leg over Wind Rider's back and kicked him into a trot. Todoh trailed along behind. The dog wouldn't have deserted his charges for anyone else. Well, perhaps Libby.

Matthew dismounted and gave me an Indian handshake, grasping forearms rather than palms while his look demanded more. One never knew when foreign eyes were watching, so we restrained ourselves until we entered the barn to take care of his mount. Wind had to wait for his rubdown until I got mine. Matthew dropped the reins and turned into me. His open lips found mine; his tongue explored my mouth. He pulled me to him, his erection pushing into my belly. What a wonderful feeling.

"Bedroom," I gasped.

"Loft. Closer," he said with a pant.

He played with my fundament all the way up the ladder. At the top we stripped. He was naked before I could get out of my cumbersome boots.

The next turn of the hourglass was what made his absences bearable. We cared not that he'd spent days in the saddle or that I had been laboring in the fields. Our aromas identified us ... one to the other. Matthew gave me no time to spread a horse blanket. He pushed me down between his legs and thrust his strong, straight cock between my lips. He must have been near to coming when he withdrew, spun me around, and bent me over a hay bale.

His arms went around my chest. He hugged me to him and whispered the word "Lover" as he began to thrust. The violence of his hips gave voice to his urgent need. He poled me like a bull spearing his cow. The slap of his thighs against my backside could likely be heard halfway to Yanube City. Certainly his cries were far-reaching.

"Take my cock, Eagle! It's hungry for you. Take everything I've got. I need you."

Sometimes Matthew fucked, and sometimes he made love. This was fucking. Raw, urgent, demanding sex. Taking what he wanted. How he wanted. Claiming me. Possessing me. Knowing that his needs fed my needs, made it all the more exciting. In the midst of his whoops and hollers, I felt my own coming explosion. He erupted in a flurry of frenzied humps, groaning as if at death's door. His hand found my rod and started pumping. Before he was through his own orgasm, mine began. I came. Fast, quick, intense. The muscles of my fundament worked his rod, drawing more cum and more groans from him. At last, he collapsed atop me, pressing my torso down onto the scratchy hay. But I was content.

"Beautiful way ... to say hello," I gasped.

"There is ... no better."

We went silent as we sought to calm our breathing.

"I've missed you Night Sky Hair," he said when he could speak steadily.

"I have a new name."

Sprawled over the hay bale with Matthew still inside me, I related the events of the last few days. He grunted at the mention of Raven Strongbow. Then he pulled out of me and went to fetch water from a bucket in the corner. As he cleaned both of us, he told me he'd heard of the Cheyenne's reappearance in the Pine Ridge area.

We dressed and went down to take care of Wind and send Todoh back to the range. We talked as he brushed and fed the gray. Finished with that chore, we walked the fields, so he could note the condition of the crops. Matthew – when he was Bear – maintained he was a warrior not a farmer, but he'd spent thirteen years at Teacher's Mead after Otter brought Matthew to us following the slaughter of his mother and brother by the militia back in the days when the North fought the South. So it was an expert eye that ran over the acreage.

"Be ready for harvest soon," he noted. "It'll be a decent crop."

"Aye, and will require your back to bring it in."

He flashed a smile. "That's why I'm here."

We returned to the cabin where I fed Matthew the best meal he'd had since he left, according to him. After we finished eating, he rooted around in the cabinet where I stored our pitching horseshoes. We'd taken up the game after our Uncle Christian gave up on home ball – what they were calling baseball nowadays – and took up horseshoe pitching. Like with everything he did, Christian was so enthusiastic he got us fired up about it, too.

Matthew was deadly at the game; I was only fair. So when I made each of us a balanced pitching set of shoes in the forge, I made the opening on his a wee bit narrower than mine. It took him a year to notice the difference and make me remedy the difference. Now, I watched him hold up the horseshoes and compare the openings.

As usual, he skunked me. I've tried mimic the twist he gives the quoits as he releases them, but it doesn't work for me. My joy at having him home rendered his thrashing harmless.

Once the novelty of the game was worn out, we went to our *okinare* on the south bank of the crick for a good sweat bath. We sat naked in the tight little shelter while restless waves of steam caressed our flesh and cleansed our systems.

In the dim light of the medicine lodge, I admired my mate's hard, naked body. I had considered him handsome beyond comparison since childhood, yet four years ago something had happened to enhance his comeliness even more ... something sinister, something that threatened to take his life. On the road from Fort Robinson, the renegade sergeant's bullet had split his forehead open in a passing blow. The hermit healer, Blood Mark Boy, sutured the wound in such a way that the resulting scar resembled a tribal tattoo. The sight aroused me in my stones. Matthew noticed and laughed.

"You look upon my scar as I look upon your hair. Perhaps they both have medicine."

My pole pulsed in the hot air. "It's medicine for me. I've missed you so much."

"As I have you."

My throat tightened. "I'll wager you took comfort in softer arms than mine."

"Then it's a wager you would lose. I want no one but my brawny blacksmith. That is who I love."

My rod jumped at his words. "That is good to know. I lie in bed after working the fields and think about you. Inevitably, some young maiden seems to hang in the background. And then when Raven ..." I bit down on my tongue.

He sat up, his interest excited. "When Raven what?"

"He's a sly one. He taunted me when we met on the trail to Trickling Water. He asked how often you ran away to spend time with your other family."

"And you gave that dog's words weight?" He started to rise.

"No, Matthew. But his words infected me. I knew where your love lay, but my imagination had played with my heart even before he spoke those hateful words."

Matthew settled back. "Sometimes I am tempted. But then I'll see your speckled head in my mind's eye, and I'll call up an image of your torso. Your groin. Your face. You. And I know I can wait."

I cleared my throat of whatever was threatening to clog it and asked about his trip. He told of locating an aunt and uncle and three cousins. His father, a Brulé Teton, had died fighting for the Union against Stand Watie's Confederate Indians, and Matthew occasionally went looking for relatives. His mother had been Yanube, my band.

"Did you see Sitting Bull?" I asked when he paused.

"Aye. He's a fine man, Eagle. Impressive. Not in the way Crazy Horse was. Crazy horse was energy and action. Sitting Bull is intellect and planning. But he can inspire others, bend them to his will. He fought for a long time to keep his people from becoming dependent on the white man. Warriors from many fires flocked to him. When you meet him, it is easy to see why he inspires such confidence."

"I heard that when he came back from Canada to give himself up, there were only a hundred and fifty or so people with him. What happened to the others?"

"He took only the Hunkpapa with him to Canada. And some of them stayed behind under Chief Wanbli Gi. Sitting Bull came back with near 200 of his people."

"Warriors?"

"Warriors and their families."

"So he's no threat to the army. I guess the days of thousands of warriors are behind us."

"Confining us to different reservations makes it hard to gather warriors. But when the time comes, he will put out the call, and we will respond."

"Firm Foot told me every time a blood leaves the reservation the army calls it breaking out."

"That's been true since '76, but they're serious about it now. Every Indian not on the reservation is declared hostile and fair game for the army."

My blood went cold in the midst of hot steam as I recalled Gideon's brief visit last Tuesday. "This is serious, Matthew. When Gideon asked about you the other day, he must have known you'd left Standing Rock. Maybe he came to take you back."

Matthew rubbed sweat from his face. "Maybe he just wanted to warn me I'd been missed."

31

"Possibly. Is there talk of confining everyone?"

"They're imprisoning the tribes and bands and any blood Indian belonging to a fire. I don't think they'll bother you or Pa and the family at Teacher's Mead."

"There's many a white who'd like to get his hands on the Mead. It's a valuable piece of property. How better to do it than send Pa to Pine Ridge?" I asked.

He shook his head again. "They think Pa's a half-breed. And the Mead's title has been upheld in court. Besides, Ma's white. I think they're safe. And if they believe Pa's half-blooded, then they figure you're a quarter blood. You're a land owner. So you ought to be safe, too. Besides, there's no band, no *tiospaye*. Hasn't been since they murdered ours thirty years ago."

"Tribal membership usually passes through the mother, so you ought to claim you're Yanube."

"I do, but you remember that piece of paper you got from the captain defending me against charges at Fort Robinson? The one saying I was innocent? It pegs me as half Teton Sioux and half Yanube. That might come back to snag me one day." He rose and started for the entryway. The steam had almost dissipated. "Maybe I ought to go look up Gideon and see what he has to say?"

"No!" I spoke sharper than usual. "I believe in meeting trouble head-on, but on this thing, we keep our distance."

"*Kay.*" He used the Creek word he'd adopted when agreeing.

I sent a pigeon to the Mead bearing the message Matthew had returned safely. Thereafter, we went to check on the cattle. Both of us kept half an eye out for any sign of Raven ... or for a cavalry patrol.

Troubled times had descended upon us again.

CHAPTER 6

Knowing Raven was alive and possibly still in the vicinity forced a change in my plans. I'd hoped to leave the fields to Andre's care while Matthew and I undertook a quick trip to Teacher's Mead. Now we agreed I should go while my mate stood guard over our homestead. He could make the trip once the harvest was in.

After our physical passions were sated – which took three days – I mounted Arrow before sunup on a Thursday and began the fifty-mile trip, packing two gray homing pigeons bonded to Turtle Crick. Mid-morning, I grew uncomfortable and reined in to take a good look around. Was Raven dogging my trail? Nothing gave cause for unease. Still, there was something. Arrow sensed it as well. His ears swiveled to the north where a deep ha-ha-cut the prairie.

As I watched, a score of tribesmen rode up out of the gully and approached at a steady walk. As they neared, one man gave the open-handed salute. I returned the gesture. The group was mostly young, although the one who seemed to be the leader was a man of about thirty-five years. A stiff roach crowned his shaven head. He had festooned his palomino's mane with eagle feathers.

The stocky man gave the customary Lakota greeting and introduced himself as Howling Wolf of the Teton Brulé fire. The short lance he carried bore fetishes I associated with a shaman, so this was likely a *pejula wacasa*, a medicine man from Matthew's own tribe. The butt end of a rifle protruded from a fringed and beaded saddle holster at his right knee.

I responded with my American and earth names as I removed my hat and rested it on the pommel of the saddle. A twitter went through the group.

Howling Wolf pursed his lips. "You are Medicine Hair?"

"Some call me by that name. And one is among you. I see you, Winter Bird. I am glad you made it back to your people."

The young warrior smiled and stepped his horse forward. "I see you, too, Medicine Hair. The beef you provided helped our village."

Howling Wolf made a small movement with his lance, and Bird back-walked the gray I had given him into line with the other men. I took a moment to scan the group facing me. I recognized none of the others. The Brulé's voice brought my attention back to him.

"I understand there are many more cattle on your range."

"Aye, and if you are as smart as I believe you to be, they will remain there. In a moon or two, I will take them to the white man's sale barn in Yanube City and sell them to him. Then I will buy more calves to raise and sell the following year. You can take them all now, but there will be no more after that. But if I grow the herd, I can donate five head a season.

33

In that manner, your children and your children's children will have a source of food."

Interest sparked Howling Wolf's eyes. "This is something to think about."

"You understand the five head is for all fires, not just yours. Else, the thing will fall apart."

"Have you seen any blue coats this morning?"

I shook my head. "Not a sign of the army, but there will be patrols. Of that you can be certain."

"Aye, especially since news of our break-out at Standing Rock."

"You broke out in force from one agency?" I asked.

Something akin to a smile creased Wolf's heavy features. "Nay. We came from several, one at a time, but our departure will be known by now."

A man with the long, sad face of a hound dog spoke up. "Announced by smoke from the fires we left in our wake."

My eyebrows climbed despite my resolve to be stoic. "You are renegades? You are raiding?"

"Aye. We intend to make the white man pay for the injustices we suffer," Wolf said.

I steadied my voice. "The time for that is past. There are too many foreigners among us now. Even at the agencies. I hear there are Indian police who do their bidding."

The Brulé shaman nodded. "True. But some of us remember the old days. Warriors are raising the hatchet all across the country. They have no right to pen us into prisons they call reservations."

The chorus of exclamations punctuating his words let me know preaching to them would accomplish nothing. Even so, I tried. "Howling Wolf, at the beginning of my nineteenth summer, I had my *hemblecha*. My Spirit Dream showed me things I struggle to understand to this day. I saw great joy and dancing as a prophet made promises to the people."

I drew a breath. "I can only assume they were false promises because after that, a big man – one of us – was murdered. Then I saw a scene of bloody carnage. Hundreds of bodies lay in the snow with blue coats walking among them. We had lost a terrible battle, and I saw no future beyond that tragedy."

Wolf's palomino pranced restlessly, likely responding to the medicine man's own emotions. "So we are to forget the wrongs against us and our families?"

"No. But small groups of warriors razing the countryside is not the way. Unless whole tribes take up the hatchet, what you do means little. The blue coats will hunt you down and kill you off, one-by-one. And what will you have accomplished?"

The Brulé sat tall astride his horse. "Perhaps we will have stirred those tribes you speak of into answering the drums."

My appeal had failed. "Since the time of my grandfather, marauding bands have used the breaks on Trickling Water as a sanctuary." I nodded to the hump of hills lying in the distance over my shoulder. "The little Islands are better. They are not broad, but they are deep. There is water, and even a little game."

"That puts an American fort between us and home."

"True, but you are nimble. The advantages far outweigh that disadvantage. And know this, the farm at Teacher's Mead is owned by my father, who is Yanube. He will defend what is his against all odds, but as he is a tribesman, I pray he will not need to do so. The farm to the east of the Mead is owned by my mother's brothers. They are white men, but fair. The people at the Mead will give aid and sanctuary to their kinsmen."

"We know of Dog Fox and the Mead," Howling Wolf said.

"My farm lies on Turtle Crick, and my neighbor, Andre Tiller, is a mile to the west. His land is stained with the blood of his wife and two sons. He has paid. He lends me assistance when I need it, and I give mine in return."

"So he has your protection?"

I hesitated. If Howling Wolf had taken umbrage at the sharing of my vision of destruction for the tribes, a claim of protection might prove a challenge. Nonetheless, I nodded. "Aye. He is under my protection. I would be offended if he and his are molested."

Howling Wolf grunted. An acknowledgment rather than a commitment. I continued. "Your Brulé kinsman, Shambling Bear, is at our farm now to keep watch over things. I am on my way to Teacher's Mead for a short visit. Now I will tell you something you already know. The army at Fort Yanube has good trackers. They will read your trail like ashes drawn across white doeskin."

"We know. A Crow, a Miniconjou, and a Mandan."

"Aye, those are their Indian trackers, but don't undervalue their own. Some of the soldiers can track a scorpion across a rock."

Howling Wolf snorted in derision and kicked his pony forward. His party flowed around me like a stream of dark water. I dismounted and blurred my trail to the point where Howling Wolf's party had passed south. I wanted my hoof prints covered by theirs when Crow or one of the other scouts read the signs. Then I scribbled an account of the meeting on a small piece of ledger paper I habitually carry in my saddlebags and attached it to one of the two gray pigeons. I felt easier as the bird lifted into the air and turned to the northwest. At least Matthew would be aware of what was going on.

The family was happy to see me when I dragged into the Mead later that evening. I'd pushed Arrow a bit after the delay with the party of Indians I'd encountered, so he was glad to have a home for the night. After the pony was taken care of, everyone gathered in the big room at the stone house to listen to my news between bites of the stew Ma put before me. Because of the homing pigeon I'd sent in advance of my visit, she'd baked fresh bread in my honor. I loved her yeasty loaves and hoped she'd send a few with me back to Turtle Crick.

My news of Howling Wolf and his raiders wasn't a surprise. For years now, the Mead had been a way station for the stage. Outgoing to Fort Ramson on Tuesdays and incoming to Yanube City on Thursdays. The drivers kept the family up to date on the goings-on in both the big world and our own little part of Turtle Island. Pa told me at least two farms in the shallow valley skirting the Yanube River had been burned out by renegades. One of the farmers had lost his life in a skirmish. Nowadays, the army regularly patrolled the river.

Alex, my only blood brother, wanted to talk crops and crop prices. Two years older than me, he pretty well ran the farming operation at the Mead. Curtis Appleton, a rosy-cheeked Englishman and his wife, Jane — equally rosy-cheeked — worked in the fields and in the kitchen for pay. They and their two fry seemed surprisingly well-content to be working for Indians. Of course, Ma's family came from Denmark, but the red blood was obvious in the rest of us.

To the world, me, my brother, and two sisters — Rachel Ann and Hannah — were quarter bloods. In a scheme to leave the Mead to my father, Billy Strobaw had passed Dog Fox, the son of Cut Hand, the last chief of the Yanube, as the natural son of himself and his dead wife, Butterfly, who had been Cut Hand's sister. The scheme had worked — barely — and so Pa was known as Cuthan Strobaw, a half-breed. In truth, his children were of that blood quantum. To look upon me, a stranger wouldn't know I had any European blood at all ... but for my ma's golden hair dotting my scalp. Alex and the girls could pass easier than I.

Three years back — that would be in the spring of 1880, just months after Matthew and I returned from our ordeal at Fort Robinson — Alexander had married Minnie Killpenny, the daughter of a farm family located four miles to the west of the Mead. She'd been the valley's temptress but now looked downright matronly. The reasons for that, little Jacob and Hans, crawled over everyone's feet and up onto any lap available. Two and one, respectively, they were placid, happy children, reflecting their father's nature more than their mother's. Alex's family now occupied my old cabin west of the stone house.

The big news of the moment had nothing to do with renegades or crops or the like. Rachel Ann was proudly wearing a modest ring with a diamond chip. Captain Gideon Haleworthy had finally worked up the courage to ask for my sister's hand. With the open declaration of his intentions, my mother's reservations had melted away.

She had always feared the West Point graduate would be loath to bring a dusky girl from Indian country back to Boston. But it seemed not all Bostonians were Brahmins or black Irish. The elder Haleworthy worked in a shipyard. In truth, from a financial standpoint, Gideon was probably marrying up. Billy Strobaw had left his family well-fixed, and Pa had only increased on it. At any rate, Gideon had showed up last Saturday and formally asked Pa for permission to marry his older girl. Then he'd made the fifty-mile ride back to the fort to report for duty.

After the excitement of that telling was past, I revealed my new name and how I came about it. Everyone was amused except Pa. His gold-flecked black eyes held a warning.

"Take care, John." I knew the use of my American name was deliberate. "The responsibilities of a shaman are heavy."

"I'm no shaman. Each time someone tries to tell me I am, I disabuse them of the notion. I told Crow Hop and Firm Foot I knew of the strange events we've been experiencing only because of the white man's telegraph."

He nodded. "Yet you got the army to leave the wounded man at your house unmolested. You got them to hunt for Raven. To many, that would look as though you made the army obey your will."

"Not any man who thinks for himself."

Pa's lips drew firm. "Sometimes, I believe you are too schooled in the white man's ways."

"Why? We live in a white man's world."

"Nay. We live with a foot in each world, and sometimes you do not pay enough attention to that other foot."

I spent the night in what had been Alex's old room and got up before sunrise the next morning to help with the chores. The incoming stage had come and gone yesterday before I arrived, leaving a team of relief horses needing a couple of shoes. As the Mead had neither blacksmith nor farrier at the moment, I lit the kiln and started replenishing the farm's stock of spare shoes.

Pa had induced Crow Johnson to return to his old job as blacksmith, but his enlistment in the army scouts had not yet expired. Crow getting shed of the military was good. The way things were heading, he'd have ended up tracking down some of his own kin.

Midday, Hannah came to the forge saying Pa wanted me outside. My younger sister stood at risk of becoming an old maid. She was twenty-and one now and pretty as a peach in bloom, but no one had showed much interest in her except for Min's brother, Esau Killpenny. He was likely enough. Esau was my height, an inch or two shy of six feet, but he had me by twenty pounds. Wasn't fat; the 180 he carried were solid.

I went outside to find Pa on the porch of the stone house looking south toward the river through his long glass. When I trotted up, he handed over the telescoping instrument and nodded with his chin toward a group of twenty or so riders on the south bank of the Yanube. It looked like Howling Wolf's party.

He whistled to catch everyone's attention as soon as the riders began to stream across the bridge at a pace that would rapidly eat up the mile between us. "What you suppose they want?" he asked.

"It's the same bunch I ran into yesterday. The spokesman's a Brulé named Howling Wolf. Medicine man, I'd guess. He probably wants to get the lay of the land. He knows we're kinsmen."

"Wouldn't be the first time a man has taken a kin's blood."

When all of our people arrived at the porch, he sent Curtis and the women and children inside the stone blockhouse. The rest of us waited on the porch until the group arrived. One skirted the house and rode out of sight. He'd likely climb the hollow hill at the back of the house to act as scout.

"*Hah-ue.*" Howling Wolf greeted my father before turning to me. "I see you, Medicine Hair."

"And I see you, Howling Wolf. This is my father, Dog Fox. The whites know him as Cuthan Strobaw."

The Lakota nodded. "We know of Dog Fox, son of Cut Hand, last chief of the Yanube. I am happy to cast eyes on you."

There was no expression on Pa's face, but I knew he was angry. Either the Brulé was careless enough to leave a trail to our front door, or he had done so deliberately. "There is fresh water for everyone. We do not stock whiskey on the farm, but my wife can find pemmican or jerky for you all. Why does the famous medicine man, Howling Wolf, appear at my farm?"

Until yesterday, I'd never heard of Howling Wolf, so unless my father knew something I didn't he was indulging in hyperbole.

Wolf took it in stride. "We have bait, but ammunition for our long guns would be welcome."

My thoughts slid to the cases of bullets resting in the hidden cavern beneath the hollow hill at our backs, but Pa didn't hesitate. "We stock only enough ammunition for the farm's needs. But we will give you what we can spare. John, Alexander. Bring the bags hanging in the entryway."

We exchanged glances before moving to obey. When I lifted the nearest buckskin pouch there could not have been more than thirty or forty cartridges. The one Alexander carried looked to be the same. That wouldn't last very long in a battle with the cavalry.

From Howling Wolf's expression as he weighed the bags in his hand, he shared my judgment. A whistle from the hill interrupted whatever response he was preparing to give. When he ordered his men up Strobaw's Crick, Pa stopped him.

"Do not ride your men through the Mead again, Howling Wolf. If you have business with me, come alone. You'll meet no treachery here, but neither will you find support for raiding and killing."

The Brulé allowed his palomino to dance a little as he gave Pa a cool look. Then he rode after his men.

"John, go up the hill and see what the lookout spotted. If it's an army patrol, whistle."

Halfway up the hollow hill, I gave a sharp whistle. There must have been a full platoon of troopers riding east along the south riverbank. Because of the size of the detachment, it was clear they were searching for Wolf's party. A series of shots startled me as I scrambled back down the hill. When I arrived in the yard, a big sow and a milk cow lay dead and bleeding. Pa'd shot them and taken out one or two window lights in the house to give him a tale to tell.

When a lieutenant who was strange to me halted his men in our yard, Crow rode at the edge of the group. I motioned north, and he immediately spotted the trail left by the riders. He disappeared behind the hill as I turned back to the others in time to hear the officer introduce himself as Second Lieutenant Schwartz. They were, indeed, on Howling Wolf's tail.

The young officer, a baby-faced blond whose brass bars weren't yet riding comfortably on his shoulders, listened as Pa explained the party had tarried just long enough to demand ammunition. When we were only able to give them a few rounds, they grew angry and killed a couple of our animals and shot out a window pane or two. He was careful to weave into his fabrication that none of the raiders raised their weapons to us. They fled when their lookout warned of the patrol's approach. Crow reappeared and confirmed the war party had gone up Strobaw's Crick toward Trickling Water.

Pa failed to inform the lieutenant the old cow had stopped giving milk and the pig was about to be slaughtered for pork. Window lights didn't come cheap, but if they distracted the army, they were worth the sacrifice.

#

On my second day at the Mead, a pigeon brought a message from Matthew informing me Raven had galloped through the Tiller's yard firing his weapon and frightening Libby. Her father had been in the fields, but the Cheyenne made no attempt on him and was gone before Andre arrived. The attack was no more than harassment of someone I'd placed under my protection.

Matthew ended the note by saying he was leaving to track Raven. Andre would watch over our fields until I got home. That, of course, ended what had been a pleasant family visit. I said hasty goodbyes and mounted up. Ma had time to press half a dozen freshly baked loaves of bread on me before I departed with the white pigeons from the Mead's cote.

The sun stood high in the sky by the time I skirted the western hill on a diagonal toward Turtle Crick, so I'd need to snatch a few hours of sleep on the way. Near midnight, I removed the leather from Arrow and made a pillow of his saddle. After a bite of jerky to settle my empty stomach, I lay back to regard countless pinpricks of light in the clear night sky. Some were blue, some reddish, a few green, but they were overwhelmingly white.

I recalled lying with Matthew in a wagon bed years back watching those stars and realizing that Otter and Billy and Cut Hand and all who had come before them had enjoyed that same heavenly display. Tonight, Father Sky was dressed in his finest regalia.

I drifted off to sleep with the taste of beef jerky on my tongue, the smell of saddle leather in my nostrils, and the distant yelp of coyotes in my ears. A slight breeze teased my face.

Arrow's soft neigh woke me. He stood nearby, looking off to the north. I eased to my feet and recovered my Henry from its scabbard. The pinto pawed the ground. I snatched my hat from my head and threw it down on the saddle after arranging the blankets as if they might cover a man. Then I backed away to the south and went prone in the dirt. I heard nothing, but Arrow Wind certainly did.

I waited half the turn of an hourglass, but nothing happened until my pony became restless again. Unhobbled, he moved toward me while his ears pointed north. Someone or something was there. It could be a painter or a bear drifted up from the Little Humps, but either would have had to swim a river and cross a couple of roads.

As watchful as I was, I didn't see the creeping figure until he was almost upon the saddle with my hat lying across it. The moment he discerned the trap, he threw himself sideways. A fraction of a second later, my rifle barked and the bullet fanned pure air. Flat of his belly, the intruder was now invisible to me.

"Don't shoot, Eagle. It's me. Raven."

I fired a second shot at nothing to let him know I was serious.

"I just want to talk," he called.

"That's why you were sneaking up on me?"

"To prevent this." His voice echoed hollowly over the prairie. "I'm going to get up now."

"You do, and you're dead."

A long pause. "Like your lover? Like Bear?"

My blood ran cold. My hands shook. I swallowed hard and steadied myself. "He's not dead. But he's not far behind. I promise you that."

"Oh, he's dead. I shot him from the saddle half a sun back as he followed me."

His voice was so firm and sure, I dropped the Henry in the dirt and lowered my head onto the warm barrel.

"Don't you want to know how I found you?" The hated voice had moved to the west. "I watched as he sent word to you by the messenger bird. I knew he was summoning you, and I knew you'd come by the quickest route. This is how you always come. I know. I've watched you take this trail before. After I dealt with the Teton, I just had to wait for you to show up."

The sound of his voice, striving to be patient and reasonable while telling me he had slain my Other Self turned ugly in my ears. I experienced a rush. My body flew up of its own volition. My feet pounded across the ground on a mission of their own, carrying me with them.

I caught Raven's startled glance as he looked up to see me dropping atop him. His rifle flew from his hands as my weight crushed him to the ground. I seized the hand grabbing for his knife and brought my right fist down on his chin with all the strength I had. His head snapped sideways. He went limp. I snatched his knife from its scabbard and hovered over him, the blade poised to strike.

My thirst for vengeance abated as doubts assailed me. Matthew wouldn't have been such easy prey. Still, it's not that difficult to shoot a man from hiding. My heart knew what to do, but my head betrayed me. I had enough ghosts of men I'd killed haunting my dreams. I lowered the blade and made a sudden decision.

I located his pony in a draw and talked my way to his side. Reins in hand, I led him to Arrow. After saddling my mount, stowing my blankets, and donning my hat, I turned northwest and left an unconscious Raven Strongbow afoot on the prairie without a mount or weapons. As soon as it was light enough, I would search for his trail and backtrack to find Matthew. In the meantime, I put distance between us.

At daybreak, I headed north to intercept Raven's trail along the path he'd likely taken. My heart took a leap when I found it and discovered a second set of hoof prints. Prints I'd recognize anywhere since I had made the shoes the animal wore. I'd put subtle imperfections in all of our shoes so one could easily recognize the trail of the other. Raven had lied. Matthew was alive and hot on his trail. I turned and rushed to catch up with my mate.

I found him at the site where I'd confronted Raven. He was standing with Wind's reins in his hand watching my approach. He'd been reading the marks in the dirt before he became aware of my presence. He waved.

"I see Raven found you. That's his black trailing along behind Arrow."

"Aye, and I have his rifle and knife, as well."

"Where is his body?"

I flushed. "I left him here, unconscious."

He raised an arm and pointed. "He recovered and made south for the river." A reproof hid in his voice.

"To hide his tracks in the water, I suspect."

"To waylay some traveler and get himself a horse and weapons is more like it."

Matthew's building anger stabbed my soul. "He told me he'd ambushed you and left you dead. I had but one thought, and that was to find you and learn the truth."

"Now you have found me and left me vulnerable to a crazy man who thinks he can claim you by killing me." He swung aboard Wind. "*Hoppo*, let's finish what you should have done."

Stinging from the rebuke, I followed him south toward the Yanube. Raven had made no effort to cover his trail. His moccasin prints indicated

41

he was running, or at least trotting. A fit warrior could keep up that pace for the better part of a day. The fact he'd not come after me said he was aware Matthew was on his trail and didn't want to be squeezed between us.

As we entered the thin screen of trees on the north bank of the Yanube, Raven's tracks became more elusive. He had gone to some trouble to mask his movements. Rather than try tracking him, Matthew went upriver while I turned east. A few minutes later, I heard three gunshots, our agreed signal.

A mile up the Yanube, I came upon Matthew standing over a body. The air deserted my lungs when I got close enough to see the slain man was Mr. Killpenny, Pa's neighbor to the west and Alex's father-in-law. What had I done? I knew how ruthless, how murderous Raven was. I'd failed to put an end to him, and Mr. Killpenny had paid the price.

Matthew held his tongue, but I knew his judgment was the same. He avoided the issue by looking around to read the signs. "Raven dropped from a tree on Mr. Killpenny and killed the man, probably with his own knife. Then he made off toward the next walk-across."

"Do you think he headed for the Little Islands?"

"That's the logical thing to do, so he probably went downstream, came out, and headed north again. He doesn't want to be far from you ... or me."

"Matthew, I ..."

"Let it go. Raven did this, you didn't. Do we take Killpenny home or to the fort?"

"Probably to the sheriff, although I don't relish the prospect," I said.

Matthew nodded over my shoulder. "Won't have to. There's a patrol."

He unsheathed his rifle and fired three shots into the air. The column across the river came to a halt, and then headed in our direction when we waved our hats. I was relieved to see Gideon leading the troop. They forded the river at a walk-across two hundred yards to our right and came up the bank to confront us.

Gideon looked over the body of the farmer as we explained what had happened. He speared me with his eyes.

"John, what's the matter with you? You knew that Cheyenne was wanted by the army as a deserter. How come you didn't bring him straight to the fort?"

My face went hot. "He'd just told me he'd shot Matthew. I didn't have time to take him to the fort. I had to go find my brother."

"So you just declawed him and set him loose." Gideon slapped his hat against his leg. "And Mr. Killpenny paid the piper."

Matthew jerked around to face him. "We told you Raven was back. Why didn't you do your job? You're just as responsible for Mr. Killpenny lying there as we are."

Gideon grimaced. "There's enough guilt to go around. My men will take the body to the fort, and I'll ride to inform his family."

42

I let my anger get loose. "No! I'll do it. And I'll tell it like it is."

"No, you're not," Matthew said, his voice firm. "I'm going to inform Mrs. Killpenny and Esau. You're riding to the Mead to let Min and Alex know."

"And I'll set after Raven," Gideon said. "As I recall, Mr. Killpenny rode a mule, is that right?"

"He had a paint mule he claimed was as good as any riding horse," Matthew said. "From the size of the hoof prints, I'd say that's what Raven's aboard right now."

Gideon sent one squad back across the river to look for tracks leading to the Little Islands and a second patrol northwest to the breaks on Trickling Water. The rest of Gideon's men loaded the body on Raven's horse and prepared to set off for the fort.

We took a moment to bring each other up to date. I congratulated the newly-minted captain on his engagement. He confided they'd had no luck running Howling Wolf's renegades to ground, making me wonder what would happen when Raven and Howling Wolf found one another, as they surely would if they continued to elude pursuit.

CHAPTER 7

I headed for my childhood home, traveling part of the way with Matthew. As he left the wagon track to cross the river to the Killpenny place, I tried again to accompany him. He rebuffed me. He was right, of course. Given my state of mind, I would have taken too much blame for the farmer's death.

When I rode into the Mead's yard at nightfall, my appearance caused a deal of surprise. Surprise soon turned into consternation as I delivered the tragic news. A shocked Min insisted on setting out for her parents' farm right away. Little Jacob and Hans remained behind under Ma's watchful eyes.

Matthew showed up later that night, and while he enjoyed the attention the family bestowed upon him, he was anxious to be on the hunt for Raven. Ma would have none of it. After a short, restless night, she put both of us to work, me in the forge and Matthew in the barn tending the spare stage team.

An alarm from Andre by way of one of our messenger pigeons drew us back to Turtle Crick the next day. His note informed us someone had been hanging around, and he was fearful the intruder would torch the cabin. We rode hard and got home at the edge of nightfall. I checked the house and barn while Matthew scouted for sign and went to look in on the Tillers. I found nothing amiss, and Matthew reported our neighbors were fine, as were Todoh and the cattle.

After a midnight meal, I moped over my "humanity" in giving Raven his life back. In truth, it had been pure squeamishness ... cowardice, if you will. I eyed Matthew and went weak in the vitals imagining him lying dead at the hands of the Cheyenne.

"Matthew ..."

"It's all right. We'll get the snake. I'm riding out of here tomorrow to make Raven think I've gone off on another trip. I'll circle around and set up camp in the grove north of us for the next few days. I'll sleep during the day and keep watch at night. Give him a nasty surprise when he shows up again."

I sighed and accepted his intent. "Can't make it for too long. We'll need to start harvesting soon."

"Raven won't be patient for long. He'll be back, if he isn't already nearby." Matthew hesitated. "John, he thinks you're afraid to kill him. You've had your chance, and you backed off. He'll have no fear of you now."

I dropped my gaze to the tabletop. "I'll not make that mistake again. Mr. Killpenny's already paid for my cowardice."

Fire lit Matthew's eyes. He came half out of his chair. "Quit that kind of talk. When you understand what you're fighting for you're as brave any

45

man as I know. You stood up to the army for me. You rode through a prairie fire for me. And when that army deserter shot me from the saddle, you fought him until he was dead. You're no coward." His lips softened. "But you're sure slow catching on sometimes."

"I didn't understand a man coveting another man could be deadly. By the nature of the thing, sex should be about love," I said.

"I don't doubt Raven set out with affection for you. But that changed when you rejected him. Rape is not about love. He seeks power over you. What perverseness drives him, I don't know. But it's there and it's strong. It dominates him and makes him as deadly as a rattlesnake."

"I understand now. If I get him in my sights again, I'll not hesitate to pull the trigger."

"I'll take that as a pledge and hold you to it." Matthew laid his fork on the empty plate in front of him. "There's enough trouble coming without Raven Strongbow. The tribes are restless, John. The army's getting aggressive about confining everyone to a reservation."

"Then why do you keep going back to one?"

"There are ways to leave. Especially one man."

"Yet it is a danger you need not court."

He sighed. "I'll never make you understand."

Yet, I did. At least, in the main. Just as I was drawn back to the Mead, he was drawn to his people, even though he had no close family ties with the Teton. If they were in danger, he wanted to help. Such was the man I had married.

For the next two days, I labored in the forge and the fields alone. I dared not travel the short mile north to the pine grove where Matthew sheltered during the day, yet I imagined him lying dead, the victim of Raven's treachery. I shook off the image. Matthew would not be so easily taken.

Thursday morning, I saw a column of smoke to the west. Concentrated, not dispersed like a wildfire. The farm five miles up Turtle Crick occupied by a widowed man named Stubblefield from down Texas way was likely aflame. Not long afterward, an army patrol passed south of the crick, heading in that direction.

Along about high sun, I noticed another tower of smoke rising well to the south. That looked to be old man Jepsen's farm. Matthew and I had faced him down years back and recovered Otter's war pony and Deere plow. Jepsen was undoubtedly one of James's and Otter's murderers, so he'd be no loss if these were renegade attacks. Howling Wolf's band? If so, he'd split into two groups. The raids were timed too closely together to have been the work of the same party.

Gideon paused his patrol at Turtle Crick on their return from the Stubblefield farm to report the Texan had been burned out but escaped with his life. The renegades were gone by the time Gideon and his men

46

arrived. He'd followed no more than ten raiders into the breaks country, but lost them there. So Howling Wolf had, indeed, split his band for the raids.

Then Gideon asked about Matthew.

"He's around. Been back for better than a week."

"I need to talk to him. Maybe he knows something about the raiders."

My spine went stiff. Was he implying something? "He went out hunting this morning. You want him to come find you when he gets back?"

Gideon frowned. "Probably be on patrol. There are several bands raiding in the area."

Like a fool, I stuck my nose in. "Actually, they're one band split into two to make it harder to catch them. It's the same group that shot up Teacher's Mead when we didn't give them ammunition. Crow will already have told you that."

"Matthew hasn't joined up with them, has he?"

His question drove me back a step. "No, he hasn't. He's out doing his best to run Raven to ground. Something you should have done."

"Matthew hasn't what?" My mate stepped around the corner of the house, leading Wind by the reins."

"Gone out with the renegades. Our almost brother-in-law thinks you're burning farms and killing farmers."

Red-faced, Gideon looked down from his cavalry horse. "I didn't say that. I just asked if he might be."

"Not sure you're ready to marry into the Strobaw family. You don't even know who we are," I said.

Gideon gave me a scorching glare and started to ride off. Matthew stopped him with a hand on Blackie's snout.

"Hold on. Let's not get crossways here. I don't know what John told you, but I've been hanging around out of sight trying to catch Raven if he makes another run at us ... or at the Tillers. Only came in because I saw the smoke. Figured a patrol might have come by, and John could let me know what's happening."

Gideon glanced at me. "Sorry if I stirred dirt in your honeypot, John. I do everything I can to let the army know the Strobaws and the Brandts aren't troublemakers. Best way to do that is to know where they are. Especially the menfolk."

Not convinced that was the whole truth, I nodded my head in acceptance of his apology. "Makes sense."

Matthew watched him ride away and then shook his head. "John, you are a wonder to me. Smartest man I know, but you let a killer walk out from under your gun sights, and then you pick a fight with a man who can do more for us than anybody else. Sometimes, I wonder if you don't have a warrior's heart after all, and you're itching to raise the hatchet."

He followed me into the forge, closed the door, and bent me over the anvil to fuck me until my fundament was sore.

47

Matthew gave up hanging out and trying to catch Raven by surprise, so the next day I rode into Yanube City for supplies while he kept watch on the farm. Halfway to town, I spotted a smudge of smoke far down river, which made me think of the Killpenny place. They'd had enough trouble with the death of their patriarch. Nobody had sent a message letting us know the arrangements, so we'd missed the old man's funeral.

I felt a change of atmosphere as soon as I entered the town's limits. Timo Bowers, the blacksmith, was friendly enough when I stopped by to jaw a little, but as I rode down Main Avenue later, the atmosphere was as thick as the smoke hanging over the upper reaches of the valley. Otter had often complained about dirty looks he'd gotten when Dull Lance was raiding and killing back when the militia was riding. That's what I felt now. Hostility. Toward Indians. Any Indians. Even one who'd grown up around them.

Sheriff Landreth, standing on the stoop of his office, gave me a good going over as I rode by. Caleb Brown at the Emporium treated me as usual, and I appreciated his genuine welcome. He sold me what I needed without a qualm. But when I went to the gun shop, I thought for a minute the Hawks brothers would balk at selling me the lead I wanted. The skin on my back didn't stop puckering until I was halfway home.

Matthew and I discussed the growing hostility in town and concluded there was little we could do about it. One thing worried me, perhaps more than it should. Winter Bird rode with Howling Wolf's renegades, and if he were caught, Gideon might remember him as the man I'd sheltered and nursed back to health. How would that cut with the military?

The ground beneath my feet started to feel slippery.

CHAPTER 8

Over the next few weeks, Matthew and I brought in a poorer harvest than anticipated. I could not explain it adequately, but it seemed that the volcanic eruption halfway around the world last summer had somehow affected our yield. Of course, that might not have been the entire story. Last winter – that of '82-'83 – had been colder than the prior year by a considerable measure, which made for a shorter growing season. By tasting the air, Matthew predicted this one would be harsh, as well.

With Todoh's help, we gathered the cattle from the free range and herded them into the hundred acres behind the worm fence in preparation for taking them to the sale barn later. The Thunderbird and Bear brand on the left flank of each animal still brought a thrill of pride, evidence – at least to my mind – that War Eagle and Shambling Bear were doing well.

Andre returned from town after delivering the combined reap from our two farms to Theo Tussler. Tussler Farm Products had bought our harvests for years, and while I anticipated no trouble from him, allowing Andre to do the haggling over prices seemed the prudent thing to do in view of the heightened resentment Howling Wolf's marauders had engendered. Despite our short reap and the financial depression that had hit the Northwest, our handsome neighbor returned with a combination of specie and bank drafts that made our work worth the effort. However, the sale of our cattle would be required to make it a profitable season.

Andre also brought other news. Two squads of cavalry had run Wolf's renegades to ground at their camp in the Little Islands. Almost caught them flat out, but not quite. The Indians ambushed one squad, but the other one came up behind them and scattered the renegades. Killed four of the Indians and wounded two more. The rest scattered and managed to get away.

"Captain Haleworthy figures that should break the back of the band," Andre finished the telling.

"You jawed with Gideon?" Matthew asked. "Was Raven with the raiders?"

"The Captain never saw hide nor hair of the Cheyenne. The medicine man who led the group skedaddled clean away, too."

"They'll slip back to the reservations and lick their wounds. Probably seen the last of the raiders until spring," my mate said.

Although I felt easier after that, I worried over the fate of Winter Bird. He was too likely a young man to wish a bad end. He didn't belong with the likes of Howling Wolf. When I spoke those thoughts to Matthew after Andre had departed, my husband flared.

"Who are you to decide who can fight for his people?"

Taken aback, I said that I merely feared for his safety.

49

"His hide is his to risk, not yours to protect." He snapped his mouth shut, but I could clearly hear the unspoken words ... "as is mine."

"Don't lecture me. I fret over him as I would you or Andre or anyone else of my acquaintance. Useless death and wanton destruction sicken me, Matthew."

He held his tongue until his flush passed. "Come with me to the reservations. Come and spend time among my ... among *your* people ... and say those words. You would choke on them."

The wall of ice between us did not thaw until we turned into bed that night. After a moment, he reached over and drew me to him.

"You are a reasoning man, and I am a feeling man," he said into my ear. "A reasoning man has got to have all the facts before he can make his conclusions. A feeling man just has to see what's there in front of him. What I see makes me afraid for our people. The white man wants us gone ... dead. And the best way to do that is to herd us together and pen us up just like those cattle in the pasture out yonder. If we feed the cattle, they survive. If we don't, they die after eating every weed in that hundred acres and chewing the bark off fence poles and trying to break out."

He sighed and rolled on his back. "The tribesmen are cattle in the white man's pasture. Sometimes he feeds them. Sometimes he doesn't. The Indian police think they're *akicita*, soldier societies keeping the peace. But they're no more than Todoh guarding the herd for their masters until it's time for the slaughter. The only difference is, we gotta keep the cattle healthy to lead them to their doom. The weaker the human herd is from hunger and disease, the easier it is for the whites."

As he fell silent, my intellect cried out that what he had said was not logical. Yet, I stilled my tongue. After all, what did I really know of the situation? Until a few years back, I had considered myself more or less white. Perhaps even a station above most whites because my family were landowners and educated. I blended two bloods equally and saw through the eyes of both. Surely, a superior position. It was not until Matthew was arrested and hauled away to Fort Robinson for trial as a renegade killer that I realized I was little different from any nameless tipi Indian in the eyes of the conquerors.

He spoke again out of the darkness. "While I was gone this summer, I took part in a big buffalo kill. Probably the last one there'll ever be." He stopped again to remember. "There were some whites with us. One of them was a man named Theodore Roosevelt. And they think we have funny names. He was looking to kill a big trophy bull, but he wasn't a bad sort. Different from most of his kind.

"Roosevelt told me some U. S. Senate bigwigs are trying to open part of the Lakota reservation to white settlers. Sitting Bull is fighting them, but they'll get it done." Matthew's bitter laugh cut through the room. "They pen us up, and then they reduce the size of the pasture."

I thought my mate had fallen asleep until he rose and returned from the eating room with a smear of butter. Without speaking, he tore away the covers, raised my legs, and about drove me insane playing with my fundament with his slick and slippery digits. Then he straddled my chest and placed his tumescent male member on my lips.

"Take my manhood, *wastelakapi*." He knew calling me beloved stirred my blood and drove me to great heights. I did not disappoint. With the fresh memory of his long, strong fingers probing my most private place, I took him to the root before vibrating my voice box and then expelling him slowly. That set off an excited assault of my mouth. The hardness of him, the clean, soapy smell of his curly bush, the weight of his silky bulk sliding over my tongue gave me as much pleasure as it did him.

I was near to coming without either of us touching my cock when he withdrew and placed his erection where his fingers had been minutes before. From his abrupt entry, he was rushing toward climax. Still, he held off, resting for a moment as he leaned down and kissed my lips. I imagined I heard the pounding of his blood match mine in that sweet moment. Then he fucked me. Hard. Brutally. Yet, with a volume of loving whispers as exciting as anything else he was doing.

He exploded deep inside me, froze for a moment, and then reached to bring me off. As soon as he wrapped his strong fist around me, I erupted, catching him by surprise. My seed gushed in a parody of that monstrous volcano that had blown away most of an island. And indeed, I felt as if a part of me had been blown away, as well. Matthew lifted a semen-drenched hand.

"Damnation, you were loaded for bear!"

"And I got one, too."

He roared with laughter and rolled over on the bed. I bestirred my weary self and cleaned us both with soap and water. As I patted him dry, he began to engorge again. I kissed the monster and told it that was all for tonight.

#####

There had been no further raiding and no sign of Raven when the time came to drive the cattle to Yanube City. Some ranchers drove herds right down Main Avenue, but something over 150 head, including the Tillers' animals, would have left the town a mess, so the four of us – Andre and Libby hazed right along with Matthew and me – came into the cattle barn from the west.

The era of long cattle drives to Dodge City has passed with the summer of '81. The Hagstone brothers, who owned the Yanube City Cattle Barn, had learned they came out ahead selling steers to the farms up and down the river. The brothers and their handlers showed no overt hostility to Matthew or me, but they preferred to do their bargaining with Andre, who took his cues from the nods and shakes of my head. When the trading was over, we came out with a decent price.

Matthew and Andre wanted to stop by the Rainbow House to celebrate, but an Indian likely wouldn't have been welcome, and Libby's dour glance put a halter on my neighbor. He did, however, go inside long enough to buy a couple of bottles for home consumption.

# # # # #

There was work to be done the next morning despite villainous bowels and heaving stomachs. I did not fare too badly since strong drink sickens me quickly. Hence, I did not imbibe beyond a cup or two. Andre and Matthew had no such strictures placed upon them and celebrated far beyond my capacity. While the two of them stumbled around trying to toss horseshoes and pitching over into the dirt, Libby grew disgusted with the entire thing and went home, taking Todoh with her for company. The dog, at loose ends with no charges to guard, was happy to go with his playmate.

The result was that I was past my queasy gut by the time the sun rose over the horizon while the other two were in the full grip of Lady Alcohol's revenge. I was not the most popular man in the cabin when I roused them to consciousness from where they slumped over the eating table snoring out of sequence and in discord. Neither a pretty picture, nor a harmonious melody.

I don't know about Libby, but I got little out of Matthew that day. Still ill, he eschewed dinner that evening. I ate gustily, and then spent a pleasant evening reading from a book of poetry by Robert Browning. After perusing "Porphyria's Lover," I considered strangling him, although I didn't possess convenient long golden tresses to go around his neck. But when we went to bed, the poet's "Love Among the Ruins" inspired me to crawl atop him and fuck his manly belly. His groan was most assuredly not one of ecstasy.

CHAPTER 9

Hard on the heels of a mediocre crop, the winter of '83-'84 came roaring up. Matthew and I always saved a host of indoor tasks such as mending clothing and repairing leather gear for the winter months. Sensing the length and severity of the winter, we went easy on our store of firewood and other fuels, preferring an extra layer of wool across our backs to throwing a spare log on the fire. We also nursed our supply of peat to keep a modicum of heat in the outhouse for our animals' wellbeing.

Early in the cold season is a time for lovemaking and rediscovering things about one another. Later, the winter is for fucking and trying to stay out of one another's way. I wondered if this was how other couples lived. While truly and deeply in love, before the season ended we were filled to the gullet with enforced intimacy, yet I did not remember ever being sated with my lover's proximity during seasons not piled high with frigid snow. I put it down to human nature.

When we got onto one another's nerves too much, we strapped on rackets or snowshoes – each had his own name for them – and ventured out into a blinding white landscape. Yet, as Matthew was fond of pointing out, that white expanse held an amazing range of colors ... blues, greens, dark shadows, even a rose when sunrise hit the snow just right.

Wolves, not normally a problem, followed game driven down from the Canadian territories by bitter cold and lack of forage. At night, they prowled the yard and scratched at the barn doors. Todoh growled at their appearance while sharing the house with us but howled boldly when he was locked in the outhouse with Arrow and Wind and the trace mare.

As if we were in the grip of a new ice age, this winter proved harsher than the last one, which had been more severe than the prior year. The cold that descended upon us ultimately became known as Starvation Winter. Almost 600 *Sihaspa* on the Blackfeet Reservation in Montana died of cold and starvation in camps near the Old Agency.

The Blackfeet, a warlike confederacy that extended up into Canada had been among the last to brook the interference of the Americans. The agency man under whose care they had been given had a well-known reputation for selling off provisions intended for his charges. No wonder then that every blood in the territory refused to believe the whites failed to realize their desperate straits. After the facts were known, the civilized people marveled that savage Indians had died rather than molest cattle whites illegally grazed on reservation lands.

Although they came late, mighty spring winds blew the winter away and the season of rebirth claimed the land. The Moon of the Red Grass succeeded the Moon of the Snow-blind as March slid into April. Despite the glorious, lengthening days, the sunlight was yet filtered. Would the Indonesian volcano affect the coming growing season, as well?

A poor crop foretells higher prices, and this new year of 1884 was no stranger to this concept. Fortunately, we had held over seed for most of our planting, else we would have needed to delve into our carefully hoarded store of spare gold and silver coins – and might still have to do so when it came time to buy steers.

Todoh kept us company during most of the planting, but would occasionally abandon the farm to go hunting varmints on his own or to sneak away to play with Libby. Andre's daughter was fourteen now and worked beside him in the fields, but she could always find time for our errant Blue Heeler.

In the midst of the planting, a gray pigeon arrived from Teacher's Mead with a message saying everyone had survived the winter in good form. It also let us know my sister Hannah had advantaged a traveling Methodist minister to marry Esau Killpenny. If I read things correctly, Mrs. Killpenny had practically gone into her dotage upon the death of her husband, and my little sister now had the responsibility for running the household. No doubt she was capable of handling it successfully, but I hoped this thing was not merely one of economic convenience and that the new couple held a modicum of love between them.

Not being present for their nuptials stung a little, perhaps made a little sharper by missing Rachel Ann's and Gideon's wedding a few weeks earlier. I'd not stood alongside when any of my siblings wed. Nor, of course, had they been present when I took Bear as my mate.

Although his fiddle foot was beginning to twitch, Matthew remained at the farm until we bought our steers in early May. Crop failures had been more widespread than thought, so many of the small ranches in the area couldn't afford to buy calves. So in this sense, the thing rebounded to our benefit. I was able to purchase 175 steers with the funds put aside from the sale of last year's cattle. Andre bought fifteen and immediately put them under Todoh's care.

More weeks passed as we went about plying our Thunderbird and Bruin brand and castrating the male calves. Finally, the day arrived I knew was coming.

"Think I'll visit the Pine Bluff Agency," Matthew said one morning over coffee at the breakfast table.

"Isn't it too dangerous?"

He fluttered a hand, dismissing my worries. "I'll be careful. I want to see if I can sniff out Raven's trail. See if he's resurfaced. You've got a handle on the farm and the cattle now."

I sighed my resignation. "Todoh and I can handle things. When will you leave?"

"Tomorrow morning. Anything I need to do before I leave?"

"Nothing other than fuck me near to death."

"I plan on doing that tonight," he said.

"I ought to give Wind new shoes before you take off."

"He'd appreciate it."

The day passed with few words between us even though we remained in close proximity. He helped me fit Wind with new horseshoes before checking his gear and calling in Todoh to spend a little time with him. The dog sensed what was coming and practically ignored me to spend his time wrestling with Matthew. Except he wasn't Matthew any longer. He was Shambling bear, a twenty-six-year-old Teton warrior in his prime.

And that night, he confirmed in a very physical way how potent his powers were. We were no sooner in bed than he reached for me.

"I will miss you," he murmured into my mouth as his lips teased mine.

"And I you. Sometimes when you leave, I don't think I can stand it."

Conversation died as he sucked my tongue into his mouth. Then he pushed me down his body. No clothing inhibited us. We slept naked as soon as the weather allowed. My tongue slid down his taut, smooth skin. He tasted fresh and clean. I took my time reaching his loins. His manhood jutted hard and thick into the air, a dew drop of moisture already wetting the end of it. I steadied him with my hand and pulled back his foreskin to run my tongue around the satiny glans.

He endured it as long as he could, and then pushed me down on him with a groan. I opened my maw and took him clear to the root. His massive bulk nearly dislocated my jaw, but I held him there, vibrating my throat in the manner he liked so much. Then I came out to the end, moistened my tongue, and rode down him again. His fingers played in my hair as I set up a rhythm. I expected him to stop me before orgasm, but his body went taut, and I felt the force of his explosion against the roof of my mouth as he came. He threw his legs across my butt and shivered and shook for an inordinately long time.

"*Wastelakapi*," he moaned. "Beloved."

I tongued him until he began to soften. Only then did he pull me up to meet his lips in a tender kiss. After a long moment, he rolled me over until he rested atop me, giving me a warm, safe feeling. One which turned to ecstasy when he slipped down to suckle my nipples, each in turn. Then his tongue invaded my navel. I gasped when he slid lower and kissed the tip of my erection before slipping me into his mouth.

He did this only rarely and was not as expert at it as I, but he sent me to that place the real Indians – the *East* Indians – called Nirvana. I was a mindless, boneless puddle of pudding awash in electrical currents by the time I finished my orgasm. I doubtless could have made one of Mr. Edison's light bulbs glow had I held it in my mouth.

Giving me no respite, he flipped me over and inserted his reinvigorated tool to deliver the fucking of my life. He kept at it until I squirmed and wiggled beneath his hard body, coming to climax as he shot semen into my fundament.

He lay atop me for the better part of the night.

#####

Todoh shared my sense of loss as we watched Wind Rider disappear down the south side of the crick as he bore my mate westward. I kept the dog with me in the forge for a bit before sending him back to the range to guard the steers.

A fortnight after Bear's departure, when the Moon of Good Cherries or June had just arrived, Todoh set up a howl in the distance. Howling was the voice he used to warn of strangers, usually, although not always humans. I dropped my hoe where I stood and grabbed my Henry from the porch before mounting the stubby knoll behind the cabin for a 360 degree view of the countryside. Todoh and most of the cattle were west northwest of me. I saw no sign of intruders, but in the far distance, the dog made a series of darts to the east. His way of letting me know whoever it was lay in a small ha-ha that stretched between him and the shaded glade a mile north of me where Otter and Bear's mother and brother lay.

I backed down the hill a pace or two and sat down to await the appearance of whoever or whatever had excited the blue's interest. A stray antelope would be appreciated; a stray human might not be. Eventually, a lone horseman topped the rise and pulled to a halt, waiting. I recognized the gray gelding and stood to give a wave of my hand. Winter Bird lifted his arm in response and kicked his mount forward.

My friend looked no worse for having lived as a renegade last year. He was thin, but as clear-eyed and handsome as ever. After our greetings, he let me know he'd broken out of the reservation alone to forage for his family. The poor crop harvest last year had made provisions for the reservation more valuable to the agent; therefore, he sold more of them to others. I sighed inwardly. Given his nature, Bear would likely try to do something to alleviate the situation for his kinsmen. I hoped that did not include raiding.

After he accepted my invitation to overnight, I called Todoh to accustom him to the stranger's appearance and smell. Bird instantly transformed into a fetching child. He threw sticks and ran hopeless races against the excited animal. Before I sent the dog back to his station, they even wrestled around on the porch with sometimes Bird and sometimes Todoh on top.

Once the dog was gone, Bird reclaimed his dignity. He tried to help me in the fields, although he had no farming skills. After he chopped down two healthy corn stalks by mistake, I sent him to feed the horses.

When we paused for pemmican and cold milk from Andre's cow sometime after high sun, he chatted about friends and family at home as if they were familiars of mine. My initial fondness for the young man grew into friendship. If I were honest, I'd admit his trim hips, narrow waist, and flaring rib cage hastened my liking of the man. He was altogether comely.

Before the sun slipped into its brilliant setting plumage, we prepared the *Okinare* and stripped naked for a medicine bath. As we allowed the sweat to strip the dirt and grime of the day's labors away, Bird revealed a lively curiosity, asking questions about the purpose of the farm tasks we had done. As he talked, I tried to keep my eyes from his well-endowed groin, even though he eyed me frankly from time to time.

The jump into the melted ice that filled the crick to its brim – runoff had come late this year, as well – nearly froze my heart into stopping. Bird gave a yelp and submerged himself to wash away the clean sweat raised by the heated rocks in the lodge. I did the same, and then raced him for the warmth of the cabin. We laughed as we shivered through the toweling that raised a modicum of heat within our systems. Then we huddled in blankets and stared at one another until I broke the tension.

"We will need a meal before retiring."

"Jerky will do."

"Nay, I have a stew on the stove. A few minutes will bring it ready. Tell me, do you read the white man's language?"

He waggled his hand back and forth. "I can make out some of the words and little of the sense."

"We live in a white man's world. You should learn as much about him as you can."

"This is true. It might help take our land back from him."

I swallowed the urge to preach. My young friend would never accept the truth simply from my giving voice to it. Only the blunt force of violence would convince him of that. I prayed he would not be slain in the process of learning the bitter lesson. I confined myself to saying that learning was good, whatever the aim of it. He listened with interest when I broke out one of Mr. Poe's books and read a story from it.

Winter Bird offered to throw his blankets by the stove, but I invited him into my sleeping room. Although I am convinced I had no ulterior motive in doing so, I found myself aroused by the warmth of the body lying next to me. I had almost achieved slumber when his hand brushed my groin. Wide awake again, I froze. Perhaps the touch had been accidental, but after a long moment, he muttered two words.

"*Tanka. Suta.* Big. Hard."

I swallowed with difficulty and forced the words through my throat. "Mayhap I have misled you, my friend. Shambling Bear is my mate, my Other Self."

Likely embarrassed, he started to rise. "I will sleep by the stove."

"Nay. We will sleep here as friends, nothing more."

He settled back and muttered something that sounded like an apology.

The hours passed slowly for me. From the sound of his breathing, Winter Bird had flown quickly away to the Land of Slumber.

The morning brought no unpleasantness or awkward moments. Without vocal expression, I believe we both understood that absent my devotion to my mate, we would have welcomed one another's touch. The fact he honored my love for Bear made him a bigger man than Raven Strongbow, who had chosen to ignore it and press himself upon me.

After I invited him into my cold room in the cellar beside the house to pick out some supplies for his family, he worked the fields with me for another day before taking his departure the following morning. Astride his gray, he fixed his stare on my left earlobe as he asked how I could be a man of peace in the midst of such misery.

"Because I see with eyes that show me what is, not what I want it to be."

"But your own Spirit Dream tells you trouble is coming."

"And I can do nothing to stand in its way. But I do what I can. I help my brothers when they come. I will not risk what I have for them, yet I give what I can."

A smile built across his features, stretching his lips, creasing his cheeks, lighting his eyes. "You are much man, *Hin Phejuta*. I think your prowess is squandered as a win-tay."

He turned his gelding to skirt the hill behind the house, leaving me panting at the hint of the role he would be willing to play. Yet, even then the manly image of Matthew Brandt, Shambling Bear, rose in my mind to fill me with love and chase away thoughts of betrayal.

CHAPTER 10

On my first trip to town in the spring, I passed a sign reading, "Yanube City, Pop ~~1760~~, ~~1737~~, 1702" Puzzled over the crude, hand-lettered changes, I stopped to visit the town's blacksmith and farrier. Timo Bowers was a good source of gossip.

The smith had been the first man to touch me back when I had but eighteen summers. I'd been apprenticing with him, and on my last night there, he entered my darkened sleeping room and put his mouth to me. After I delivered my seed, he departed without uttering a word. This morning, he made sense of the altered town limit sign. Some of the settlement's population, especially Sesesh settlers from the south, were pulling out to seek warmer climes in Texas or returning home. The long depression was taking a toll on the town.

Timo had no other worthy news, so I left for Brown's Emporium to pick up supplies. I was near to self-sustaining at the farm, but there were a few things I bought rather than fashioned.

As I rode down Main Avenue, I encountered little of the hostile, frightened looks I'd garnered last summer. A long winter without depredations had eased the townsfolk's anxieties about Indians. The yin and yang of inflation and crop failures had given the good citizens of Yanube City more pressing worries than a lone tribesman riding down the street. Other than the military post, there was little to sustain the growth of the town beyond the farms and small ranches stretching up and down the river. Mayhap the entire populace would pull up stakes. No, the hard fact was they'd never cede this territory to its rightful owners.

The moment I set foot inside the big department store that occupied an entire block on Main opposite the Rainbow House and the Swinging Door Saloon, Caleb Brown, the proprietor, appeared and shook my hand.

"John, I've been wanting a word with you. Will you join me in my office?"

I followed him upstairs to a closet-sized room holding his desk, what looked to be an upright chest for his papers, two chairs, and little else. One window faced out onto the upstairs salesroom with its racks and counters of denim clothing, bolts of cloth, pails and rakes, and a collection of goods that almost defied description. A second pane of glass gave a view of the stairway and the main entrance to the store downstairs. Both admitted a little light, but it required a lamp's glow to see well, and that made the small room stuffy. Caleb seated me in a hard, sturdy chair opposite his desk and offered a drink, which I declined. Strong spirits clog my stomach and fool with my head.

The merchant came right to the point, which is the single advantage of speaking to a white man. I've spent many an hour discussing nothing of real interest before some Indian decided he'd been polite enough to ask for what he wanted.

"I sense an opportunity for both of us," he opened. "And coincidentally, it might favor your kinsmen out on the reserves, as well. I've heard stories of hunger and deprivation."

I knew – not from his telling but from sources on the reservations – Caleb occasionally sent goods to be distributed either at his cost or for free. I knew of no one else who cared enough to undertake this sort of generosity.

"There is a demand for certain Indian goods back east. Things like lances, bows, arrows, quivers, native-made blankets, drums, rattles, flutes. And war bonnets, especially war bonnets.

I laughed. "Those are ceremonial and seldom worn. Usually, they're treasured pieces of a family's past, handed down from father to son."

He took a sip from his glass. "You and I know that, but folks back east think every brave wears one, especially when making war. The public is fascinated by Indians. They fear a tribesman mindlessly yet covet things he crafts and uses."

"They've coveted him out of his land," I said with a bitter bite.

"Yes, and that's a tragedy. One I don't see being set right in my lifetime. But if people are willing to pay, perhaps we should see they have the opportunity to spend their money."

"Is this the time for such an undertaking? Things seem hard right now. I saw people leaving in wagons packed with their worldly goods as I rode into town."

"True, crop failures and the depression have hit us hard, but it's not so desperate all over. I have contacts back east who have asked me to find a source of such items."

I mimicked my grandfathers and sat in silence for a period of time considering Caleb's proposition. The more I thought on it, the more I believed the idea had merit. I could see no harm and perhaps some benefit. No Indian would sell his family treasures, not when he could fashion something new to sell to the white man. To be an Indian was to be a trader. It might work.

So I struck a business bargain with Caleb Brown just as my putative grandfather, Billy Strobaw, had once done with this man's uncle. Billy and the original Caleb Brown had entered the beaver trade together over fifty years ago.

I spent the entire seven miles back to the farm thinking about what I'd just committed to do. I would buy the articles from natives and had an option to receive payment upon delivery for a small mark-up or receive half my money back and share in any profits equally. Rachel Ann and Hanna were both blood and capable of making things like dolls and toys and womanly things. But the most coveted items would doubtless be more warlike in nature.

Mark Wildyr

A week later, a wandering tribesman stopped to beg some jerky. Upon learning he was on the way to Pine Ridge, I gave him provisions in exchange for delivering a message to Winter Bird, whom he claimed as a kinsman. He also promised to give the same message to Shambling Bear if he saw him. The message was simple: "Need to see you soonest. Bring lances, bows, knives, headdresses, etc. Will explain when I see you."

Then I returned to working my farm and firing up the forge for things Andre or Libby or I needed. Between these chores, I showed my face out on the range to visit Todoh and his herd of cattle. The dog handled the larger number of animals as well as he had last year's charges. He worked hard to limit the beasts range, allowing them to stray farther and farther from the farm only when they exhausted forage in the immediate vicinity.

He joined me in the saddle, riding on my lap as we checked the steers, pausing occasionally to examine a limping calf or a scabbed wound. When necessary, he would help me throw a skittish animal by grabbing a switching tail and hanging on, careful to dodge flying hooves, while I twisted the steer's head until he went down. After medicating whatever had caught my attention, we'd both let go and allow the aggrieved animal to lumber to its feet and trot away.

My next visitor not the one I was expecting. In the stead of Winter Bird, Howling Wolf showed up with fully a score of men on a Wednesday at mid-morning. They came in from the east, so I had little warning. Todoh was far to the northwest and had not been disturbed by the riders. I experienced the same sense of irritation Pa had exhibited when the medicine man had led his party through the Mead. A careful examination of the group as they trailed single file down the north bank of the crick told me Bird was not among them.

I stood on the porch so as to be at a height with the Brulé medicine man perched on his palomino. I confess a prickling of the skin at the sight of him. He seemed a thoroughly unpleasant man, although his horse was as attractive as ever. We exchanged open-handed greetings.

"How are things with you, Medicine Hair?" His voice was courteous enough.

"Passing," I replied. "Are you raiding or foraging?"

"Some of both. I am here to collect the levy of beef you agreed to last year. Once the steers are safely on the way, we will make the Americans feel our presence."

"It is not a levy, Howling Wolf. It was something I volunteered to help my people. I'll honor my word, but I counsel on waiting. The animals are not yet heavy enough to provide much food."

"It is more than our families have now. So we will take them."

61

"You will take them when I say so. But I will strike a bargain. Take three of the animals now, and I'll provide three – not two – additional beeves when they have put on more weight."

Judging from the deep frown puckering his dark face, not many stood up to Wolf. But after considering the matter, he nodded.

"I will go with you to select the animals, so my dog does not stampede your horses." My attempt at humor did not sit well. "But first, let me say again, my neighbor to the west is not to be molested. Nor is the fortress at Teacher's Mead." I used the word "fortress" apurpose, to remind him there were many rifles to protect the farm and the Jacobsen place adjacent to it.

As I stepped from the porch on the way to the barn, I removed my hat and ran fingers through my hair. A ripple went through the warriors. My speckled head would likely be the making or the breaking of me one of these days.

Todoh was distressed by the presence of so many strangers, and once again, I had to coax him up into the saddle with me to ride among his charges. Howling Wolf chose three animals, but I ignored him and chose three different ones. He couldn't be allowed to feel he was in control of the situation. Actually, the animals I chose carried more weight than his selections.

Once two of his party were herding the three calves toward the breaks along Trickling Water, I sought to ease things by asking about conditions on the reservations. He painted a grim picture of hunger and misery. There had been a baker's dozen die over the winter from freezing and starvation.

Howling Wolf unbent enough to tell me he had seen Shambling Bear four or five suns back. My mate had seemed to be in good health, although despondent over conditions he found. Of Winter Bird, he had no news.

Before he took his leave, I tackled a ticklish situation head·on in the full hearing of his party. To reinforce the shaky authority of my unearned reputation, I removed my hat and spoke more animatedly than usual in order to make the sun catch and blaze in the yellow hair hiding among the black on my scalp.

"Howling Wolf, it does not serve any of us well for you to bring a score of men to the farm. I am of no value to your people if the Americans consider me either a renegade or a supporter of your raiding. It would be better to come with a small party the next time you visit."

The man did not respond. He merely lifted his hand in a casual farewell and rode away, heading east, where he likely planned on fording the river and setting up a stronghold in the Little Islands to plan his coming raids. I immediately sent a pigeon to the Mead to let Pa know trouble was coming.

Winter bird rode up on the south bank of the crick leading a pack horse the next day. He gave a great smile and shouted a greeting as the two animals thumped across my wooden bridge. I helped him care for his horses, placing them in stalls with a full feed trough and ample water. He stowed two heavy packs in the corner of the barn and then settled with me on the porch for a drink of water.

Bird was old-fashioned enough to indulge in the small-talk ritual, speaking a little of riding with Howling Wolf last year. He'd had a near miss during the battle in the Little Islands with the cavalry. He showed me the healed scar where a bullet grazed his left arm and told of nearly being captured. He'd escaped that fate by sending his gray gelding wading down a small crick to the east, away from the direction the soldiers expected him to run. He'd made his way home to the reservation alone.

Finally, I stood on the edge of the porch and whistled for Todoh. The beast hit the porch at speed and almost tumbled Bird from his chair. The next five minutes were given over to play-wrestling between the two.

Once I sent the blue back to the range, I explained the Yanube City merchant's plan.

"Your white friend ain't the first to come up with this idea," Bird said as we headed for the barn to sort through his packs. "The Indian agent's got somebody picking up things for him."

Bird had brought short bows, quivers, and arrows, as well as flint knives with beaded and fringed sheaths, scrapers, a few headbinds, and one buffalo-horned headdress. He'd also brought several pairs of moccasins.

When we started bargaining over prices, I learned I'd been right. Bird was a trader. We arrived at what he would pay the owners for the items, and I added ten percent to that for his benefit. He had only a loose concept of what that was, so I showed him how to calculate the sum by removing the figure at the right of the column. Bird was elated at the weight of the silver and copper coins when I paid him.

After a night of tossing restlessly, my thoughts constantly turning to the handsome young man sleeping in the other room beside the stove, I dressed Bird in some of my white man's clothes. Distracted by the depression or not, white folks might not be ready for the sight of a nearly naked Indian in a flap, and I wanted him to go with me to meet Caleb Brown.

The merchant was pleased by the goods we brought and reviewed the prices I'd paid for each item. Despite a frown over the cost of the headdress, Caleb declared himself satisfied and told Bird what he would like for his next run. As expected, the list was heavily slanted toward war items. While Winter Bird prowled the two floors of the store, I closeted with Caleb to finalize our agreement. I elected to receive half my funds up front and then the second half upon receipt of the sale to the merchants back east plus half of the profits.

When I went back downstairs, I discovered how clever a trader Bird was. He had purchased a number of items, metal utensils mostly, to give to his providers. Doubtless he gained a penny here and lost one there.

Still, I knew I was trading with a man who would deal fairly with his people.

Upon our return to the farm, we heated some rocks and indulged in a medicine bath. Our physical attraction to one another already revealed, we both had erections before we worked up a good sweat.

He eyed me sharply before fixing his stare on my left earlobe. "If this is too painful, I'll leave. I know it ain't gonna be, but I sure do want you."

I swallowed hard. "If I weren't married to Shambling Bear, I'd accept you, Bird." My sweat glands opened, and moisture rushed down me like a cataract. All of it wasn't from the heated stones. Some of it carried the odor of excited perspiration.

"I know. But I'm glad you don't get your back up when I look at you. It's a pleasure just to see you. To know you." He swiped sweat from his eyes and went on before I could answer. "But I'm here whenever you need ... uh, want me."

It was an odd thing to hang upon a hard-bodied, battle-bloodied Sioux warrior – and certainly nothing I would say to any brave's face lest violent reaction be provoked. Nonetheless, one of Ma's expressions leapt from my childhood to ring in my ears. "What a sweet man he was."

CHAPTER 11

Columns of smoke announced the commencement of Howling Wolf's raids the morning Bird set out for home. The Brulé apparently had split his force into several smaller bands. Four distinct smudges rose into the cloudless blue sky: a fire far to the east, answered by one to the south, near the Little Islands, and one virtually at the edge of Yanube City. The black cloud rising from west of Andre's looked to be the Stubblefield place again. The burly widower was probably finished this time ... if he hadn't perished in defense of his property.

A squad of cavalry passed south of the crick at high morning, too late to be of any aid to the Texan, although I worried Bird's passage near the farm would be noted and misunderstood. I was in the loft of the barn retrieving a gray pigeon from the cote with Pa's reply to my warning when I heard a number of horses approaching on the north side of the crick. I sneaked a quick look at the message, which cautioned me not to reveal any contact with Wolf's band, and then scampered down the ladder to greet my guests, the squad returning from Stubblefield's farm. To my relief, Gideon led the patrol.

"Trouble?" I asked.

"Hell's broke out all over. They wiped Stubblefield out. Chased him off and emptied out his stores then burned everything. He's lucky they didn't take his scalp. We tracked them to Trickling Water where they entered the crick. No telling which way they headed from there." He removed his campaign cap and rubbed his scalp. Sweat glistened off his fair skin. I noticed a heavy circlet on his right ring finger. "They've hit at least four farms so far. Must be a hundred of the bastards."

"More like twenty, I'd guess. That's how many showed up here the other day."

My brother-in-law shot me a sharp look. "They were here?"

"It's most likely the same group that came by. They were foraging for provisions for their families, and I donated three steers."

"You know who they were?"

"The same bunch that shot up the Mead last year."

"Howling Wolf? Be careful. He's a snake. They might take after this place before it's over."

"They were looking for ammunition at the Mead, and Pa didn't give them enough for a good hunt, much less a battle. That made them mad. They were after provisions from me, and I shared."

Gideon straightened in the saddle. "Don't feed them, John. Don't give them any provisions at all."

"I do that, they'll kill or drive off the whole herd. As it is, I give them a few head and keep the rest of my cattle. They've got some respect for me because Otter's shadow still hangs over this place. That and we share some blood." I didn't see the need to explain the power my hair represented to the tribesmen, but Gideon had already tumbled to that.

"That speckled head of yours might come in useful after all." He was tired. It showed on his features. "Keep an eye on the Tillers. They don't have that protection."

"Howling Wolf knows I'll come shooting if they hit his place."

"Hope you know what you're doing."

"I'll be careful." I nodded to his hand. "I see you have your West Point ring back."

Soon after he'd been assigned to Fort Yanube, Gideon had lost his ring to Matthew in a wager on a horserace. I'd not seen it since ... until today.

He lifted his right fist and glanced at the ring. "Matthew sent it to the Mead by one of the pigeons with a note it was a wedding gift. Cuthan gave it to me the last time I was there. Generous of Matthew. I figured he'd traded it years ago."

I watched Gideon's patrol almost out of sight on its way back to the fort before digging out the message from Pa and reading it again. I'd ignored his advice for two reasons. I'd seen the Mandan scout eyeing a few tracks left over from Wolf's visit. Gideon would have known soon enough I'd had visitors. Plus, I wanted to be open and honest with him. He was the only man inside Fort Yanube kindly disposed toward us.

Andre showed up on Gideon's heels. He'd started the mile trek with his daughter in tow, but I saw her out playing with Todoh.

"You think I oughta board Libby with the minister's wife in town?" he asked right off the handle.

"Your decision, not mine. Howling Wolf promised to leave both of us alone, but I don't know how long that will last."

"You put any stock in his word?"

I paused. "Some. If the blood lust gets too high, his warriors might forget about his promise. But I think he keeps them under control." Clearly, my neighbor wasn't satisfied, so I went on. "Andre, do you know what they call me?"

"War Eagle, if I remember right."

"I have a new name. Medicine Hair."

His glance went to my head. He grimaced. "So my daughter's safety hangs by a hair?"

"A hair's pretty strong. If you weave enough of them together, you have a rope."

Actually, I was pretty sure my protection would hold with Howling Wolf, but there was that other thing. Libby was on the cusp of becoming a woman, and some randy warrior's carnal lust might overtake his fear of retribution. Although neither of us gave voice to these thoughts, I suspected his mirrored my own.

"Why can't they just let us be? I don't bother them none."

My temper rose, but I swallowed it. "Take a trip to the reservations ... any of them ... and then ask me that. They're starving, man."

"So are some of ours. Hell, there's people leaving Yanube City every day because they can't support their families."

"Yes, I saw it with my own eyes on my trip to town. But that's the difference, Andre. My people are penned up under guard on the reservation. They can't leave and go find a better place. They have to stay put and starve."

"But the government provides them with everything they need. They're better off than we are."

I hadn't realized until then that's exactly what most Americans believed. What a deal the savages had. Give up a little land and get taken care of for the rest of their lives. Yeah, until they froze or starved to death or died of some white man's disease.

I steadied my voice. "That's true. Unless the provisions the army sends are short. Or don't arrive at all. Or have gone rotten. Or aren't sold to outsiders by the Indian Agent. Or they aren't shot by some settler for trying to steal a calf to feed hungry families."

Andre flushed. "Sorry. Didn't mean to stir you up. It's just that ..."

"I know your wife and two sons were killed by renegades. But I also know that Dull Lance lost two wives and children to the Americans before he ever laid eyes on you. Doesn't make it right, but maybe puts a little perspective on it."

Andre studied Libby and Todoh playing in the distance. "Will the hate ever go away?"

"Not as long as people are penned up on reservations and starving to death."

He turned sad eyes on me. "I expect we'll be pining for snow squalls before the summer's done."

"I think you're right."

# # # # #

Things settled down a bit for the next two weeks. I saw evidence of fires far to the east, which made me anxious over the Mead, and especially the Jacobsen place. I sent a white pigeon streaking east with a request for news. A gray bird showed up the next day informing me the Killpenny place had been attacked, but Esau and Hannah and Widow Killpenny had holed up in the cabin and fought the renegades off.

Pa and Alex had set out as soon as they saw smoke rising, but when they arrived, the cavalry was already there. They took shots from the troopers until Esau and Hannah were able to explain who they were.

The raiders had fired the outhouses and tried to set the crops ablaze. The fields were too green to burn, but my sister and her husband lost all their fodder for the farm animals. Almost as a footnote, Pa informed me one of the raiders had been killed, and Esau was certain they'd winged at least two others.

How could I have been so stupid as not to warn Howling Wolf clear of my brother-in-law's farm? Well, he and Hannah had delivered their own warning. I was willing to bet my sister – still little more than a girl to my mind – had drawn her share of blood in the fray.

I stayed clear of town as much as possible because of raids throughout the summer. Teacher's Mead, my boyhood home, regularly received news of the outside world by stagecoaches that stopped there twice a week, but Turtle Crick had no such connection. Andre went back and forth a few times, either bringing Libby over to stay with me or taking her with him on the seven-mile trip to town. Upon his return, he usually stopped by to share news.

One interesting bit he related was that the man who'd been with Matthew on his last buffalo hunt had come to Dakota Territory, apparently to stay. According to Andre, Theodore Roosevelt's mother and wife had both died on the same day last February, just two days after his wife delivered their only child, a daughter named Alice. Roosevelt – I took the name to be of Dutch origin – must come from a wealthy New York family, as he was said to have purchased the Elkhorn Ranch in the northern Badlands country. I wondered if Matthew knew. He had apparently liked the American.

During high summer, another visitor brought disturbing news. One of the army's scouts, the Mandan called Sharp Eyes, showed up alone and spent an hour on my porch drinking coffee before he told me Winter Bird was in the fort's guardhouse. A patrol had intercepted him west of the Stubblefield place leading two pack horses carrying weapons. The lieutenant in charge arrested him as being a part of Howling Wolf's raiders. Bird protested that the renegades were armed with rifles and short guns, not the bows and lances he was carrying, but his reasoning had fallen on deaf ears.

I accompanied Sharp Eyes back to the fort but decided my word would carry no weight. When Gideon, the only officer who might have listened to my plea, proved to be on patrol, I went into town and informed Caleb Brown of events. Together we secured an audience with the fort commandant, Lt. Colonel Dabney Irons, the same man who had sent Matthew in chains to Fort Robinson back in September of '79.

Irons, a thickset man made even thicker by the passage of time, had managed promotion from the rank of Major, but he was well over fifty now, so I imagined he would end his career at Fort Yanube. He apparently thought so as well, as his disposition had not improved. He was courteous to Caleb as the leading merchant in town but dismissive of me.

Caleb explained our mission. Irons heard him out and then seemed to retreat inside himself to think.

"All right," he said at length. "I'll not press charges as being a part of the murdering bastards who're killing and raiding up and down the valley."

Caleb stood. "Good. If you'll do what is necessary, we'll take him and his horses with us as we leave."

"You'll do no such thing. You can have the horses and packs, but the Sioux stays right where he is."

Caleb dropped back into his chair. "Why? I've explained things to you."

The officer's eyes slid over to fix on me. "He's a tribesman caught outside of the reservation where he's been assigned. Under War Department standing orders, he is therefore declared a hostile."

"But I induced this man to leave the reservation on a perfectly legitimate endeavor. You can't hold this against him."

Irons stood, obviously indicating the meeting was at an end. Caleb would have none of it.

"Dabney, you can be such a damned martinet sometimes. I demand the release of my employee. Upon the conclusion of our business, he's returning straight to the reserve."

"My hands are tied. Those are my orders."

"Do I have to go to Bismarck with this?" Caleb asked.

The Territory's capital had been moved from Yankton to Bismarck last year.

"I don't answer to the Governor. I'm army, not a damned militia man."

"Col. Irons," Caleb's voice got tight. "I don't want to start a war with you or the U.S. Army, but right is right. This man you're holding has done nothing wrong. If he technically violated one of your blessed rules, then you damned well have the power to overlook it. I told you he's returning to the reservation within a day or so."

Irons turned a muddy, mottled color. "This means that much to you?"

"It does. And furthermore, I expect him to bring me another load of goods in a few weeks and would appreciate his not being molested again."

"It might be safer to employ ... uh, Americans for your enterprise."

"Americans won't get me what I want. Are you going to release him?"

"Very well." Irons stalked to the door and bellowed for his adjutant.

A man with captain's bars raced up the stairs and presented himself. As soon as he received his orders, Irons turned to us and nodded stiffly. As we exited the room, I sensed his eyes on me. Perhaps it would have been smarter to let Caleb do this alone. If Irons carried grudges, Brown's Emporium would not be his target.

Caleb and I picked up a clearly relieved Winter Bird, his packs, and horses and returned to the store. As we unloaded the packs and examined the goods the Lakota had brought, I let out a groan. Some of the beautifully decorated pots were broken. A few of the bows had been destroyed as well. The packs had apparently been dropped to the ground where a horse had stepped on one of them.

The merchant reassured the stone-faced warrior-turned-trader that because none of this was his doing, a fair price would be paid for everything. Winter Bird loosened up upon learning this and haggled for each piece as if it were in perfect shape.

He grew recalcitrant again when Caleb and I asked him to bring another load. I am not certain he believed Caleb's reassurances. Finally, I removed my hat and addressed my friend.

"Winter Bird, have I not protected you when you were injured by Raven Strongbow and the army came for you? Have I not secured your release when you were wrongfully taken while on the way to me?"

Bird, his eyes fixed on my hair, nodded.

"So long as you do not take part in depredations against the settlers and continue to bring the goods that Mr. Brown wants, I will extend my protection. Remember that your trades buy things your people desperately need. Do you believe me on this?"

The young man shifted his stare to my right lobe. "I believe you, Medicine Hair. I will do as you wish."

After Bird received his payment, he went into the store proper and started buying supplies. Caleb and I went upstairs to settle up. He had received payment for the first shipment, and once we had an accounting, my share of the broken goods hadn't injured the enterprise fatally.

His packs now laden with goods his people needed, Winter Bird seemed intent on heading straight home, but I prevailed upon him to remain overnight at the farm and start out early the next morning. On the way back to Turtle Crick, he complained of a loose shoe on his gray, so I became a farrier and reshod his gelding. Afterward, we took a steam bath and a dip in Turtle Crick.

A bit of awkwardness arose when time came to retire. He resolutely threw down his blankets beside the cooking stove although we both wanted him in the sleeping room with me. But I dared not insist. I could not have kept my hands off him.

Once abed, my erection refused to be ignored. I tried. Lord, how I tried. But my throbbing tool pushed sleep away and presented me with a problem. Throwing back the covers, I tore off my sleeping shift and caressed the length of my torso. Every nerve reacted to the stimulation of my own touch in a different, sensual way. I brushed my nipples, giving me a shock that almost brought me off the mattress. My belly fluttered at my caress. My ballsack, full like an overripe love apple, tingled at my touch. My cock, as hard as I'd ever experienced it, pulsed to my heartbeat. I took the solid bulk of it in my right hand, pulled the foreskin back, and traced the glans, already wet from want, with the fingertips of the left. I shuddered at the thought of the comely, desirable young man in the other room.

My mouth opened to call to him, but I shut my eyes and the room was immediately filled with another presence. Matthew ... Bear. He came to me in my mind. His strong, naked image etched on my closed eyelids. It was as if he became a living, moving being. I slowly stroked myself. He smiled encouragement. He disappeared from my blinded eyes, but his broad hands caressed my arms. My beat became more rapid; my breath more shallow. Now his wet mouth warmed my nipples ... first the one and then the other. I gasped and stroked my cock faster. His palms feathered the inside of my calves, moving up my thighs until they cupped my scrotum.

"M ... Matthew," I whispered aloud. "Oh, Matthew."

My body tingled. The pressure built. Rational thought deserted me, and I gave myself over to raw passion. I dug my heels into the mattress, arching my body as my own volcanic eruption occurred. Hot lava spewed forth, shooting into the air and splattering my chest and belly. I froze for a moment as my body continued to gush. Then I resumed pumping until my seed ran dry.

Finished at last, I settled my butt back on the bedding and lay still and silent as waves of goose bumps washed over me. I opened my eyes and slowly returned from whatever enchanted place I'd been. I lay panting and wondering at the power of the experience. I masturbated occasionally during Matthew's prolonged absences, but it had never been like this.

Finally, I bestirred myself enough to stagger to the wash basin on the chest holding our personal clothing and with clumsy, near-dead fingers washed myself with my dampened sleeping shift. Then I eased open the door and peered blindly into the other room. Through the gloom, I made out the still form of Winter Bird lying motionless in his blankets. Suppressing a sigh, I noiselessly closed the door and returned to bed.

A chill seized my body and my mind. Matthew's presence had been so real, so strong that I became frightened. Had something happened to him? Had he died and come to say goodbye the only way he could? Had I been visited by a ghost? I folded my arms over my chest and held myself through the long, sleepless night.

The next morning, a handsome and clear-eyed Winter Bird thanked me for rescuing him from the army and for the provisions I gave him out of my cellar. Still shaky from my experience of the night, I pressed him for a commitment to return with more goods for Caleb. He gave in, albeit reluctantly, before riding northwest toward Tricking Water breaks. His choice of routes let me know he was nervous about running into a cavalry patrol.

I watched him out of sight before turning to what was going to be a busy day, made even harder by lack of sleep and an unsettled mind.

CHAPTER 12

The next day, I made arrangements for Andre to tend my fields, loaded four caged gray pigeons homed to Turtle Crick in the buckboard, and headed to town. I double-teamed the buckboard, strapping an unhappy Arrow beside the trace mare. Pa's note had said the Killpennys had lost their hay supply, so they could probably use a little help.

On the way to Yanube City, I intercepted Gideon leading a patrol back to the fort. He looked haggard as he told me they were on their way to collect fresh mounts before heading out again, this time to patrol east along the Yanube River. I don't know how much damage Howling Wolf was doing, but he was sure running the army ragged. Strange, considering the Brulé had only a score of men while the troopers numbered something over two hundred. There was a lesson in that fact I'd have to consider. When I told him my mission, he sent his good wishes to Esau and Hannah.

Unwilling to endure the sour looks cast at me from the boardwalks, I kept my eyes fixed on the road as I rolled down Main Avenue, but I could feel the hostility. The raids had stirred the Americans considerably. I halfway expected to be accosted; however, I reached the feed store without incident. A hand lettered sign to the right of the door advertised hay at $30 a ton. Last year, it had been $45.

The owners, James and Hugh Milne, with whom I'd dealt amicably over the years, greeted me not with a hello but with unwelcoming glares.

"What you doing here?" James, the older brother, demanded.

"Came to do business."

Hugh spoke up. "We don't deal with hostiles."

My eyebrows climbed, along with my blood. "What do you mean? You've known me for years. When have I ever dealt trouble?" Even as I asked the question, my mind slid back over the years to when I'd stalked and hanged the false pastor who had excited a crowd into lynching Otter and burning up James. But these men had no knowledge of that affair.

"You ain't hearing me, Injun. Get outa here. We don't want your kind in our store."

I hung onto my temper ... although precariously. "All I want is to buy some hay. I'm paying hard money for it, not paper money. Sell it to me, load my wagon, and I'll be on my way."

James lifted a hand and silenced his brother's retort. "All right, put $60 on the counter in gold or silver, and we'll sell you the hay."

"The sign says thirty."

"To the likes of you, it's sixty."

"Then I'll take my leave. The farmers along the river will sell me a few bales."

"Hold on." James's protest revealed that business wasn't good. "Forty-five, and that's my last offer."

Without a word, I spun on my heel and walked outside. James was right behind me.

"All right, John. Fork over $30, and it's a deal."

"No. You've demonstrated you have no principles, so I won't show you a dime until the buckboard is loaded with a full ton of fodder. Then I'll lay $25 in silver on the counter."

By the time I pulled out of the feed yard with a wagon full of hay, I'd recovered some of my aplomb. Turning things back on the brothers had mollified me a bit. I shook my head. They'd always been fair men. What was this warfare doing to us? All of us?

I took the stage road south of the river to the Killpenny place. Hot weather and a dry spring and summer had wilted the grass. Fields in the distance looked puny. If something didn't happen, we'd have another poor crop. The second in a row.

I took a look around and found the air clear of smoke. Perhaps the army had Wolf and his men on the run. While I'd started the trip early, stopping to buy hay and making my way in a buckboard had slowed me enough, so I would likely spend the night on the road. But I would cover as much distance as possible.

Early afternoon, I raised a dust cloud ahead of me. Likely the stage bound for Yanube City, which came in on Thursdays. Sure was raising a storm. I kept an eye on the coming vehicle as we closed the gap.

When we were close enough, I realized Dusty – if Dusty Skediver was still driving for the coach line – was running his horses to death. Out of caution, I pulled off the right side of the road onto the prairie. The lead horse ran with an uncertain gait. Dusty was bent over the reins, his shotgun messenger, Barnaby Bates, knelt backwards, trying to maintain his balance while keeping watch behind the coach.

As he rumbled past, his animals slick with sweat, Dusty bellowed one word. "Injuns!"

Once his dust cleared, I saw four riders bearing down on me. Given the condition of the brace of animals pulling the stagecoach, it wouldn't take them long to catch up. I flicked my reins and pulled the wagon athwart the road. Removing my hat, I stood in the wagon well with both arms raised. The four Sioux would either shoot me out of the buckboard, swarm around me to continue the chase, or stop to deal with me. It all depended on how high the blood lust was.

The man in the lead slowed his horse and faltered a moment before approaching warily. I stood stock still. The other three fell in beside him, their animals blowing noisily. The leader rode so close his animal's muzzle nearly touched my chest. At the last moment, he turned his mount to the side. The warrior wore only a breechcloth and moccasins. His head, shaved but for a roach, was painted black with red and white lightning bolts slashing the cheeks. Beneath the paint, I discerned features as ugly

74

as the man's demeanor. His heavy chest heaved from excitement and exertion.

"Why does Medicine Hair bar our way? Are you standing with the Americans against us?"

"Who asks?" I said with false calm.

"I am Blackhawk."

"Nay, Blackhawk. I waved you down to stop you from riding into a trap. As I left town this morning, a full company of soldiers was preparing to leave to patrol the river. They cannot be far behind me. I suggest you take to the water and wade downstream to a walk across. After that, go where you will."

"Will you betray us to them?"

"If you mean will I tell them which way you went, yes. They won't need a scout to follow your trail, so it would render me false in their eyes if I claimed not to know. But I won't tell them who you are."

"I want you to tell them. I want my name known to them. I want them to fear me."

Perhaps he was younger than he looked beneath all that paint. He spouted pure nonsense. Nonetheless, I obliged. "Very well. I will tell them I recognized the warrior, Blackhawk."

He nodded, turned to his men, and waved toward the river. After debating with myself a few minutes, I climbed down from the buckboard, unhitched the horses and led them to water. By the time I had them back in the traces, Gideon's patrol was approaching rapidly up the road. I was standing in the buckboard again as he reined in.

"Are you all right?" he asked. When I nodded, he went on. "What happened?"

"Once Dusty passed me, I planted myself in the road and waited until the Sioux came up. Then I convinced them to give up the chase."

Gideon did not look pleased. "By telling them we were on the way, I suspect."

"It seemed prudent. Else they'd have run down the coach and killed everyone on it. When Dusty passed me, his lead horse was limping. He couldn't have outrun their ponies much longer."

My brother-in-law unbent a little. "He was already down to a trot when we came across them. Which way did they go?"

I answered his question and volunteered the raiders were led by a man known to me as Blackhawk. Gideon sent his scouts to find which way the Indians went once they reached the river and turned back to me.

"Rachel Ann would appreciate a visit."

I clamped my hat back in place to cover my surprise. "She's living at the fort?"

He nodded. "Yes. Been there since spring."

"How's she faring?"

He understood my question and answered slowly. "It was awkward at first, but after Colonel Iron's wife learned how educated Rachel Ann is, she took her under her wing. That helped a lot. Still, she'd take comfort in seeing family now and then."

He put a finger to his hat and led his detail away as I resumed my journey.

At nightfall, I guided the buckboard a distance off the road nearer the riverbank. My caution was not from fear of being deliberately attacked, but in the darkness I might be taken as a danger to anyone coming upon me.

Neither the horses nor I heard anything disturbing during the night, so I slept reasonably well atop the hay bales in the buckboard. Early the next morning, I settled for jerky and river water to break my fast before moving on down the road.

Killpenny Farm was set closer to the river than most spreads up and down the valley, making irrigation of its fields possible. While Esau's crops were hardier than other fields I'd seen, they still did not promise a bountiful harvest. The Killpenny outhouse had not been built double-walled with a tabby of clay for insulation like my buildings, so it had pretty much burned to the ground during the recent raid.

Hannah was working the fields. Esau hammered on something over by the ruined outhouse. My sister spotted me first and ran out to meet me as I turned off the stage road. I hopped down and hugged her to me before holding her at arm's length to inspect her. She looked healthy and happy with a gentle bow to her belly and a special glow.

"Does he know?" I asked quietly.

"Of course, I know." Esau walked up behind her with a goofy grin on his face. "It's a boy."

We all laughed. "So you've decided that, have you?" I asked.

"It's probably not anything yet." Hannah glanced at the ground shyly. "It's too soon."

Esau slapped dust from his hat against his right leg. His blond hair shone in the sun a thousand times brighter than my few twigs of gold.

"I heard your barn went up with all your hay supply, so I brought some to help out," I said.

"Mighty grateful. Tell me the cost, and I'll repay you."

"You can repay me when my barn burns and I need fodder. Surprised you haven't started rebuilding the outhouse."

He motioned over his shoulder. "That's what I was working on. The frame. The family's coming tomorrow bringing your uncles along with them. We're gonna raise the new barn."

"Good, I can lend a hand to the enterprise. Tell me where you want the bales dropped."

Hannah went inside to see to the making of a meal while her husband and I unloaded a ton of hay. After that, I helped tie a tarp over the stacked bales even though there was no indication of weather. I appreciated Esau's caution.

Mrs. Killpenny had regained some of the weight she lost after her husband was killed, but there was something missing from her eyes. They saw but didn't register. A tremor ran though me. I was responsible for her loss. I should have killed Raven instead of granting him clemency. He advantaged my mercy – nay, weakness – to kill the farmer for his mount.

Despite my deep-seated sense of guilt, we had a decent visit before I ventured the four miles downriver to the bridge that led to the Mead. I'd let the family know I was on the way with the last of my white messenger pigeons. Once the greetings were out of the way, I put the gray birds I'd lugged along with me – all homed to Turtle Crick – in the Mead's cote. Upon returning home, I'd reclaim the white ones since they considered the Mead as home. Matthew had devised this message system a few years back, and it had served us well, even though we had to occasionally replace and train new birds for those lost to hawks.

After not seeing my family for almost a year, I took stock of them, as they did me. Ma looked the same. Slender, almost thin, with a head of spun gold hair. Threads of silver among the yellow had diminished its brilliance, but she retained her fire. As usual, she had a hot meal awaiting me.

We all gathered at the kitchen table while I brought them up to date on my life and provided what little news I had of Matthew between spoonsful of venison stew. Pa had surrendered a little to time. The gray streaking his hair was nearly as startling as my speckled mop. Yet it remained thick and lustrous. A few creases lined an otherwise youthful and handsome face.

Otter had always said Pa looked exactly like Cut Hand. Of course, Timo Bowers said that of me. A bright intelligence lit Pa's coal black eyes peppered with tiny flecks of gold, a trait we all three shared – father, son, and grandson.

Alexander was as wiry as he had always been. At twenty-seven he was settled in a comfortable family home doing the only thing he wanted to do ... farm. I was a farmer, too, yet there was a difference between us. His life was bound to the Mead's six-hundred odd acres. Sometimes, I yearned to feel closer to him, yet he seemed content with the way things were.

Min, his wife, had turned decidedly matronly, although she showed no sign of carrying a child at the moment. Little Jacob had attained three, and Hans had just turned two. They were lively children and would likely grow up to be honest, reliable men like their father.

The Appletons looked the same, all four of them, and appeared happy with their station.

The sight of Crow Johnson brightened my day. The Absaroka had completed his obligation as a military scout and returned to run the Mead's blacksmith shop and care for the coach company's spare teams of horses. He'd built a cabin convenient to the forge for his wife and her two half-grown children. My friend had respected the customs of his tribe and married his dead brother's widow and adopted his nephews.

My telling of interrupting the raid on the stagecoach prompted a warning from Pa to steer clear of both sides of this conflict. "In the end, you'll be crossways with both the renegades and the army."

"I should have stood aside and let the raiders take down the stage?"

Pa thought for a long minute. "No, you couldn't do that. But you take a powerful chance relying on the strength of your hair."

"And my blood."

He shook his head. "Indians have been killing Indians back into history. Don't count too much on your bloodline sparing you."

The following day was as happy a one as I remembered – save for when Matthew returned from his sojourns. My uncles, Jacob and Christian, joined the rest of us at the Killpenny farm to restore the barn. Christian, my favorite, brought his sense of humor along with him to liven the day.

Crow and the Appletons remained at the Mead to work and keep an eye on things. The women prepared food and ran herd on the little ones while the rest of us set to work on the outhouse. Esau already had the framing for the four sides ready, so we merely had to hoist and hammer them into place on the existing foundation. Things progressed quickly. We raised the gambrel roof before the sun went down and had time for a round of horseshoe tossing. Christian whipped us all, but Esau tossed a mean shoe, as well.

My limbs were tired by the end of the day, but my heart was lifted because I could see my sister had a good marriage with Esau. So far as I could tell, Alexander was pleased with his union, and Rachel Ann was certainly in love with Gideon. For all the traveling Matthew's warrior's heart demanded of him, I was satisfied with his love. Each of us was settled into the life he or she craved.

Saturday morning, I was later beginning the trip back to Turtle Crick than planned. Ma hung on too tightly, finding things to keep me a few minutes longer. By the time I crossed the bridge over the Yanube, my buckboard was filled with venison from the cavern in the hollow hill, pieces of clothing Ma and Min and Jane Appleton had made for both Matthew and me, and other odds and ends, including two cages holding four white pigeons.

The air was clear of smoke or any other evidence of violence, so I set the team at an easy pace and enjoyed reliving my visit to the Mead. I quit the road after darkness fell and settled down for the night with a meal of pemmican and river water. I even ate half of one of the four small cakes Ma'd sent home with me.

Before sliding into sleep, I decided to stop at the fort and visit Rachel Ann as Gideon had suggested. It would be a Sunday, so if Wolf and his men weren't wreaking havoc, it might prove a good time to catch both of them at leisure. Sad that the state of our lives depended upon the whims of a Brulé medicine man.

CHAPTER 13

I arrived at Fort Yanube around high sun the next day. As the sentry box was not manned, I drove the buckboard straight onto the post without challenge. Howling Wolf could have led his party right up to the headquarters building without much trouble. Of course, he'd stir up a nest of blue-coated wasps to sting his backside if he tried it.

A man with three stripes told me where to find Captain Haleworthy's billet, and I was lucky enough to catch the couple at home. Rachel Ann came flying through the door and clasped me as if I were a lifeline, but after we disentangled and I'd given her husband an American handshake, I discerned from her rush of words that she was happy in her marriage and coming to grips with her environment. Nonetheless, she hankered for the sight of a familiar face and made me promise to come by and pick her up the next time I decided on a visit to the Mead.

Like our sister Hannah, Rachel Ann was with child, although in a more apparent way. We managed to still her chattering tongue sufficiently for Gideon to tell me he hadn't caught up with Blackhawk's party the other day. Since that incident, the renegades had been quiet. Chased off, he surmised. Resting up and planning for the next round of attacks was my judgment.

Upon leaving the fort, I headed straight home. Unless I saw something requiring urgent attention in the fields or with the cattle, I intended to put away my supplies from the buckboard and indulge myself in the sweathouse. As I neared the bridge over Turtle Crick, I glanced over at the little structure and pulled to a halt. Wisps of smoke rose from the pit I used for firing the stones. Closer inspection showed where two individuals had entered the enclosure, which yet radiated warmth from the heat of the rocks. I followed their tracks to the crick bank where they'd taken a dip to clean away the sweat.

I glanced toward the house with my heart leaping in my chest. Matthew was back! I started for the wagon but halted in my tracks. Who was with him? Maybe it wasn't my lover but stray tribesmen taking advantage of my absence. Or ... and the thought raised chill bumps on my back ... maybe Raven had returned. Such brazen behavior would fit his nature.

After retrieving my rifle from the buckboard, I left the wagon where it was and crossed the bridge afoot. Nothing looked amiss in the yard. I crept up on the porch of the house. The door was locked, as I had left it; the cellar door, secure.

I turned my attention to the outhouse. The door was shut, but I hadn't padlocked it so that Andre or Libby had access to any supplies they might have needed in my absence. The hay doors in the loft were closed, although someone could be watching through gaps in the wood.

I stole across the yard and flattened against the barn. Reaching around with my left hand, I tugged the door open enough to slip through. As my eyes adjusted to the gloom, I relaxed. Winter Bird's gray stood in the stall beside my pinto. Why had he returned? He'd left for home less than a week ago. His two pack horses were missing. Had he been set upon and robbed? Was he hurt?

A groan brought my eyes to the ceiling. He was in the loft. Another noise. I went to the ladder and opened my mouth to call out to him when I remembered the second set of footprints at the sweathouse. I snapped my jaws shut, placed my foot on the first rung, and quietly ascended the ladder enough to poke my head through the opening.

The sight that met my eyes brought a tangle of emotions. Winter Bird stood naked, his head bowed, his pelvis thrust forward, a look of utter bliss on his handsome features. Andre, also without a stitch of clothing, knelt before him, swallowing the young Sioux's large, rampant cock. I should have left, but my muscles seemed frozen. As I watched, Bird placed his hands behind Andre's head and began to thrust, fucking his companion's face, uttering "uh" with each movement. He lifted his head, his black eyes shining in excitement. A roar passed his throat as he thrust deeply and froze against Andre. Then with a great shudder, Bird began pumping rapidly, straining to empty his sac. His eyes rolled upward as he worked through his contractions.

After a long moment of silence, the young man fell on his back atop a hay bale. Andre loomed over him, the glans of the big tool I remembered from our times together slick and shiny with the colorless, tasteless, odorless lubricant that sexual excitement brings to men. He lifted Bird's strong, slender legs and presented himself. Both men grunted as his cock slid home. Fascinated by the roll of muscles playing in Andre's back and buns and thighs, I watched him fuck the Sioux. His excitement was such that it did not take long. He soon jabbed Bird's fundament savagely, drawing closer and closer until he came with a muted cry.

A cloak of sadness descended over me as the exclamation sounded suspiciously like "Otter!" My murdered kinsman had been Andre's first encounter with a man, and the only one until we mutually satisfied one another before I knew of my love for Matthew.

I silently descended the ladder and slipped through the door. Once across the crick, I climbed into the wagon's seat and rumbled across the bridge. When I dismounted, both men were both standing fully clothed in front of the barn to greet me with welcoming smiles. I gave Andre an American handshake but clasped Bird's forearm in the Indian fashion.

"What are you doing back here so soon?" I asked.

His grin faltered. "Too many soldiers on the road."

I said nothing about his missing pack horses.

"How was everyone at the Mead?" Andre asked.

I brought them up to date on my visit, and my neighbor shared the information that all had been quiet along Turtle Crick. At the edge of my vision, I caught sight of Todoh standing on stiff legs in the distance, his attention centered on us. I whistled and braced myself as he came running. True to form, he leapt from the ground and landed against my chest. Laughing, I hugged him close and let him lick my face. After a moment, I dropped him, and he transferred his attention to Bird.

Andre and I left them roughhousing while we walked the fields. He and Libby had done more work on the plants than expected. They looked healthier than those on the valley floor along the river. I should get a decent reap if nothing came along to set things afoul between now and harvest.

I returned to the house alone and sent Todoh back to his charges. Bird and I sat on the edge of the porch. His demeanor had changed.

"I come back with news. And it ain't good. I just got home and paid everyone off for their goods when Raven Strongbow showed up."

My heart lurched. "Was Shambling Bear in the village?"

He shook his head, easing my mind. "Nay. They say he's gone north to visit the white man who went on the last buffalo hunt with us."

My eyebrows climbed. "Theodore Roosevelt?"

"I think that is the name. Bear was much impressed by the man when we hunted."

"Good. It's near the time he should return, so maybe he'll come straight to Turtle Crick from there." I paused. "Did you speak with Raven?"

He shook his head and switched to Lakota. "No, but I listened while he talked to others. He says he came back to see how his brethren were faring."

"More than that, I think."

"He's gonna join Howling Wolf if you ask me," Bird said.

"Not good news. Had he left by the time you started back for Turtle Crick?

"No. I came right away to bring you the news. If you'd send some of those birds you use for messages with me, I wouldn't have to ride so far. I'll get some, so you can send me messages, as well."

"Good idea." Switching to English, I asked if he'd ever braced Raven over attacking him.

Bird frowned, and I noticed how fetchingly he wore it. "Nay." He fell silent for a moment. "I ain't afraid of him. But I'm not ready to kill a man, and that's what I'd have to do if I faced him down."

"Aren't you afraid he will paint you as a coward?"

"His claim won't mean nothing to them who know me. And I don't care about the others. I know who I am."

An unusual attitude for a prideful Sioux warrior, but one I appreciated. "Did you not kill when you rode with Howling Wolf?"

"I don't know. I shot at men, but I don't know if I killed any of them. I hit one farmer, but it was in the shoulder. Another one ... perhaps."

"Why are you not riding with Wolf now?"

"He ain't a good man to ride with. He thinks more about his own skin than anybody who rides with him. But I gotta admit I was thinking on joining him when I got your message about trading."

I stowed the items from the wagon bed and forgot about a sweat bath for the moment to hoe the fields. Bird joined me, speeding my efforts considerably. He had learned from helping me on his last trip.

After putting in half a day, I said I needed a good bath, and he joined me. He grew rampant again, but perhaps it wasn't as intense this time. No wonder, given what I'd observed earlier. I kept my hands off myself with difficulty. Nor was it easy to sleep alone in my bed.

The next morning, we rode into town, and ignoring stares from the townsfolk, I stopped at the place where Matthew had bought our last homing pigeons. The proprietor of the junk shop where a man could find about anything if he wasn't too particular about how clean it was, hesitated before selling us more birds. I chose a darker gray than the ones I already had and bought a second set of four with a brownish cast. The slovenly man probably envisioned us setting up a message system whereby murdering, pillaging renegades could communicate with one another.

We headed back to Turtle Crick as soon as our purchase was complete, but the gossip mongers had been at work. As we neared the Sheriff's Office, Landreth stepped into the street and held up his hand.

"Can I help you, Sheriff?" I asked as we drew abreast of him.

"What's this buck doing in town?"

"This is Winter Bird. He lends Caleb Brown and me a hand in buying some items for trade."

"He ought not be off the reservation. I got a right to shoot him outa the saddle just for being here."

"Mr. Brown received approval from Colonel Irons for him to come into town to deliver his goods. I'm usually with him. Then he returns to the reservation."

"Which agency you from, boy?" The Sheriff's tone was not pleasant.

"Pine Ridge ... sir."

"Sheriff. You call me Sheriff, you hear?"

"I hear, Sheriff."

"Go on. Git outa town. Don't wanna see your red hide again."

"You'll have to take that up with Mr. Brown," I said.

"I don't gotta take it up with nobody, boy."

But there was a tone to his voice that let me know he wasn't as sure of himself as he tried to sound. Caleb Brown was about the most influential civilian south of the Missouri River.

We arrived at the farm without further incident. Nonetheless, the confrontation had bothered Bird. I don't think he could figure whether he was angry or shaken by the sheriff's warning. Likely both.

I sought to distract him by explaining the pigeon training procedures. Being a bright young man, he absorbed my instructions and then, despite the lateness of the day, departed for home.

I put the new dark gray birds in the cote. I'd get Libby to start training them tomorrow. She had more patience with that sort of thing than I had.

# # # # #

That night, Todoh woke me from a sound sleep. I bounded out of bed and pulled on clothing before hitting the door and making for the barn. The blue was still raising a ruckus by the time Arrow and I raced along the edge of the fields on the way to the range. A near-full moon had risen, albeit it was a hazy orb, so the night was not as dark as the last time I went on the prowl for Raven. And there was no doubt it was the Cheyenne spooking the dog.

As I neared, Todoh stopped barking. Moments later, he appeared at Arrow's side, panting and looking nervously over his shoulder. Then pandemonium broke out. A distance to my north a shrill yell followed by several shots broke the night. The sound of hooves began to build.

The bastard was stampeding the cattle. I jerked my rifle from my scabbard and raised it to my shoulder. After he fired more shots, I led him and sent three bullets in his direction. Things settled down after that. I heard fading hoof beats, which meant some of the cattle were still running, but a scattered herd was harder to stampede than animals grouped closely together where they fed off one another's panic.

I opened the gate and herded as many animals as I could find into the hundred-acre pasture. In the morning, Todoh and I would go on the hunt for the rest of them. Realizing I'd be unable to sleep, I remained where I was and propped my naked back against a fence post to catch a nap when I could. Which wasn't often. A loincloth doesn't offer much protection against a chill night. Todoh had disappeared. Probably out looking for the rest of his charges.

As soon as it was light, I spotted three dead animals. Raven had cut the throat of two, and one had fallen to what was probably my own bullet. Ignoring them for the moment, I took a count of the cattle in the penned pasture and then mounted up to ride northwest, the direction the stampeded cattle had been heading. Within half a mile, I saw Todoh nipping at the heels of a score of half-grown steers, herding them back to where he wanted them. I figured that left about twenty-five head missing.

By high sun, I'd recovered all but one of the missing animals. The beast would either return on his own, be brought down by predators, or roam free and grow wilder than he already was. I spent the rest of the day butchering the three dead steers. When I returned to the barn for the buckboard to load up the meat, I discovered the real reason for Raven's raid last night.

Medicine Hair

A broken tree branch stood upright in the yard before the stoop of the cabin. Affixed to the top was a scalp with long black hair. Scratched in the dirt was a version of Cheyenne erotica, three stick figures. One, with a bird hovering above his head had a fading erection. A slash across his neck and X-ed out eyes indicated he was dead. The second was clearly Raven, given the crow over his head. Displaying a massive rod, he held a scalp dripping with blood. The third man – me from the dots in the sand at my head indicating my strange hair – was on his knees in front of him.

My heart froze. Had the murdering rogue killed Winter Bird just because the Lakota was my friend?

CHAPTER 14

I snatched the scalp, kicked the stick away, and scuffed the sign language from the dirt before collapsing onto the porch. Why didn't Raven kill me? Why come after those near to me? Had he known of Winter Bird's attraction?

That drew a grunt. He'd been watching us. He'd seen us emerge from the spirit lodge, our erections leading us to the crick. My muscles tightened so much I shivered as if in the grip of ague. Cold? No, fear. Not fear for myself but for those I held dear.

Finally, I bestirred myself enough to glance at the thing in my hands, seeking something of my beautiful young Lakota friend. It did not speak to me. No part of his spirit lingered. Only then did I examine it closely. My heart sped up. This was not a fresh scalp. The flesh had dried and curled, yet Winter Bird had left this very yard only yesterday. I took a deep breath and exhaled slowly. This was not Bird's crown.

I dropped the thing in the dirt and mentally shook myself. I couldn't let Raven get into my head. He had lied to me before. Claimed he shot Matthew from the saddle and left him dead in the dirt, but that hadn't happened. This scalp from some unknown warrior was aimed at unsettling my mind. And Raven had succeeded. For a moment.

Reassured that reason had won over illusion, I fetched a spade and buried the trophy on the south bank of the crick where I would be unlikely to walk over it. After packing the earth back into the shallow pit, I said a few words for the soul of the man who'd lost a battle sometime in the past. How had Raven come by the trophy? Such a prize conjured the image of honorable combat. Something beyond Raven's capability.

Now that I'd expunged the Cheyenne from my head, I returned to work in the fields. As I plied my hoe, I considered what to do about him. If he watched me closely enough to discern affection between Bird and me, he had gotten close enough to do real harm. If so, I'd be helpless unless I figured out his movements.

Once I reached the end of the row, I put away my hoe and fired up the flame in the forge. After sorting through bits and pieces of metal, I hauled out a beaver trap Matthew had bought years ago when there were a few of the animals along the crick. A careful inspection of the contraption convinced me I could recreate just such a device on a bigger scale. It took most of the rest of two days for the project. The hardest part was constructing a steel spring that did not snap under pressure. Finally, I fashioned one that held.

How to set the trap without killing or maiming Todoh with the thing? A foul smelling salve from Otter's Pandora's box mixed in some ragweed produced a strong, noxious odor natural enough not to raise suspicion.

Near dark, I called in Todoh and shut us both in the blacksmith shop. First, I rubbed his nose in the foul-smelling mixture and uttered warnings in a strong voice. Offended, he rubbed his snout with both forepaws and whined. Then I spread a film of the mixture over the big trap before setting it. Using a stick, I tripped the plate. As the thing snapped shut with a ringing clang, the dog jumped back in alarm. I repeated the process several times until Todoh appeared wary of the trap. Doubtless, he would associate that ragweed odor with danger.

Twilight was giving way to darkness before I ventured up on the hill behind the house and noticed a slight depression where Raven might have lain in hiding at the apex of the mound. The spot gave a good view of the yard, outhouse, forge, and fields. The Cheyenne had likely watched me from this very place over the past few days.

When darkness shrouded my movements, I dug a shallow pit and fit the big trap into it. I set the trigger, scattered sand and weeds over the device, and showed Todoh where it was. Then I backed down the hill and set Matthew's beaver trap, similarly smeared with the smelly unguent, on the north bank of Turtle Crick in a spot with a good view of the front of the house. Once that was done, I sent Todoh back to the range and went inside to clean up and eat. Maybe I'd do a little reading before bed.

For three mornings thereafter, I resisted the urge to mount the hill and check my trap. Mid-afternoon on the third day, Todoh commenced barking. Given a good excuse, I climbed the stubby hill to check the undisturbed trap and to see what had claimed his attention. A line of five horsemen approached from the north, giving the dog a wide berth. After a moment, I decided the riders were Crow Hop and Firm Foot along with three companions. They approached at a walk so as to not appear threatening.

After I gave the open-handed sign, one rider detached from the party and headed for the hill to stand guard against an army patrol. I signed a warning about the trap and descended to await the others in the yard.

As greetings and introductions went around, it became clear they were scavenging, not raiding. After water and coffee on the front porch, Firm Foot, who seemed to be the leader of the group, let it be known there were other Indians in the area.

"Aye. Howling Wolf's band has been causing trouble," I said. "He's stirred up enough dust, so the army shoots at any Indian it sees."

"Seems to me they did that the last time we were here," Firm Foot said.

"That was Raven's doing. He hid in the rocks and shot a trooper from the saddle just as they met up with you. The army thought you'd fired on them."

"That man's a snake," Crow Hop muttered.

I took off my hat and rubbed my head. "He's come back. Winter Bird saw him at Pine Ridge on his way to join Wolf somewhere around here."

None of the group had seen Shambling Bear, but Firm Foot repeated what Bird had told me about my mate going north to visit the white man, Roosevelt. After I opened my cold room so they could have a meal of jerky and root vegetables, Firm Foot asked me to donate an animal or two for their families back home.

Before heading out to the range to select the animals, I wrote a note on a piece of ledger paper saying the band had purchased three head of Thunderbird/Bear branded animals from me and was returning to the reservation. If shooting broke out, the note would mean nothing, but if they were merely stopped, perhaps it would provide safe passage. Then Todoh and I watched my friends haze the steers away.

For some reason, I was nervous that night. Todoh must have felt the same. He woke me in the wee hours with a long howl. I lay abed wondering if it could be Howling Wolf signaling me. Yet when the animal's voice rose again, it was Todoh feeling his ancestry. As it was not an alarmed sound, there was little reason to worry, but still I rose and went out onto the porch dressed only in my sleeping shift, which was little protection against the cold night. Nonetheless, I held still in the shadow of the overhang while chill bumps played over my flesh. Finally satisfied my mind was playing tricks on me, I returned to bed.

I rose early the next morning and had started for the barn to tend the animals when the flap of black wings on the north side of the crick caught my attention. Damnation, had Matthew's beaver trap caught some animal as food for the crows?

The device was sprung all right, but there was nothing in it. The trigger plate and the jaws were awash with blood, but the trap was empty. I stood and considered a minute. Then my mind's eye replayed what must have happened.

Someone, most likely Raven, had walked into the thing. He'd muted his cries, but made enough noise for Todoh's sharp ears to pick up the sound. He must have stood in agony while I was on the porch, sniffing out the night. Then when I went back inside, he freed himself and limped away into the darkness. There was little doubt these images were something close to what had happened. It had taken human hands to release the trap's ragged jaws.

I retrieved my rifle and tracked bloody footprints until they disappeared into the crick. Farther down the waterway, he'd come out of the water and recovered his mount. The hoof prints were larger than a pony's. Raven was still riding Mr. Killpenny's paint mule.

I tracked him back across Turtle Crick and up into the Trickling Water badlands before giving up. There had been no blood on the ground for the last several miles, so Raven must have managed to stop the bleeding.

#####

The Moon of Brown Leaves was on the cusp of giving way to the Moon of Changing Seasons – meaning September was slipping into October – when Todoh's joyous yipping brought me to the top of the hill. He was racing for a lone horseman riding south. I didn't need the dog's confirmation to know Shambling Bear was home, although he'd be transforming himself into Matthew Brandt with each step closer to the farm. I recognized the erect carriage, the way he tilted his head slightly to the left, the width of the broad shoulders long before his beautiful features were clear to my eyes.

I grew so excited, I came near to stepping into my own bear trap on the crest. As I watched, the dog cleared the ground and leapt into the saddle, almost spooking Wind Rider. And that's the way they rode into the yard, both of them on the gray's back. They dismounted on opposite sides of the horse.

Matthew, handsome as the devil in buckskin trousers and beaded shirt, rushed forward to grasp my forearm. I nearly succumbed to the urge to kiss his broad, laughing mouth, but dared not for fear of unseen eyes. We stood for a moment without speaking before he released me to give Todoh the expected attention. While he satisfied the dog with some rough and tumble, I went inside the cabin to wash the fields from my hands and face. I had intended to start a meal for him, but he entered and walked up behind me to clasp me in his arms. The groin pushing against my buns felt warm and alive ... and promising.

"You should be naked by now, Wife," he growled in my ear. When he nipped my earlobe, my cock sprang to attention. Laughing aloud, he moved his hands down to grasp me.

"Give me a moment, and I'll achieve a state of utter nakedness."

"Nay, I'll do that for myself," Matthew said.

He ripped buttons from my shirt and tore the garment from my torso. I hastily pushed down my trousers lest he do the same with them. Naked on the bearskin rug before the fireplace hearth, I watched him pull the shirt over his head. His chest was weightier than I'd last seen it; his stomach flat. When he slipped off his trousers and stood before me in all his glory, I admired again at the slight flaring of hips below his incredibly narrow waist. His cock, engorged with blood, jutted skyward as straight as an arrow. The bulbous glans reminded me of a steel point set in the end of his shaft.

I rose to my knees and grasped him. "This is the arrow that pierced my heart. This is what I wait for. This is why I deny all others."

His delighted laugh changed to a groan when my lips closed over him. But he permitted my ministrations only briefly before pushing me over and lying atop my body.

"*Wastelakapi!*

There was that beautiful word again ... beloved. It moved me as no other. He paused to consider its significance before continuing. "I have missed you so much. Each time I come home is special to me ... to us. I want this one to be even more so."

He kissed me deeply and then moved down my torso. He suckled my nipples as if drawing mother's milk. Then he worked his way down into my bush. Finally, his lips kissed my throbbing tool, wet now with the fluid that precedes intercourse. I shivered when he took me in his mouth. Even though he'd done this on occasion before, he was still inexpert at the act and choked. He came up and tried it again.

This time, his mouth and throat closed over the entire length of my hot cock. I felt him try to vibrate his throat, as I did for him, but it is not an easy thing to do, and he couldn't manage it before he had to come up and take a breath.

I spread my arms and legs wide on the rug and gloried in his attention. All too soon, he rose up to kiss me and murmur into my mouth. "Really special, John."

He rolled over, taking me with him, and opened his knees. I fell into place, my excited prong probing his buns as he raised his legs."

"Are you sure?"

His voice came out in a rasp. "You seem to take such enjoyment in my fucking you, I want to try it for myself." He closed his eyes and managed to look like a dusky angel despite the excited flush on his features.

Hesitantly, I stroked his crack with my hard cock. I'd dreamed of this unlikely moment for a long time, yet I was afraid. If the act proved revolting to his warrior's nature, he might decide to have nothing more to do with me.

"Ah, that feels good. Do it, War Eagle. Make love to your Shambling Bear."

Reason abandoned me, taking my fears with it. I dipped my fingers into the crock of butter he'd placed beside us, found his sphincter, and pressed. He winced. I paused. He bit his lower lip and nodded. My entry into a place no other human being had ever been was difficult, made more so by my reticence. Finally, the entire length of my cock filled his dark channel.

He opened his eyes and the pain melted from his features. "Now show me how much of a man you are."

I began slowly, often reaching down to kiss his lips. No need to hurry. Make this good for him. Oh, no! All too soon I felt the lava rising. I slowed to prolong the moment, but he urged me on, his face flushed, lips open, eyes centered on mine. So I bucked like a bull. Short and jerky. Long and hard. Thrust after thrust into that tender sheath. My heart raced; my blood sang. Sweat popped out on my brow and dripped onto his broad chest.

The world went away. Turtle Island consisted of nothing but the two of us. Matthew beneath me, receiving all I had to give. Me atop him in unimagined bliss. I thought my heart would burst as I erupted and spewed hot, life-giving seed into him. I shouted aloud, proclaiming my love and devotion as exquisite contractions spurted semen deep inside Matthew. My Matthew. My beloved. My *wastelakapi.*

When my orgasm was finally spent, I grasped his cock, but he brushed me away.

"Stay inside me," he gasped. "Play with my *aze.*

So I gazed straight into those dark eyes and stroked his nipples while he excited himself. The desire, the ecstasy in his face revived me. I hardened and thrust against him as his fist rose and fell, slowly at first, and then faster and faster. At the first spurt of his seed, he clasped me around the neck and brought my lips to his in the sweetest kiss I'd ever experienced. My second, unexpected ejaculation took me completely by surprise.

We lay still, panting and fighting for breath for long minutes before his right thumb touched my numbed lips. "*Le mita ohinyan,* he whispered. "Mine forever. Never forget it."

I looked down on the beautiful man who had just bestowed his grace upon me. "Thank you. I know that was contrary to your nature ..."

He laid fingers across my mouth. "Nay. Thank you. No matter what hides in our future, I have deposited my *hiyuye,* my semen, upon you in every way possible. You have taken it in your hands, on your belly, down your throat, and in your fundament. And now, I have done no less. You are as much a part of me as I am of you. No ceremony, Sioux or American, can bind us any closer than what we did today."

He kissed me before rolling us over and fucking me so hard, so lovingly, so desperately that the future he had alluded to must surely linger just over the horizon.

Later, we pitched horseshoes before lounging in the medicine lodge, so steam could open our pores to leech away poisons collected in our systems. As sexually exhausted as I was, I could not take my eyes off his smooth, finely muscled body while he listened to the recitation of my past few months, including what had happened with Raven. I had to use all my powers of persuasion to keep him from going on the hunt for the Cheyenne. He likely acquiesced because he knew the trail was cold by now.

After he settled down, he told me how desperate the situation was on the reservations. He approved of my giving some of our cattle to be sent back to the reservations. There was talk of war. Red Cloud spoke against it, as did our friend, Touch the Clouds on the Cheyenne River Reservation. Sitting Bull sat on the fence, neither encouraging forays nor speaking against them.

The rumors had been true. Matthew had gone north to visit Theodore Roosevelt on his Elkhorn Ranch. My mate sang praises of this white man as I'd never heard spill from his mouth before. Until now, he'd viewed most Americans distantly, if not hostilely. No other man like him trod this earth, Matthew declared. He was a far-seeing man with great ideas and strong medicine. He saw into the future, and Matthew liked what Roosevelt discerned. This was an important man, my lover declared.

We spent the rest of the day and most of the night resting and fucking, although he did not present himself to me as he had upon his arrival. That was fine. I'd drunk at the Well of Bliss once, and that would hold me for a long, long time.

#####

The next few weeks were taken up with work. We had only just finished harvesting and storing the crops when *Wakinyan* washed the prairie with waves of thunderstorms. As before, we followed Andre into town with our buckboard piled high and allowed him to negotiate as if all the crops belonged to him. Thurlo Tussler of Tussler's Foods knew better, of course, and he would have gladly dealt with us, yet this subterfuge provided him cover, so he went along with it. Crops had not been good along the valley again this year, so Andre managed to negotiate a decent price for ours. It would require several more town trips to deliver the bounty.

Hard on the heels of settling up with our neighbor, we gathered the cattle ... his and ours ... and drove them to the sale barn. Despite holding another five steers back for delivery to the reservations, we did all right with the cattle, as well.

#####

Libby had done a good job working with our four new gray pigeons, so they were trained by the time Winter Bird showed up with packs of new goods for Caleb, bringing his newly homed birds with a brownish cast. The depression was still raging back east, so prices were not as good as on the prior trip, but Bird would still be able to provide some relief for his people. When he overnighted with us, Matthew made noisy love to me while Bird slept in the other room beside the stove. My lover looked upon this as staking his claim, but mayhap he merely inflamed the handsome young man behind the door.

93

CHAPTER 15

Once the pressing matters of the harvest and cattle sale were behind us, Matthew began to obsess over Raven. He was itching to go on the hunt for the man. He concluded the Cheyenne, likely injured by the beaver trap, was holed up somewhere nursing his wound. With any luck, he'd die of blood poisoning I pointed out.

In lieu of riding west, my mate sent a message to Winter Bird asking if there was news of Raven on the reservation. This and the fact Howling Wolf's party began raiding the valley farms hard before winter set in, kept Matthew with me.

As a further diversion, we decided to visit Rachel Ann at the fort. Distant smoke rose in the autumn air as we made the seven-mile trek. A hand-lettered sign at the edge of town brought us to a halt. A sign the likes of which I'd never laid eyes on before.

"No Injuns allowed inside the limits of Yanube City. Any offender will be arrested or legally shot dead if caught."

Sheriff Charles Landreth's name was printed below the crudely lettered board.

Matthew reached out to tear it down. I grabbed his arm.

"What if some blood enters and pays the price because you tore down the warning?"

He snatched his hand back. "How many do you think can even read the damned thing?"

"Other than you and me, not many."

"And that's who the thing is intended for. You and me. *Kay*, it stays, but it's not going to stop me from seeing my sister."

With palpitating heart, I followed him down the street. The ring of Timo's anvil filled the air as we passed the blacksmith shop. Shortly thereafter, we turned west down a broad dirt street and arrived at Fort Yanube's sentry box.

The private on guard looked flummoxed. He gaped at us when we asked for Captain Haleworthy. Appearing uncertain as to whether or not he should be pointing his weapon at us, he stammered that the Captain was out on patrol chasing hostiles.

"We're here to see our sister, Mrs. Haleworthy," Matthew said.

That deepened the private's confusion. He finally put fingers to mouth and let out a loud whistle. A corporal came running, rifle at the ready.

A lieutenant and a captain managed to straighten thing out inside a quarter of an hour. Rachel Ann eventually appeared at the gate, accompanied by the corporal. After big hugs, she led us back down the street out of hearing distance of the guard box.

"Oh, Matthew, it's been so long!" She enfolded him in a sisterly embrace and then held him at arm's length. "You look good. I thought everyone on the reservation was starving to death."

"A lot of them are. But I've been up north visiting a ranch where they eat very well."

As we chatted, I noticed the captain had remained at the sentry box. Before long, the corporal rode out of the fort and headed south.

"We've got to go," I said.

"I saw him. I'm staying right here until Rachel Ann and me are caught up on visiting."

"Come over here." My sister stepped across a ditch, maneuvering us onto the fort's property.

Before long, Landreth, his deputy, and four other horsemen rode up. The sheriff looked down on us from his mount. The way his moustache ran up into his nose hairs always fascinated me. Repulsed me was more like it. A little gray in the black made the fury caterpillar look mottled.

"You boys see the sign at the city limits?"

"Hard to miss. But I figured that since we're civilized, it didn't apply to us." Matthew's voice was amiable enough, but the way he set his feet wasn't. His rifle was near at hand in Wind's saddle scabbard.

I stepped forward. "Our family's lived in these parts and traded in this town ever since it's been a town. I have business to conduct with Caleb Brown now and then."

"Don't make no mind," the Sheriff drawled. "The law's the law."

"It's not a law," I came back at him. "It's a policy."

"Wrong. The City Council passed an ordinance." Landreth smiled benevolently, but his hand rested near his six-gun holster.

I thought for a minute. "Mr. Brown's the chairman of the council. He'd have sent word if it had passed."

Landreth's smile died. "It's before the council right now. Be a law by the end of the week." The man's pig eyes studied us closely. "Tell me how come you boys' place don't get hit like the other farms?"

"Maybe they leave us alone for the same reason you try to keep us out," I said. "Because I've got some of their blood. But I've got some of yours, too. Mostly yours, as a matter of fact."

The lawman nodded at Matthew. "You ain't. I hear tell you're gone most of the time. You riding with them renegades, Brandt?"

"I go to visit my family. My wife's at Pine Ridge."

His words hit like a blow to the solar plexus even though he was spinning a story for the sheriff. I fought for breath.

"How come she don't come live at Turtle Crick and save you all them trips?"

Matthew mimicked a white man and stared right into the lawman's eyes. "She's afraid you'll shoot her, that's why."

"Sounds like a sensible woman. I'll ask it the other way around. How come you don't stay on the reservation with her?"

I found my voice. "Because he owns part of the farm. And because I need his help. We're honest farmers, Sheriff, and you know that. Now, we'll finish our visit with our sister who's married to Captain Haleworthy. Or do you want her to get out of town, too."

Landreth tipped his hat. "Ma'am." He back-walked his horse a step or two and headed down Main Avenue, taking his gang with him.

Rachel Ann was near to tears, so we remained a while longer before walking her back to the sentry box and saying goodbye.

As we mounted, I suggested we go see Caleb Brown and determine the lay of the land. As soon as we entered the store, the merchant came flying down the staircase.

"What are you doing here? It's dangerous for you to be in town."

"We know. We just had a set-to with the sheriff," my mate said.

"Good to see you, Matthew. You're looking good."

"He's been eating off Theodore Roosevelt's plate up north."

"I hear he's got quite a spread."

"Two of them. The Maltese Cross at Chimney Butte and the Elkhorn north of Medora."

"How did you come to be up there?" Caleb asked.

"I met him on a buffalo hunt last year. So when I heard he was in the Territory, I went up for a visit."

"I see. A shame about his wife and mother. Did he really lose them on the same day?"

Matthew nodded. "St. Valentine's Day. And he's taking it hard."

Caleb turned to me. "John, you'd better send a message to Winter Bird and tell him not to make another trip until things settle down."

"When will that be?" I asked. "Landreth says the council's passing an ordnance barring the likes of us from the town limits."

"They're trying, and frankly, I'm not certain I can stop such nonsense. It's dangerous for you even in the absence of such a law. I'll send word when the issue is settled."

As we left town for home, I heard threats from my neighbors of lo these many years. Neither of us spoke on the entire trip. As soon as we arrived, I climbed up into the cote and dispatched one message to Winter Bird advising him of the situation and another to Teacher's Mead to let Pa know what was going on.

Later, as we lounged in the medicine hut, I could not still my tongue. "Matthew, you spoke of a wife to the sheriff."

He reached over and placed a hand on my thigh. "Rest easy," he said in Lakota. "You are my only wife. But I could see where Landreth's mind was heading. I thought it best to divert the path."

# # # # #

With no cattle on the range beyond the five head in the penned meadow, Todoh had little to do, so he was constantly underfoot. He gave most of his attention to Matthew, and my mate constantly brought him

97

into the house. I put up with it until the dog raised a leg against the stove, then I whopped him on the butt with a towel and sent him scooting out the door. A moment later he set up such a clamor, we both went outside to see what was wrong. He was around behind the house, so we had to mount the hill, mindful of the still cocked trap, to see what had attracted his attention. A lone rider, a tribesman given his clothing, approached at a slow walk. The man was slumped over with his forehead nearly in the mane of his black gelding.

I walked out and led the pony into the barn. No need to advertise his presence to anyone who passed within sight. Matthew closed the door behind us. At first I feared it was Bird, but this was a stranger, a thin man with a bloody shirt. His face contorted in pain, he told us he was Eagle Wing, an Oglala fighting with Howling Wolf. His leader had sent him to me for aid.

I cursed silently. "Where is Howling Wolf?"

"In the ha-ha," the man gasped. "Behind ... cabin. He waits."

"Let him wait," I muttered.

Between us, we got the warrior off his horse and up the ladder to the loft. I removed his shirt before placing him on a blanket spread over hay bales and almost gasped at the ragged tear in the man's shoulder. Matthew went for water and clean cloths while I got Otter's Pandora's box of healing herbs and medicines. I forced a dose of laudanum down Eagle Wing's throat and began picking the wound clear of bits of dirt and buckskin. I gave the young man a stick to put between his teeth and dosed the torn flesh with an astringent. If I did not stop the bleeding, he would die.

The man's shoulder was clearly shattered. He needed a real medical man for that, but perhaps I could keep him alive until he could find one. When I had done all I could for Eagle Wing, I covered him against the chills and fever that would surely come and sent Matthew to talk to Howling Wolf. I would have preferred to go, but I was needed at the wounded man's side.

"Close Todoh up in the barn when you leave," I called after him. "Give Wolf three of the steers, which I have already promised him, and tell him to go back to the reservation. I will send Eagle Wing when he is fit to travel."

Matthew's head reappeared at the opening to the loft. "If the army finds him here, they'll arrest both of us."

"I'll allow you to condemn him to death, if that is your wish."

Matthew grimaced. "He stays. I've already put his gelding out of sight in the spare stall."

"You know why Wolf sent this man to me, don't you?"

"So he'll die under your care, not his. To diminish Medicine Hair's power."

"And since I've laid hands on him, Wolf will probably insist on taking Eagle Wing with him. Then when the man dies, he can claim my medicine failed. Don't let Wolf have him."

After Matthew departed, I turned to find the young warrior already slipping into the bosom of fever. Infection was setting in. I shuddered as I remembered Blood Mark Boy and me fighting to save Matthew from burning up after he was shot near Fort Robinson.

We had lost an hour of sun before Matthew returned. He cursed his way to the top of the ladder. "That snake was coming to take his wounded man. Bringing his whole gang. There are only eleven of them left, by the way. They look in rough shape. Anyway, the only way I could prevent it was to give them all five steers. We're wiped out."

"That's all right, I kept them to send to the reservation, so we're out nothing. There's plenty of beef in the cool room for our needs. You'd better go get some rest. The next few days are going to be rough. Fever's already burning him up. Spell me sometime in the night. And bring cool water when you come."

Matthew and I took turns attending Eagle Wing for the better part of a *senight*. During that time, I was convinced we'd lost him two different times. I did not know a human being could live with such a temperature ravaging his body. Yet, we managed to bring the fever to bay and drain and pack his suppurating wound. There was nothing we could do for the shattered bones, so even if he lived, the man would likely lose the use of his left arm.

It required deviousness on our parts to keep the wounded man's presence from the Tillers. Both Andre and Libby were accustomed to free rein of the farm since they often tended the place during our absence. Indeed, Libby liked to look in on the pigeons in the cote. By various subterfuges, we avoided this until Eagle Wing regained his senses and we could hide him behind stacked bales of hay. The black gelding we explained away as an animal we'd obtained for Winter Bird. Both Tillers were aware of our arrangement with the Sioux trader.

Well into November, our guest with the wounded wing proclaimed himself strong enough to return home. Neither Matthew nor I were convinced he was fit, so we reluctantly concluded my mate should accompany him to the reservation. The lack of smoke and constant cavalry patrols suggested Howling Wolf had taken his group back to the reservations before the cold season settled in.

My heart was clogged with fear the day the two of them set off, circling well to the north of Andre's spread in order to remain undiscovered. If they ran into army patrols, Eagle Wing's wound would paint them both as renegades. And early snow squalls represented as real a danger as the military. It would be a long five or six days before Matthew returned.

Medicine Hair

The two mounted figures were no more than out of sight than I raced to send a messenger pigeon to Winter Bird advising they were on their way. He needed to know of my misrepresentation about the black pony to the Tillers should they ever ask about the animal. I likewise wanted the reservation to know Eagle Wing lived and prospered. I sighed as the brownish hued bird rose and raced to the west. Once I'd discounted the power of my hair. Now it seemed as if I were advertising it.

A man fights with the weapons he has at hand.

CHAPTER 16

After spending a week preparing the farmstead for winter, I dared to venture into town for a load of peat from the trader who customarily brought the fuel down from Canada. No one seemed to care I was invading the limits of Yanube City. Likely because there had been no recent raids. The now abandoned Stubblefield place yielded some charred timbers and a few other items for fireplace fuel, adding to our woodpile. Spring would be a long time coming.

I was beginning to fret – nay, that is a misnomer. I fretted from the day he left – but I was beginning to worry before Todoh tore off the cabin porch to joyously announce Matthew's return. I mounted the hill and watched my lover approach. My sphincter tingled in anticipation of the demand he would place upon it.

As he cared for his horse, my mate told me the trip had gone well. Eagle Wing was back among his family, loudly proclaiming Medicine Hair's skill at healing. Matthew also brought news that Winter Bird was well, his standing high among the People for providing a modest source of income and trade goods.

Matthew also told me Grover Cleveland was to be our new president, after defeating his Republican opponent in the national election. Ironic that such momentous news came to me from Indian country where the People were largely unmoved by such events. Few believed a new occupant in the White House would improve conditions on the reservations.

Matthew waited until we reached the warmth of the cabin to strip my clothes from me and do what he did so well: make love and fuck ass. After a lengthy, energetic tumble, we lay in one another's arms while Todoh scratched at the door and whimpered to join us. He became so insistent that Matthew finally rose and walked naked to the door to admit the beast. Todoh sent him into gales of laughter by giving his ballsack a sloppy lick with his wet tongue. My lover barely got back into bed and pulled the covers over him before the big dog landed in the middle of us. After we got Todoh settled down, all three of us slept.

#

While Indian troubles tended to occupy minds in our territory, back east other concerns claimed the public's attention. Something called the Federation of Organized Trades and Labor Unions proclaimed an eight-hour work day and settled on May 1 as May Day or Worker's Day. Meaningless. Farmers toiled from sunup to sunset.

The International Meridian Conference in Washington fixed Greenwich as the world's prime meridian. Of course, we did not learn these things until later, and gave them little merit when we did. After all, neither measure protected against raids nor filled an empty belly, although the time thing seemed a practical step. Local authorities could no longer proclaim the time to be whatever they wished it to be. Some sort of standard seemed useful ... if not imperative.

The news that affected us most was not news at all. The entire country was in the grip of a depression, and had been since '82. There was talk of it ending in the coming year.

Winter descended upon us, colder again than the miserable white-out of the year before. Nature apparently decided we did not have travails enough without another long, oppressive season. Although Matthew and I were snug and comfortable in our abode, we could not help but wonder what tragedies were playing out on the agencies.

For some reason, our personal relationship remained better this year than last. Perhaps it was because fear of what the future held roamed the fringes of our consciousness. Whatever the cause, we did not get on one another's nerves as usually happened before the weather loosened its grasp. The New Year passed without incident, although in February, the Moon When Trees Cracked passed without being full. Matthew searched for its meaning in prayer while I simply accepted it as a natural celestial phenomenon.

During the Moon of the Snow-blind, we began to move about and checked on the Tillers. Todoh rode with me in the saddle, and was overjoyed to see Libby. The girl had sprouted, or perhaps it was just that we had not seen her in months, but she was definitely growing into a young woman. I retained little memory of her ma'am, but my mind's eye considered that the filly resembled the dam.

With the coming of snowmelt, we began outside chores, not the least of which was a good mucking out of the barn. Matthew helped with that odious chore, and then we mounted two fat steeds and undertook a hunt. Both Arrow and Wind were pleased to be released from confinement and outdid one another in trying to break free of the reins to do a little galloping.

We ran across a party of huntsmen from Pine Ridge who told us of the hardship the People had endured and of rumors of an uprising of the Cree and Métis – mixed bloods – in Canada. Some hoped the tribes south of the border would rise and join the rebellion.

We had finished plowing the fields when a messenger pigeon arrived from Winter Bird. Its appearance surprised me. I'd assumed all of the birds had disappeared into someone's stew pot over the winter. Then I realized the white birds belonged to us, not our friend. He may well have sacrificed his own had they not rested in our cote, but he would not steal ours.

Bird's note – a mixture of crude printed English and Sioux sign language – conveyed the message he had survived the winter, but the real import of the thing was that Raven had been seen at Pine Ridge walking with a decided limp and keeping his right leg covered. Matthew's beaver trap must have caused lasting damage. Bird warned that the Cheyenne was filled with more hate than ever. If that was possible.

Bird's message caused me to check the trap on the hill, and a nosy Todoh tagged along behind me. After carefully clearing away an accumulation of months of debris, I triggered the plate with a long stick and learned it still worked. The ragged jaws bit the thick bough in half and reminded the dog to be wary of the monster.

Matthew agitated to mount up and go looking for Raven Strongbow, but I claimed to need his help. The planting was yet to come, and in little over a moon, I'd buy steers for the year. That was our busiest time, and I could not accomplish everything without his help.

As was usually the case, the lack of depredations for the last several months had eased the townspeople's attitude somewhat, so Matthew and I were able to ignore the hateful sign still posted outside of town and enter its premises to purchase whatever supplies we needed. The Hagstone brothers were even halfway civil when we stopped to check on the availability of cattle when the time came to buy. The harsh winter just passed had put the animals in short supply.

During our visit to Brown's Emporium, Caleb suggested I contact Winter Bird and ask him to make a trip as soon as possible. Once raiding started, it would be too dangerous for him to venture into town.

"I see the sign banning tribesmen is still up," Matthew said.

"Yes, but that's just the sheriff's policy. It doesn't have the force of law."

My mate grimaced. "The force of the sheriff's six-shooter is pretty effective policy. Did you whip them in the Town Council?"

"I merely stalled their efforts to pass an ordinance. If we're hit again this year, they'll get the job done."

We made it out of town without a confrontation with Sheriff Landreth or his deputies. As soon as we got back to the farm, I sent a message to Bird to make haste with the biggest load he could manage, as this might well be the only trade this year.

May brought the purchase of our cattle. The barn could only sell us a disappointing 100 head at inflated prices. While in town, we received fresh news of the uprising by the Cree and Métis in Canada, now called the Northwest Rebellion. In early April, the Battle of Frog Lake in Alberta was followed on the second of May by the Battle of Cut Knife where the Cree roundly defeated the Mounties. But on the ninth of this month, the dreams of the rebellion spreading south of the border died when Canadian government forces delivered a decisive defeat to the rebels at Batoche. Luis Rael, the Métis leader of the uprising, was on the run.

Whether Howling Wolf and his ilk had waited to see the outcome of the war to the north or not, they were late making an appearance. Winter Bird arrived at Turtle Crick leading a string of three pack horses with the first news of the raiders. On his way here, he had come across a prairie fire sparked by a burning farmhouse farther up Turtle Crick.

He'd given the stricken farm wide berth and crossed to the north side of the swollen crick in the hope no one would connect his trail to that of the raiders. He reported the fire had burned itself out at a broad buffalo wallow on the far side of the crick a few miles west of us.

I conducted him to Caleb before word of the raid roused the Americans. No one attempted to stop us as we made our way down Main to the big store. Caleb saw to the unloading and accounting for the pile of trade goods Bird had brought. When the merchant decided this was the only run we'd attempt this year ... unless things changed drastically ... I impetuously donated my expected share of the profits to Bird. After a moment's hesitation, Caleb did the same. My heart fell when the Lakota had to buy two more mounts to hold all the items he intended to carry back to Pine Ridge with him. A string of five animals wouldn't be impossible to manage, but Matthew would undoubtedly offer to go along to help control the pack horses.

As soon as we arrived back at Turtle Crick, my fears became truth. Matthew announced he would ride in aid of Bird upon his departure on the morrow. In truth, his help was needed. They'd have to overnight at least once, and twice if they did not push the animals along. Two rifles would better protect Bird's treasure against thieves in the night. They might see no one on the way to the reserve, but then again, they might run into a party of raiders or a troop of cavalry.

#

That night, Matthew came to me as I stood naked before the dressing table Otter had made many years ago. I was drying off after my bath when he walked up behind me, already rampant and slicked up with butter or a dollop of lard. He pushed my legs apart and entered me easily. I braced myself against the table as he went about fucking me in his very competent way. I arched my back and accepted his vigorous assault while watching his face in the mirror. His beautiful features, so sharp and smooth, slowly contorted with his efforts.

Toward the end, I feared for his heart as he frantically beat my fundament with his thighs. He gasped for air and loosed occasional noises that equally represented ecstasy and expended energy. I, in turn, groaned with each thrust as my cock continued to swell to the point of bursting. Moments before he ejaculated, his driving rod sent me over the edge. I sprayed the mirror and the tabletop with gouts of semen. He came right after me, filling me with hot sperm. I felt sweat on his powerful chest as he leaned over to rest across my back. He panted in my ear.

"I love you, John. I don't believe any man has ever loved another as I love you."

I swallowed words of censure saying he would not leave me for long periods if that were so and reached back to touch his face. "Yes. There is another. The man who loves you feels just as deeply."

He slowly withdrew from me, clasped me about the waist, and spoke in Lakota. "I know you love me. I ought to be angry that the man on the other side of the door comes while I am gone. I know he has a lust for you. Probably as strong as the one Raven nursed before it became a perversion. But it doesn't bother me because I hear truth in your love-words. I am content because I know the man I married."

He kissed my ear and looked at me in the mirror, his face becoming devilish. "Or perhaps Medicine Hair has worked his magic on me and sends me along, so he can have his way with whomever he wishes."

I laughed, but my heart recognized danger lay in this banter. If he dwelt upon it, he might convince himself of his words.

I turned to face him. His wet rod pressed into my stomach. "There *is* enchantment here, but that ability lies with you. Do you know when I recognized I was in love with you? The day you stalked out of the river and rode away. I called after you because the scales had fallen from my eyes, but you wouldn't listen."

He smiled as he remembered. "And the next time I came home, I took you in the glade on the south side of the river. That was a magic moment for me. The moment I realized it wasn't just a yen I had for you. It went deeper. Right straight into my soul. That was when I knew I loved you."

The next morning, Matthew and Winter Bird were not yet out of sight before I went into the fields in search of distraction lest my heart fracture into pieces.

# # # # #

Three days later, Howling Wolf visited the farm with three others trailing him. One of the men I believed to be Blackhawk, although I was not certain as his shaven head was no longer covered in black paint. Nonetheless, his ugly, pocked features led me to this conclusion. After exchanging greetings, I made a point of asking after Eagle Wing. This soured the Brulé's disposition.

"He is not with us," he answered in a curt voice. "Your medicine was not strong enough to return the use of his arm to him."

"It was good enough to give him back his life."

"I need warriors, not cripples."

"Then mend your men's wounds with your own medicine. Don't send them to me when you believe they are beyond help. Why are you here?"

My rudeness struck home. He drew himself straight in the saddle. "I come for the beef you owe me."

"I owe you nothing, Howling Wolf. But I choose to give you steers for your families back home. Once again, you come too early. The animals carry little meat, and they are fewer in number this year. Too many of them died over the winter."

"We cannot wait. We will take the levy now."

"Come back in a moon, and they will be worth your while. I will put two of the animals behind a fence and overfeed them for you."

"We need them now. Not during the next moon."

"If you wish to squander your ration, I will give you one."

The man's face turned mottled. "I will take them now. And if your dog gets in my way, I'll take him, too. He will boil up into a good stew."

"You touch Todoh, and I'll come for you, Howling Wolf. Then we'll see what your medicine is worth. But you did not come here to war with me, so it is not necessary to point knives at one another. I have given you my best advice."

The medicine man was on a spit with a fire toasting his toes. I'd faced him down in front of his men. Out of the corner of my eye, I noticed the others following the exchange closely. Only Blackhawk seemed to take it personally.

Wolf caused his palomino to dance nervously. "I will heed your advice. In the middle of the Moon When the Berries are Good, I will be busy making the Americans pay, but Blackhawk will return for three of your biggest steers."

"He will return for two, but I will choose good animals. One other thing." I might as well get this off my chest. "I hear the Cheyenne, Raven Strongbow, has returned to Pine Ridge and intends to join you. Aside from the fact he is a snake and not to be trusted, I will consider it a personal insult if he is allowed to join your party."

Perhaps I had gone too far because Hawk's face betrayed his thoughts. "He shoots straight, and I need all the men I can get. You ask too much."

"I will not unsay my words, but I'll add some more. If you permit him to ride with you, keep him close. What he covets, he will take. Regardless of who it belongs to. That applies to you, as well as to me."

Wolf and his men departed without acknowledging the truth of my statement, leaving me to wonder if I had provoked the Brulé into violating our unspoken truce. Best warn Andre of the exchange. It would cause him worry, but at least he would be alerted.

CHAPTER 17

When the spring winds ceased to blow, Howling Wolf filled the valley with fire and smoke. I stood on the hillock behind the house and looked south to where a gray haze clung to the earth like nature's fog. We were in that peculiar state where the upper air hung heavy and pressed smoke against the ground.

There was plenty of army activity. Patrols often passed in the distance. Then one day, on a Friday, if I recall correctly, Gideon led one to my door. To my surprise, Rachel Ann accompanied them.

My brother-in-law handed his wife down from her mount – careful of the small bundle she carried – before turning to greet me. "Look who I've brought for a visit."

I hugged my sister and gave her a peck on the cheeks. A broad smile brightened her pretty features as she held out an infant for my inspection.

"Meet William, your new nephew. Isn't he handsome? Like his papa."

More like his mother, although I did not express the thought aloud. There was little of the father in his dark features. Even so, Gideon grinned as though his senses had leached away.

"William like his grandfather Strobaw and William like his grandfather Haleworthy," he said.

"He'll do both of them proud." So Rachel had not shared the family secret with her husband. That was all right. It was good he continued to consider us quarter-bloods. "When did he arrive?"

"In March. On the 15th. You'd have known if you had bothered to stop for a visit."

"An Ides of March child." I slid past her censure.

She frowned. "Is that a bad omen?"

"Not unless your name is Caesar. No, it is merely an interesting observation."

"We've come to stay a bit, if you'll have us," Rachel Ann said.

"Is Matthew here?" Gideon asked.

"No, he accompanied Winter Bird to Pine Ridge with a load of supplies. I expect him to be gone awhile."

Gideon tarried only long enough to have an enlisted man carry his wife's bag into the cabin. Rachel Ann watched them ride west, apprehension clouding her dark eyes.

Several hours passed before my sister loosened up enough to speak her mind. She was generally happy with her life at the post. Most of the women had come to accept her, but when raids placing their men in danger started, resentment bubbled to the surface. Even the steadfast friendship of Mrs. Colonel Irons wasn't enough to shield my sister from covert hostility.

Having a woman in the house was good, although I had to surrender my bedroom and sleep on blankets beside the stove. The baby ... something a little over three months old ... kept Rachel Ann from joining me in the fields, but she threw herself into heavy housework. Although I believed myself a clean, tidy man, she was soon scrubbing the interior of the cabin like Ma would have done.

During the day, we spoke of the world as it was. At night after chores were done, we read books and relived our childhood. Little Ides – as I elected to call him – proved as comfortable in Uncle John's lap as he was in mother's. He delighted in twisting around and pulling my nose with his chubby little fingers.

Todoh was so enchanted by the tiny creature that he constantly slipped away from his charges and stole back to the house. Gentle with the baby, the big blue even put up with the child yanking on his ears. Rachel Ann thought tugging on the crumpled left one would make it stand tall like the right, but that proved not to be the case.

Although I enjoyed the company and companionship, I began to fret after a week went by. Before long, Blackhawk would put in an appearance to collect the two steers in the pen. While I had no doubt my sister would keep my confidence, I didn't wish to needlessly test her loyalty to her husband. The day she began standing on the porch and scouring the southern horizon, I understood she missed Gideon. When the Tillers' buckboard rolled into the yard on the way to church Sunday morning, she asked if I minded advantaging their company to return to the fort.

Andre tarried and talked crops while she scurried about gathering her things. She was unencumbered of the infant. Libby had taken charge of the child the moment she laid eyes on him. In short order, Todoh and I stood on the porch and watched the wagon –with my sister's horse tied behind it – rumble across the bridge and head south. The dog expressed his displeasure with a long whine.

Not a quarter of an hourglass had gone by before Todoh began acting strangely. He was lying on the porch, eyes still fixed on the wagon track, when he suddenly became upright and whipped his head to the right. His low growl brought me outside. As soon as I came through the door, he bounded off the porch and headed straight into the cornfield.

This was not his behavior when distracted by varmints, so I took his reaction seriously. I fetched my Henry and followed him cautiously. Although the plants were no more than shoulder high, it was difficult to follow the dog. I had not yet spotted him when he set up a loud yammer. Still unable to see him, I raced down the row as quickly as I could, coming to a halt when a loud shot cracked through the air.

I cleared the end of the field in time to see the dog disappear down the north crick bed. Moments later, a big paint labored up the south side of the stream and headed south.

Raven! The Cheyenne was back. Although I was on low ground and had but a head visible to me, I threw up my rifle and fired. It took but a moment to consider he'd likely seen the Tiller's buckboard and was heading for it. I ran for the corral, cursing aloud over being at the far end of the field. When I threw open the gate, Arrow caught my urgency. He was already moving when I twisted my fist into his mane and threw myself at his back. Guiding the pinto with my knees, I pounded across the bridge.

A distant gunshot frightened me. But Raven hadn't had time to catch the wagon. The dog must have given chase to the Cheyenne's mule. I urged Arrow into his fastest run. Before long, the buckboard came into view moving along at a walk, Rachel Ann occupied the seat beside Andrew. Libby sat in the bed of the wagon cradling Ides. Off to their right, Raven was bearing down on them. A second, smaller stream of dust was Todoh, still on the chase.

Unable to reach them in time, I pulled up and fired three warning shots in the air. To my horror, Andre reined to a halt to look around. He spotted Raven and pulled his rifle, but it was apparent he wasn't certain what was happening. To spur him on, I emptied half the shells in the Henry's sleeve in the direction of the Cheyenne.

Heartened to see Rachel Ann climb into the bed while Andre drew a bead on the approaching horseman, I kicked Arrow into a run. At Andre's first shot, Raven pulled to a halt. As he raised his rifle, a blue bundle of ferocious energy bounded from the ground and landed squarely on his back, almost unseating the man. I was close enough now to see the dog had his teeth in Raven's shoulder. Still, the renegade was able to shake him off. Fearful, he would shoot the dog, I raised my rifle to my shoulder. I couldn't hit anything while pounding across the prairie, but maybe I could frighten him into fleeing.

Andre beat me to it. I heard three loud reports. Raven paused long enough to toss a shot at the wagon before turning west and fleeing. I drew up and sent the rest of my bullets after him. Then, whistling sharply for the dog, I raced for the buckboard.

Everyone was all right, although Andre's trace horse was down, shot through the side. Ides was letting out one howl after another until Todoh hopped into the wagon bed and poked his nose in the baby's face. Instantly, my nephew shut up and grabbed the dog by his ears.

"Raven?" Andrew asked as we unhitched the dead horse.

I nodded. "In the flesh. And he's still not ready to kill me."

"He's going after those close to you, instead."

I put a noose around the downed horse's neck and used Arrow to pull him off the road. By the time we hitched Rachel Ann's pony into the traces, I'd given up the idea of setting off after Raven, so I sent Todoh back to the cattle and escorted the wagon all the way to the fort.

Upon arriving back at Turtle Crick, I located Raven's tracks and read the story. He'd lurked about on the north bank of the crick near where I'd caught him in the beaver trap last year. He'd obviously seen Rachel Ann and the baby. Andre must have passed within feet of where he lay hidden, so he was well aware my sister and her child were on the wagon. That was likely why he'd gone after it.

But why was he in my cornfield? That's where Todoh had headed when he first caught scent of the Cheyenne. Before losing the light, I carefully walked the field and discovered the reason. He'd set his own steel trap, something larger than for beaver. More like a wolf trap. He'd hoped to snare me or Todoh.

I snapped the trigger on the device and lugged it to the outhouse for storage. Mayhap I'd set it and catch him in his own snare.

When I went to check on the cattle, I noticed the two steers in the enclosed pasture were missing. I investigated and found horse tracks, not mule prints. Blackhawk and another brave had been here while Todoh and I were gone. None of the other cattle seemed to be missing, so it was well and good I'd not had to confront the big warrior. He seemed an unpleasant man.

The next morning, I rode into Yanube City and battled sullen hostility long enough to buy two half-grown pups of indeterminate parentage. They sported massive paws, so they'd be large beasts in a few months. Yet they were still young enough to train. I experienced some difficulty getting them home, but they eventually got tired of being dragged along behind Arrow and kept up. They tried attacking his heels once or twice, but sharp kicks soon cured them of that. When we arrived at the farm, I gave them water and a little raw meat before taking them out to acquaint them with Todoh.

This was the real test. The two, one a shaggy black and white and the other a coal black with a white muzzle, got along with one another, but how would they react to Todoh? More to the point, would he tolerate them? After a little stiff-legged growling and snapping, curiosity got the better of them. Before an hourglass had run, they were playing like juveniles.

When they were comfortable with one another, I led them around some of the steers, whacking them across the butt with a rope when they nipped at the animals. Another hour elapsed before they understood the cattle belonged here.

Then I rode to the Tiller place and offered Andre his choice of the two. Libby, who had no fear of strange animals, went down on her knees and immediately chose the black with the white muzzle.

"Now I'll have two White Patches," she said, stroking the beast's silky back. "Course, we can't have a pony and a dog named alike, so I'll call this one White. You know, because he isn't."

Ah, the female mind at work. She'd made a good choice. The short-haired cur had a better disposition than the shaggy one. After hearing of the trap Raven had set, Andre promised to work with White to instill fear of a snare's jagged jaws, just as I intended to do with my new canine.

Although the farm demanded most of my time, I worked daily with the new dog, which I named *Heyoka Sapa*, or Black Clown because his patchwork coat reminded me of a drawing of a clown's suit I'd seen in a book. In the lazy way of talk, he soon became just Sapa, or Black. Despite his penchant for running off to play with Todoh on the range or with White at the Tillers, I managed to eventually train him to remain in the vicinity of the house and fields. So confined, he was less self-sustaining than the blue heeler, but I didn't mind feeding him jerky. He also developed a liking for vegetables, so he shared most of my plate.

Sapa grew territorial and had to be restrained when strangers tried to enter the yard. I smiled inwardly at the welcome Matthew would receive upon his return home but then thought better of it and sent a message by pigeon to Winter Bird, asking him to warn of my new sentry.

#####

One day that must have been in the middle of July, I was working in the vegetable fields when Sapa began acting nervous. His whine alerted me that something was not right. After a good look around, a cloud of dust south of me sent me to the house for my spyglass. From atop the hill behind the house, I made out distant, indistinct horsemen. It took several minutes of study to discern a number of tribesmen, likely Howling Wolf's raiders, fleeing before what seemed to be a full platoon of cavalry.

As they were headed directly for the farm, I got my Henry and fired three warning shots into the air, hoping the Tillers would hear and take cover. Then I moved my two horses from the corral into the barn and locked Sapa in the building with them. Todoh, I left to his own devices. He would be all right provided he didn't try to protect his cattle too vigorously.

I settled on the porch with my rifle to watch. Before long, I heard the muffled thunder of pounding hooves and an occasional gunshot. In a few more minutes, things became more distinct. Then the Indians disappeared over the edge of a ha-ha. A moment later, Howling Wolf, if indeed it was his group, showed his genius. A cloud of smoke erupted from the gully as his men took cover and turned their guns upon the enemy. The line of charging blue coats faltered and came to a halt. The officer leading them must have been a shave tail. He let his men mill around before getting control of them and charging the gully.

Everything fell silent as the troopers poured over the lip of the depression, telling me Wolf had split his men, going both up and down the ha-ha. A moment later, the troopers came up out of the ditch and paused on this side. More confusion as an officer and a sergeant split their force and rode both east and west.

The blue coats were no sooner out of sight than Wolf's band came up out of the ha-ha where they'd originally disappeared. The wily medicine man had anticipated the lieutenant's move and reassembled in the depression. Now he pounded north. I feared for a moment he was coming to the farm, but instead, he stopped short of my bridge and led his men single file into the crick. Three of his number went into the water on the left – the east side of the bridge – leaving an obvious trail. Moments later, they returned to blur the tracks of their companions and waded upstream to join Wolf.

I hoped the war party came out of the crick short of the Tiller farm. I had little fear of an attack on my neighbor. Wolf would not wish to attract the attention of the cavalrymen in the vicinity. But if he got too close, Andre might fear himself under attack and open fire.

After a quarter of an hour passed without alarm, I released the dog from the barn and returned to hoeing the vegetable field. Not long after that, Sapa set up a racket, and I saw the Mandan and another army scout at the bridge examining marks in the dirt. Shortly thereafter, a young officer left the bulk of his troops on the south side of the crick and led four men across the bridge into my yard. I went out to meet them.

"Mr. Strobaw?" the shave tail asked, uncertainty clouding his eyes. Apparently, he was new to the command and no one had told him the Strobaws were a blood family.

I introduced myself and learned his name was Ryerson. He wasted time explaining the situation I'd seen for myself, but I let him talk. The sergeant at his elbow looked as pained as I was. He was a mean-looking three-striper. A veteran. A veteran hater.

In response to his question, I told the Lieutenant I'd bolted the door to my cabin and closed the shutters when it appeared the raiders were headed for the farm. By the time I realized they'd turned off, all I saw when I stepped onto the porch was the tail end of the party, three warriors wading the crick downstream.

The two scouts were tricked for a crucial half hour, but a careless hoof print at the edge of the water revealed the deception. Sharp Eyes appeared and informed the Lieutenant that Wolf had gone upstream.

"You knowed that, didn't you?" the Sergeant asked with a snarl in his voice.

"I know precisely what I told you. I went to the barn to tend the animals after that, so they must have passed while I was there."

"A whole passel of hostiles pass with just a barn wall between you, and you don't hear nothing?"

"If you'll examine that barn wall, you'll find it's double thick and filled with clay tabby. An army could have passed, and I wouldn't have known it."

The NCO's eyes shifted to the dog standing stiffly at my side, but he didn't speak his thoughts. The dog would have heard even if I hadn't.

In moments, the Sergeant led a squad of men along the north bank of the crick while the bulk of the command followed the Lieutenant on the south side. They'd undoubtedly find where the Indians came up out of the water, but Wolf should have reached the badlands by then. I wondered at the casualties of the battle I'd witnessed. The army would have already sent theirs back to the fort, but some of Wolf's men may be lying wounded out on the prairie.

A bit later, I prowled the area aboard Arrow's back and discovered a single dead tribesman, pierced by army bullets. There was little I could do for the warrior beyond covering him as best I could with a thin layer of rocks and saying a prayer for his safe journey along the Western Road.

CHAPTER 18

I spent an uneasy night. Nothing else untoward had happened yesterday except the military patrol passed on the south bank of the crick late in the afternoon on its way back to the fort. I saw no evidence of casualties, so it was unlikely they had caught up with Wolf and his warriors.

As I walked to the house for something to eat after early chores, I stood on the porch, as was my custom, to sweep the landscape with my gaze. In these times, it was better to be aware of what was going on lest something nasty catches you unawares by the seat of the pants. Sapa lay with his chin on his paws, so nothing was alarming my sentry. But just before I turned into the house, I caught a flash of light well out onto the prairie. Immediately, Otter came to mind. Just before they came for him, he'd been aware of someone watching the cabin. That flash was probably a binocular lens carelessly catching the sun. I was under surveillance.

Clearly, the army suspected me of aiding Wolf and his raiders. That would not have bothered me unduly except for two things: If the Brulé invited himself to my doorstep again, the army would place its own interpretation on our meeting. And when Matthew returned, I had no fondness for strangers keeping eyes on us.

Yet if Raven was bent on mischief, a witness to his hostility would be helpful. Some bored soldier might decide to shoot the Cheyenne as he slunk around the premises. No, I'd not be that lucky. I spent that day working the fields as if unaware of foreign eyes.

The next morning, I was feeding the horses in the corral when Sapa's bark alerted me to a squad of troopers proceeding apace up the road. I shut the dog in the barn and walked out into the yard to greet the men ... and found myself facing a pistol leveled by the same sergeant who'd been with Lt. Ryerson two days earlier. Nielsburg if I remembered correctly.

I raised my hands, palms out to show they were empty. "What's going on?"

The three-striper threw a leg over his mount and hit the ground, his gun barrel still leveled at me. "That's what we aim to find out. All right, boys. Take a look around. You know what we're looking for."

"If anybody goes through the barn door, that dog'll tear his leg off. Let me go put a noose on him."

"He do, and I'll shoot him." Nonetheless, the Sergeant waved me toward the barn, keeping a respectful distance between us all the way.

I opened the door and grabbed the dog by the ruff as I yanked a short length of rope from a peg and slipped it over his neck. He was only half-trained, so my instructions to settle down were virtually useless. When Sapa stopped yanking on the rope, I gave Nielsburg the once over.

"What's this all about?"

"It's about a cold-blooded killer, that's what it's about." He threw an arm toward the crick. "I got a man down not more'n two hunnert yards from here. Throat slit. Weapons, horse, and binoculars missing. Taken right offa him after he was murdered."

"I don't know anything about it. What was he doing out there? Was he headed here?"

"I'm askin' the questions. Did you do that to my man?"

"No. Why would I?"

"Maybe he seen something he oughtna."

"Nothing to see except me working."

"Hear tell there's another Injun lives here."

"My brother, Matthew. But he's at Pine Ridge visiting his wife ..." I had to stop and swallow. "Been there a few weeks now."

"Why don't you jest tell me where Private Bangler's horse and gear is, so I can get on about my business."

We argued back and forth for a good quarter of an hour while the sergeant's squad of nine men took my house and barn and forge apart. Finally, a corporal came and reported they'd found nothing.

Sgt. Nielsburg rode out of Turtle Crick Farm an unhappy man, and it wasn't hard to figure he'd lay his unhappiness at my door. I hadn't mentioned my brother-in-law because overusing Gideon's goodwill might rub it thin. I likewise didn't share my suspicion that Raven Strongbow had killed the man Nielsburg had set to keep watch on me. That was personal business. I have no idea if the army put eyes on me again, but I saw no more flashes of light on the prairie floor. Of course, that didn't mean someone wasn't there.

A week later to the day, Sheriff Landreth, breathing fire through his moustache-clogged nostrils, pounded up the wagon track with a posse of six men. Without a word, he dismounted and shoved me up against the barn. He was manacling me when Sapa lunged for him. Landreth reached for his six-shooter, but a deputy dropped a lariat around the dog's neck and dragged him away.

The Sheriff leaned against me and put his mouth to my ear. "Where's Brandt?"

"Pine Ridge," I grunted from beneath his weight. "Visiting ... wife."

"I'll just bet he is. Riding with them raiders is more like it. You'd be, too, if you had the sand for it."

The big man was just settling down to punching me out when Gideon and a squad of nine troopers rode up. My brother-in-law rushed to my side.

"What the hell's going on here?"

"I'm gonna finish this conniving bastard's spying for them raiders once and for all."

Gideon pushed the man away. "You'll do no such thing. He's got no part in what happened."

I drew a breath and turned around, my hands still pinioned behind me. "What happened?"

"You know, you lying bastard," Landreth started for me again, but Gideon stepped between us and told me what had set the sheriff off.

Howling Wolf had stomped on the Americans' toes this morning. He attacked Yanube City. I don't know what he figured to gain from it besides a whale of a lot of trouble, but he did it anyway. From Gideon's telling, Wolf and most of his men had swarmed the south end of town and set fire to everything they could before Yanube's fine citizens woke to the danger. When the army rode out of the fort to confront them, three of the Brulé's warriors fired on the column from ambush near the sentry box. Then they fled on their tough little Indian ponies.

None of that hit me, personally, so long as Rachel Ann and Ides were okay. But that changed when my brother-in-law said the three braves on the north side had shot down Timo Bowers when he came out of his forge to see what was going on. Timo was a friend.

"Is he dead?" I wiggled my shoulders in the hope Gideon would release me from the irons.

"The doctor was still working on him when I left."

"Take these things off," I shouted at no one in particular. "I need to go see about Timo."

Gideon leveled a finger at my chest. "You don't set foot in town. Not right now. Someone's liable to shoot you on sight."

"Things is changed now, Strobaw," Landreth said. He jerked me around roughly and unfastened the manacles. "That sign applies to you and Brandt now. Stay outa my town."

I rubbed my wrists. "Sheriff, that blacksmith has been a friend to the Strobaws longer than I've been alive. If he's hurt bad, he needs somebody to take care of his business. I'm a smith, so I'm going to go to his aid. If that earns me a bullet, then so be it."

Gideon pulled a frown, but he stepped up to aid me. "Bowers will have orders from people needing things. John's about the only other man in this part of the territory who can be of aid."

It took another hour for things to sort themselves out, but after the posse and the patrol left for town, I sent a pigeon to the Mead to let Pa know what had happened and ask him to send Crow to help out in the forge. Crow was an Indian, but he'd worked for the army for a couple of years, and everyone in town knew him to be an honorable man. I closed up the place and started for town, leaving my home in the care of my two dogs.

Smoke still rose from the south end of town as I approached the limits. If I had to guess, the feed store and its supply of hay were gone. A second column of smoke rose over where the cattle barn lay. Had Wolf gotten away with some beef for his people? Likely not. He'd be too busy running for his life. Maybe it was because everyone was seeing to their own skins, but I didn't encounter many angry looks by the time I dismounted in front of the doctor's office. Mrs. Doctor Helgren let me know Timo would survive, but he'd been transferred to the care of the sawbones at the fort. Her husband hadn't returned from there yet.

Gaining entry to the fort required a quarter of an hour and involved a private, a corporal, and a captain. Even so, I eventually stood beside a recumbent figure in a long low building filled with at least a dozen beds ... all occupied. I garnered more hostile stares here than I'd endured all morning. Understandable. These were casualties of Howling Wolf's running battles with the army. I began to reconsider the Brulé's effectiveness. He was likely dealing more misery than he was receiving. Even so, he was fighting a losing battle.

Timo was conscious and in obvious pain. For the first time, the weight of his sixty or so years was stamped on his features. He was in such magnificent physical shape – thanks to his profession – that it was easy to ignore the silver hairs among the black on his head and dotting his beard. But now, he was revealed. Here lay a man who had outlived most of his peers and still wielded a smith's hammer until renegades' bullets laid him low.

He started when he saw me. For a fraction of a second, he reacted to a tribesman rather than to a friend. Then reason gained control, and he smiled as I spoke.

"Hello, Timo. Decided to take a few days off, did you?"

He swallowed. "Forced on me, I'd say."

"I came by to see if there's any work you need finished before you're back at the shop. Wouldn't want your customers left waiting."

Relief washed his pinched features. "Thank you, John. I've been fretting over that. Big relief."

Speaking haltingly in the manner of a man in pain, he told me where to find his orders, how to complete them, and even confided some of his clients' peculiarities. He unhesitatingly told me to take the keys to his shop and home from his trouser pockets hanging on a peg beside his bed.

"Just finish them up," he ended the conversation. "There likely won't be any new orders coming through till folks know I'm back in the forge."

I told him that Crow Johnson was on his way from the Mead to fill in until he was back on his feet, and he gave instructions the Absaroka was to live in his house until that time. After that, I left the fort and headed for Bower's forge.

# # # # #

The smithy seemed a different place without Timo's presence. I located the board where he wrote down orders and found a half-finished reflector for a Mrs. Timmerplate's fireplace. Easy enough to finish according to the specifications he'd written. The rest of the items were within my skill level, and certainly Crow would be able to complete them. I lit the fire and located the materials needed to finish the reflector while the flames reached their desired temperature. Then, I went to work.

Half an hour later, the doors burst open as Sheriff Landreth and two deputies stormed inside, guns drawn. I froze lest they find an excuse to pull triggers. Then I carefully laid the smith's hammer down on the anvil.

"You in my town, Injun. Broke into a man's private property. Likely robbing him of his life's work. Tell me why I ought not gun you down right where you stand."

My brow was already heavy with sweat, so he'd not be able to see my pores open up to anxiety. Honest sweat from a man's labor held no aroma, but the sweat of fear bore its own odor.

"Hold on, Sheriff. We already straightened this out. I told you I was coming to help Timo, and if you'll look over on that peg, you'll see his keys. He gave them to me, so I could fill his orders while he's laid up."

"That's your story. Mine'll be different."

"Why are you so bent on getting rid of me? I've dealt you no grief. I'm law abiding. And right now, I'm trying to help a man who's laid out on his back."

"Yeah, by a kinsman of yours."

A deputy brought over Timo's keys and dangled them before the lawman. "Keys was right where he said they was."

"Ride for the fort and make sure his story meets up with Bowers's. We'll just stay right where we are till you get back. Go on. Strobaw, you get back to work."

I watched the deputy disappear outside. "No thanks, I'll just stand right here until he confirms Timo's accounting. Wouldn't want this thing to go catawampus. That might give you call to mistake the hammer for a weapon."

"Balderdash, boy. I was of a mind, I'd just shoot you and put the hammer in your hand after you was dead." He paused. "At least you got horse sense, even if you are uppity."

I kept my uppity self absolutely still until the deputy returned and said I had both Timo's permission and thanks for helping him out. The Sheriff seemed disappointed, making me wonder what kept a halter on his trigger finger. The only thing I could think of was that Billy Strobaw cast a long shadow from the grave he'd occupied for the last twenty-four years. That and the fact the Strobaws would all rise as a man. And they'd likely carry any tribesmen in this part of the territory with them when they did.

As Landreth walked out of the forge backward so as to keep an eye on me, I told him Crow Johnson was on the way to work the forge and watch over Timo's property until the smith was back on his feet. It was obvious the news didn't sit well. Crow, as a recent scout for the army, had the goodwill of the officer corps at the fort, so Landreth would be less likely to shoot him on sight. When I finished work for the day, I hid Timo's keys

119

and left a note using sign language to let Crow know where to find them. It was unlikely anyone else would be able to decipher my markings.

I got back to the farm before light was gone and found a messenger pigeon with a note saying Crow would arrive sometime tomorrow. Good. I wouldn't lose any more work in the fields. After I fed Sapa, he and I rode out to the range to check on the cattle. Todoh had things under control, so I headed back to the house.

During the night, Sapa gave a nervous whine and came off the bed, heading for the front door. I slipped on moccasins and took up my Henry before easing outside. The dog hopped off the porch and headed around back of the house. Staying close to the side of the building, I followed him cautiously. After a thorough search of the vicinity, I found nothing ... especially the hour of sleep I'd lost roaming around in the chill night clad only in my sleeping loincloth.

The next morning, Sapa led me to tracks leading from the north bank of the crick up past the house toward Trickling Water. I'd have figured it was a traveling tribesman had the hoof prints not been outsized. Sure as shooting, Mr. Killpenny's paint mule had laid down these tracks.

I must have let Raven get into my head because I didn't sleep much over the next few nights.

We were deep into the Moon When Cherries Turn Black – September by the white man's calculations – before Todoh let out a howl along about noontime on what must have been a Thursday. That was his Matthew bark. I stood in the vegetable field and loosed a smile. The dog was streaking across the prairie toward a distant horseman. From the way he carried his shoulders, the rider was my mate. Shambling Bear was home.

But our time had to wait. Todoh demanded my lover's total attention for the better part of an hour. I bided my time by brushing Matthew's flea-bitten gray and cautioning Sapa to remain at my side. Wind Rider seemed content with my ministrations. Once Todoh's time had run, we devoted another precious hour to introducing Sapa to Matthew and overcoming the dog's hostility. He came over slowly, but once he got the idea Matthew was a permanent fixture, he became less stiff-legged.

The first opportunity for Matthew and me to embrace came as we stood in the kitchen after the horse and dogs were taken care of. Sapa had entered with us, and as soon as Matthew wrapped his strong, corded arms around me, the dog snarled. Despite calling him down, he continued to exhibit what I can only call jealous tendencies. So we threw him out of the house.

Despite our urgent needs, Matthew wanted both a tub and a medicine bath before becoming intimate. I came close to breaking the agreement. While toweling him off after sluicing him down in the tub, I grabbed his stiff pole. It took a moment before we brought ourselves under control and marched down to the medicine lodge. The stones were already heated, as I'd taken the time to stoke the fire while he was bathing in the house.

Before long, we lay sprawled inside the little brush and canvas structure while steam swirled around us. Fortunately, Sapa did not like the damp heat and remained on guard outside.

As was our custom, we discussed farm matters first. Then I told of visits by both the sheriff and the army. I passed on Landreth's stated belief Matthew was riding with the raiders. My mate expressed no alarm on that subject because a man from the Indian agent's office at Pine Ridge had looked him up and engaged him in pointless conversation, leading him to believe someone was checking up on his movements. Of course, he had ventured up north to visit Mr. Roosevelt again, so a portion of his time was unaccounted for. This white man from far off New York had impressed my lover in a manner no other white man had managed.

Then he told of the appalling conditions on the reservations and asked if I would be willing to contribute a part of our herd to help alleviate the widespread hunger among the tribes.

"We already help."

"No, *Wastelakapi*, I mean a real contribution. Twenty or twenty-five head."

"But that's a quarter of what we have."

"And infinitely more than what they have," he responded quietly.

"We will give them all, if that is your wish." He knew I was putty in his hands every time he called me beloved.

"Nay. Then we'd have nothing to contribute later. Let me give Pine Ridge twenty head, and we'll sell the rest to reinvest in the future."

"Done. I'll help you on the drive to the reservation."

"No need. Winter Bird and two of his friends await us on the Trickling Water. We'll take the cattle to them. They can drive them the rest of the way. Bird has a small load of trading goods with him."

"Then we must take enough silver to pay him. I'll take the load to town later."

"Good. But first, we gotta take care of one another." He stretched his wiry frame, displaying an enormous erection.

I grinned. "Let's see if you can keep that up after Turtle Crick's cold embrace."

He laughed and tore out of the sweat lodge. I was right behind him. The cold water certainly took the starch out of my rod, but his remained ramrod straight. As we ran dripping toward the house, Sapa close on our heels, I shriveled further at the recollection that just such a display had been the downfall of Otter and James. The army had had the farm under surveillance once; perhaps they still did.

Once inside the cabin, Matthew drove all such thoughts from my mind. We dried one another with towels, nearly bringing ourselves to ejaculation by our antics. But reason prevailed, and we were still strong with desire by the time we tumbled into bed.

121

He hovered over me, his face uncommonly handsome as he studied my features. He seemed to grow more Indian as he spoke in Lakota. "I am blessed beyond all men that you give me your love."

I put a banter in my voice. "You say that to all your wives, I expect."

A shadow crossed his eyes, and I realized I'd hurt him. "I have no wife but the one I hold in my arms right now. I have pledged my word to you, John. And you of all people on this earth should know I honor my word."

I clasped him to my breast. "I know. I know. But while I'm here alone, my mind plays tricks on me. I dream of you with a woman, and then I begin to believe the tales they tell of me, that my magic hair can see things other can't. Then, I don't know what's imagined and what's magic."

"I thought you didn't believe your speckled head gave you medicine."

"In rational moments, I *know* it doesn't. But here alone ..."

"You can put an end to that. I would like nothing better than for you to come with me. I would be proud to display my wife to my people. I speak of you that way, you know."

"Do you?" My heart swelled. "I'm glad. Now fuck me!"

"I have something new I want to try."

I frowned, struck by doubts again."

His laugh was like the bong of a golden bell. "Don't let that imagination of yours run off. I heard a man speak of doing it to his wife in the armpit. He swore there was nothing like it."

"I know of no special glands in the armpit for your cock to satisfy, but we can try it."

He gave an elfin smile. "I want to give it a go."

He leaned down to kiss me, and I'll swear sparks leapt between our lips just before they touched. Then the warmth of his breath on my cheek and the touch of his moist tongue on my open lips brought their own magic, infusing me with a satisfaction akin to orgasm. He spread himself down the length of my naked body. His cock nestled alongside mine. His ballsack pressed against my own. Our bellies kissed, and our chests lay heavy against one another. My nipples tingled.

"I love you in all your incarnations, John Strobaw, War Eagle, Night Sky Hair, Medicine Hair. You are all as precious to me as the blood in my veins. Your heart beats for my heart, and gives me strength."

"My husband has been taking lessons in love talk." I teased him to overcome the paralysis of my vitals occasioned by his words.

"Nay. They are inspired by my closeness to you." He presented his pulsing cock to my lips. I took him. How comfortably he fit into my mouth. Even when he pressed himself against me so that I lost the ability to breathe, my trust in him ... my need for him was all that mattered.

In moments, he withdrew and jabbed at my shoulder. I obediently clasped his turgid cock in my armpit. As he began to thrust, I got nothing from it other than the knowledge this was something he desired. That and the ability to lick his satiny skin when he pressed close. After a few minutes of this, he withdrew and frowned down upon me.

"I think it is overrated. Too much friction. Of the wrong kind. Wait!" He held up a finger and disappeared from the room. Moments later, he reappeared with his big cock made slick by a smear of butter. He jumped back in bed and assaulted my left armpit energetically.

"Ah, better," he said.

I contented myself with touching him in any place I could reach. Whether it was from the novelty of the act or long abstinence, it did not take him long to achieve ejaculation. He groaned and froze against me. His cock was so long, he delivered most of his load on the bedding beneath us. After a moment, he hunched so hard the bed threatened to collapse.

With hardly a pause, he flipped us over, smeared his own semen over my cock and pulled me into his armpit. I must admit the warmth of his flesh energized me. Soon, I was fucking his hollow as enthusiastically as he had mine. Orgasm came quickly, and I made a mess on the other side of the bed. Once through the exquisite experience, I settled my body atop his and placed my forehead against his broad brow.

"Messy," I said.

"But not unpleasant."

"No, I'll give you that. But frankly," I paused to give a thrust of my hips, "I prefer that buried in my fundament."

He smiled. "And it will be. As soon as we recover."

"We ought to change the bedding."

"Why? We'll just mess it up again."

CHAPTER 19

The next morning, we put Todoh under stress by cutting out twenty head of steers and hazing them toward Trickling Water. I fretted the animals were not yet meaty enough, but Matthew assured me they would go a long way toward alleviating hunger among our kinsmen.

My spirits lifted when I saw Winter Bird. We tarried beside the small party's campfire to bring one another up to date and to pay Bird for his wares. Matthew had claimed it was a small load, but the packs spread among himself and his two companions burdened our horses to the point I feared we might have to walk back to the farm. This was a blind transaction in that we did not take time to unload the packs and examine each piece, but I was prepared to stand any loss should I have miscalculated the value of the goods.

Before my young friend and his companions departed, I gave them a piece of paper stating that they had traded for the steers. This small group with a large number of cattle would provide a tempting target to thieves and renegades, but Matthew stilled his impulse to accompany them and returned home with me. We managed to ride nearly to the farm before the laden horses showed signs of distress, forcing us to dismount and walk the remainder of the way.

Deciding to get the trading goods to Caleb Brown promptly, we loaded the packs in the buckboard and headed into town the next morning. No one had restored the "Injuns Keep Out" sign I had torn down. Matthew and I stopped at the Bowers forge where we were cheered by the pleasant visage of Crow Johnson.

Crow wasn't particularly tall, but he was broad and heavily muscled. He confided that a sheriff's deputy had accosted him upon his arrival, but he didn't hadn't allowed himself to be intimidated. He'd visited the fort to ascertain friends there knew he'd be at the smithy until Timo returned. We tarried overlong in an excess of pleasure at seeing our old friend again. He let us know all was well at the Mead. Mrs. Killpenny had passed on, but had been replaced on this earth by Annabel, Hannah's and Esau's new daughter. I was an uncle again. The news left me feeling estranged from my own family. Upon leaving the forge, Matthew and I pledged to visit Teacher's Mead once the harvest was in and the cattle delivered.

Caleb was pleased to have an unexpected supply of trading goods, and it developed I had not overpaid for the items as a whole. Thereafter, Matthew and I gathered what supplies we required and left town without trouble.

# # # # #

Over the next two weeks, we worked the farm during the day and made love at night. Matthew fucked me in every orifice with his big log, even trying the other armpit and declaring solemnly my left was a better fit. He was more generous than usual in reciprocating and bringing me to climax in his handsome mouth. My happiness was so complete that I grew fearful fate would soon intervene to bring me back to earth. Nonetheless, the sale of the harvest to Tussler and the delivery of the cattle to the rebuilt cattle barn came and went without serious problems. When we got a decent price for both crops and cattle, I took it as a sign the long depression was easing. Still, the loss of twenty head put us short on the cattle end of the business for the year.

By the time our equipment was cleaned, repaired, and stored away, the absence of recent raids prompted us to ask the Tillers to keep watch over the farm while we visited the Mead. Libby agreed to feed the mare, our pigeons, and Sapa. Possessed of a soft heart for animals, she would likely feed Todoh, as well, even though he was capable of foraging on his own. Hopefully, we wouldn't be gone long enough for him to adapt to the easy life.

We set out across the prairie in a southeasterly direction, eschewing the roads in order to avoid travelers who might take fright at the sight of two Indians. We did not make haste as we planned on star camping that night. Experiencing Matthew beneath the stars was different from enjoying him in the closeness of the cabin. It was as if we demonstrated our love and devotion before every god-touched thing in the universe. My lover must have felt the same as he was both lusty and vocal. We brought one another to climax with the cold night air prickling our flesh and then snuggled beneath the blankets to restore heat, regain breath, and recover strength.

When we set out again the next morning, we rode in companionable silence except when one or the other commented on the scent of wild lilacs or pointed out a kestrel soaring above. Our easy mood soured when we spotted smoke even before raising the three hills behind the house at the Mead. We set the ponies into a trot. The sound of sustained gunfire put us into a run to find a group of armed men besieging the Mead's big stone house. The Appleton's cabin was afire. Crow's was already reduced to smoldering beams and ashes. Had Howling Wolf broken our tacit truce?

Without exchanging a word, we veered south so as to approach the raiders from behind. When we were in position, we pulled side arms instead of rifles. At a nod from Matthew, we kicked our horses forward and bore down on the exposed attackers from the rear. I selected two of the villains – noting they were white men, not tribesmen – and shot one down while sending Arrow crashing into the other. When the thug squirmed on the ground and tried to raise his six-shooter, I fired into his chest.

I veered left around the outhouse and forge and flushed three more outlaws while Matthew went in the opposite direction. Gunfire broke up quickly after that as the remainder of the yahoos ran for their horses. Infuriated by the attack on my family, I switched to my long gun and kept throwing lead until they were out of range. I hit at least one but did not unseat him.

Pa and Alexander came out of the house as Matthew and I inspected the other buildings for malingerers. I counted five dead men, and one so wounded he was incapable of fleeing. Then I found a body I didn't want to see. Curtis Appleton lay face down near his burning home. Fearful his family might be inside the cabin, I started to rush through the door, but Pa grasped my elbow and said Jane and the children were safe in the stone house.

Moments later, she flew to her husband's side and knelt over him protectively. Dexter, a gangly youth of fifteen, fell to his knees beside his mother and tried to console her. Ma stood at a distance clasping Prosperity, Curtis's daughter, in her arms.

I breathed thanks to the Great Spirit that Crow's wife and children had elected to visit her family on the reservation while he was tending Timo's forge in Yanube City. At least, she and her children had not been exposed to the raid.

Pa remained with Jane while the rest of us fetched water to douse the burning buildings lest sparks set off a prairie fire. As soon as Curtis was wrapped and laid in the undamaged forge, I sent a messenger pigeon to Turtle Crick. Libby would find it when she fed the birds this evening, and Andre would go to the fort tomorrow to notify Gideon of the raid. I made it plain the attackers were a mix of white men and breeds, and that five of them had been killed and a wounded prisoner had died soon thereafter. I also asked that Gideon notify the Sheriff of Curtis Appleton's demise, so he could be entered into the rolls of the dead.

Afterward, we all gathered in the big room at the stone house to sort things out – save for Matthew, who set off to track the remnants of the gang that had attacked the Mead. Pa hired Dexter in his father's stead. Despite the youth's years, Cuthan offered a man's wage to the youngster, his way of assuring Jane she still had a home and security. The family agreed to move into the stone house until the Appleton's cabin could be rebuilt.

That evening, Matthew returned to report he had tracked a dozen horses well into the Little Island Mountains on the south side of the valley. He'd found one body, so evidently the man I'd shot had bled himself to death as he fled. While I usually suffered the ghosts of men I'd killed, at least for a brief time, I'd not be bothered by any of these killers.

This was not the homecoming Matthew and I had anticipated, yet despite the tragic events, interaction with the family fulfilled our needs. Jane didn't want to wait for a minister to travel to the Mead for her husband's burial. All of us were intimately familiar with the Holy Bible, but she asked me to conduct the service. Ironic that she chose the only member of our family to have murdered a clergyman. But, of course, she didn't know that.

The next day, after Curtis was laid to rest in the family cemetery, Gideon rode up with a squad of cavalry to make a belated attempt to catch the raiding party. Rachel Ann and baby William – the infant I'd nicknamed Ides – rode at his side. Her reunion occasioned a few more tears – my sister considered the Appletons family. Eight-month-old William Haleworthy met his infant cousin, Annabel Killpenny, for the first time.

Gideon had the six dead, canvas-shrouded renegades we'd laid out in a ravine searched for identification and buried at some remove from the house. Then Matthew and I accompanied the unit on the trail of the rest of the attackers. The body of the raider Matthew had discovered in the foothills of the Little Islands had been rendered grisly by scavengers. Gideon ordered it buried, and we pressed on, following the remnants of the party until they emerged on the south side of the range and disappeared in the river a few miles beyond. Satisfied the killers had fled the vicinity, Gideon elected to return to the fort. Apparently Rachel Ann and Ides were prepared for a protracted visit.

After Matthew and I arrived back at the Mead, we went into a family meeting. Ma's brothers, Jacob and Christian, rode over to participate. The party that had attacked the Mead had been made up of whites and mixed bloods, and at least one black African. We concluded the group was traveling the countryside raiding and robbing in the hope tribesmen would be blamed. They'd likely not suffered such a catastrophe before Matthew and I rode up behind them. Seven dead out of a gang of about twenty was a heavy load. Almost as heavy as the one we bore with the taking of a single life.

Matthew and I volunteered to set out for the Maartins' Lumberyard in Yanube City for building materials, but Pa decided he wanted to replace both burned cabins with stone structures. We made a family affair out of the five-mile trek up Strobaw's Crick to the rock quarry. Ma insisted Jane and the children accompany us. The entire extended family – save for Gideon – joined in the effort of building the two cabins. Each was made a bit larger and infinitely more sturdy than the structure it replaced.

#

Although Gideon had promised to use the army's telegraph to send news of Curtis Appleton's death to his family in England, Jane wanted a written missive explaining things in greater detail. There was now a picture-taker in Yanube City, so we decided to make a trip into town for images of her and the children to enclose with the letter. Pa insisted on the trip to town, more to divert Jane from her depression over the loss of her husband than anything else.

After the stage came through the following Tuesday, we set off on the fifty-mile trip, Pa and Ma and Jane and the children in the buckboard with Matthew and me on our war horses. Rachel Ann and Ides remained at the Mead with Alexander and his family.

The long trip required an overnight, which the younger folk took to be an outing, although Dexter, acutely aware he was now a fifteen-year-old working man, struggled to contain his enjoyment.

Ma and Pa were not prepared for the hostility they encountered upon entering the city limits even though Matthew and I had sought to prepare them. The Mead was self-sufficient, so they rarely traveled to either Yanube City or Fort Ramson, one-hundred-fifty miles to the east of the farm.

We finally found the man who took images – what many tribesmen called drawing with light – at The Leather Shoppe near the livery stable. He apparently augmented his income by his picture-taking skills. The word "Photographer" appeared in modest lettering beneath his store sign.

Amos Hearth looked to be a newcomer to the territory. His first reaction to three male Indians was fear. The second was indecision at admitting us to his store. What did we want? Could we pay? All of this was clearly written on his fair face, quickly followed by confusion at finding two white women and two European children in our midst.

Pa's educated English eased his initial fears, but his confusion returned when we explained Jane's husband – the children's father – had been killed by a gang of renegades. He obviously concluded an Indian raiding party had perpetrated the deed, and we didn't correct this impression.

After he decided we intended nothing nefarious, he became quite loquacious and confided his first love was photography. The leather goods were merely to put food on the table. He used plate technology, although he explained that a man named George Eastman had developed a film for the camera, and Amos was anxious to test that technique.

It looked to me that picture-taking was hard work for everyone involved. The subject had to remain unnaturally still while Amos fiddled with the camera, his head covered by a hood much of the time. Although the prices were quite steep – half a dollar for each, we got into the spirit of the thing and sat for our pictures. Jane and the children were grouped in one; Ma and Pa in a second, and me and my mate in the third.

After we agreed Matthew or I would pick up the photographs when Amos had had time to develop the plates, we headed for Turtle Crick Farm, so everyone could rest up and start early for the Mead in order to avoid overnighting on the trail.

The Tillers and the dogs were all happy to see us. Libby's hand had settled Sapa to the point where he showed no hostility to strangers. It wouldn't do to leave either dog in her care too long, else they'd become overgrown lap toys.

Dexter's reaction to Libby was something to see. They were of an age although he towered over her petite form. Poor Dex was not just smitten, he was bowled over. His fair English skin reddened alarmingly when he was introduced to her. She acknowledged him prettily and then turned to his younger sister. Dex went from flushed to pale in the blink of an eye. His mother was still too deep into her grief to notice, but Ma did. I saw the birth of a scheme in her blue eyes.

Our little home was overfilled by the multitude, so Matthew and I decided to sleep in the loft of the barn. Dex volunteered to suffer the elements with the "men," in the outhouse. He'd apparently forgotten we'd all slept exposed to the chilled, open air only the night before. Likely, he was still addled by his confrontation with the pretty Tiller girl.

The household stirred well before sunup the next morning to break fast and get the buckboard on its way to the Mead. Matthew considered accompanying them, but Pa insisted they'd be all right. Dex, in his tremulous, breaking voice, joined in to say he was a pretty good shot in case brigands set upon them. Noting that the boy had no weapon, Matthew rooted around in the cellar, which served not only as our cool room but also as a storage area, and came up with a single shot, small bore rifle he'd brought home from his travels one day. It would be of little use in a firefight, but no one pointed that out to Dexter Appleton.

Both Matthew and I remained on edge until a messenger pigeon brought news they'd arrived home without incident.

Later that same day, Matthew rode to Yanube City to pick up the photographs and take them to the Mead. We'd discussed sending them on the stage, but the next outgoing coach wasn't until next Tuesday, and if Jane had her family portraits in hand, she could dispatch the letters to her family, including the photographs, at that time.

Not an hour after he and Wind disappeared from view, Sapa came alert at my side in the vegetable field. Before I could react, he took off around behind the barn, raising a ruckus as he went. Clasping my hoe as a potential weapon, I raced after him. Long before I got there, sounds of a struggle reached my ears. Then I heard a shot and the dog squeal in pain. After that, silence. I raced around the corner of the barn and saw nothing but my faithful guardian lying dead on the edge of the crick bank.

I raised my head and howled in rage.

CHAPTER 20

Raven Strongbow was back. No doubt about it. And without the sacrifice of my beautiful Sapa, I might not have known the Cheyenne was skulking around. Todoh had no bovine charges to watch over for the moment, and he normally would have been with me. Would that have been boon or bane? Could the two animals have dealt with the scoundrel, or would they have both died?

But this morning, the blue was out on the range playing with Libby and her mongrel, White, which placed me in a conundrum. Should I track Raven or head straight for Libby and the dogs to make sure the snake dealt them no grief? I dashed to the house to recover my Henry from the porch and took to Arrow's back, fearing any moment to hear sounds of violence north of me.

I skirted the fields and paused to loose three quick shots into the air as a warning to both Andre and the girl. Then Arrow sped to where Libby was throwing sticks for the dogs to retrieve. They paused to watch as we approached.

"What is it, Mr. John?"

Her wide velvet-eyed stare held such trust it struck me a blow to the heart. That I represented danger to her because of a twisted would-be lover was unthinkable. Yet, such was the case. I explained Raven's presence in clipped tones and pulled her onto Arrow's rump. Todoh and White followed along without a sound as I made for the Tiller place at speed.

Andre met us with his rifle at the ready. He cursed as I explained what had happened and offered to go with me to track down the skunk. I prevailed upon him to remain behind to send a message to the Mead and to protect his daughter.

Within minutes, Todoh and I raced for the spot on the north bank of the crick where my faithful friend lay dead. The blue showed little curiosity at the sight and smell of Sapa's body. I led him to recent moccasin tracks.

"Find," I ordered.

The beast sniffed the tracks and understood but was quickly frustrated. Raven had gone down the bank into the water and likely swam to where he'd left his pony despite the autumn chill. It wasn't until I discovered where the Cheyenne had emerged from the crick that Todoh was of any further value. He struck off south for a distance before looping back north again, and that told me what I needed to know. Ordering the dog back home, I forded Turtle Crick and raced straight for the breaks with my heart devoid of hope. Raven would have had plenty of time to reach the rough country and erase his tracks.

How many times did I pass before his gun sights as I roamed the breaks country? I am confident he watched me from some hidden spot. The raised hairs on my neck told me that. Why didn't he shoot me from the saddle? Apparently, he still held out hope that someday I would succumb to his persistence. My patience at an end, I reined in and filled my lungs.

"Here I am, you coward! Yours for the taking. There's no one around but you and me. Come on down. If you can whip me, you can fuck me!"

My frustrations rang around draws and canyons and echoed off baked clay walls, rushing back to me as if I were offering to bugger myself.

Suddenly tired, I fell silent and listened. Nothing. But for the soft gurgle of Trickling Water flowing down its channel, the breaks were absolutely silent. I waited for what I judged to be an hour before turning Arrow homeward to take care of Sapa's body.

#####

Early the next morning, a full platoon of cavalry approached from the south, obviously intent on using my bridge across Turtle Crick. As they drew nearer, I perceived an officer unknown to me was leading the troop. A new lieutenant from back east from the look of him. A sense of unease rippled my back at the sight of Sgt. Nielsburg riding at his side.

As they drew up in my yard, the soldiers fanned out in a defensive posture, further exacerbating my alarm. I greeted them from my front porch. The officer and the NCO remained horseback. Sharp Eyes, the Mandan scout, joined the two. The officer, who looked even younger up close, gave me a casual salute.

"Mr. Strobaw, I presume."

"That's me. John Strobaw. What can I do for you Lieutenant ... uh ...?"

"Seddon. Second Lieutenant James Seddon. We're on the trail of a party of Indians. Renegades. Can you tell us anything about them?"

"I've seen no one of late. Someone shot one of my dogs to death yesterday, but I lost him when he went down into the crick water, and I've seen no sign of him since."

"So there are no hostiles here?"

"No. I'm alone at the moment."

"I was given to understand you have a hired hand. A Teton Sioux."

My hackles rose. "You are speaking of my brother, Matthew Brandt, whose mother was a Yanube."

"And whose father was a Sioux. A Brulé, if I understand the situation. Where is he?"

"He's visiting our father at Teacher's Mead, that's fifty ..."

"Yes, I'm familiar with the place and the Strobaw family history. So there's no one else on the place. Perhaps you wouldn't mind if we had a look around."

Trying to tamp down my rising blood, I spread my hands. "By all means. Can you tell me what this is about?"

132

"Sgt. Nielsburg, see to it!" the Lieutenant said. He turned back to me. "Someone ambushed a patrol an hour back. We traced the shooter here."

As the three-striper dismounted, a shot rang out. The Mandan scout slid from his horse without a sound. The sergeant grabbed his lieutenant's leg and sought to pull him down, but another rifle report sounded, and the young officer flopped from the saddle. The troopers started firing, but it was willy-nilly.

Nielsburg crouched between the horses and drew his handgun. It took a second to realize he was leveling it at me. I staggered backwards and tripped on the porch steps as he fired. The bullet splintered the cabin door. Unarmed and unhurt, I remained prone on the porch. The NCO bawled at his men, and sent them racing in all different directions.

Another shot rang out, and one of the men stumbled backwards, clasping his right shoulder. From my place on the floor of the porch, I caught the muzzle flash of a rifle beyond the crick. The shooter was taking cover in a ha-ha. Some of the soldiers perceived that as well and returned fire. Others mounted and headed for the gully. A private kept me under guard while the sergeant saw to his lieutenant. Neither of them bothered with the fallen scout.

The sergeant cursed when he found the officer dead. He bounded up on the porch and gathered my shirt in his fist, half pulling me to my feet. "So that murdering Brulé's at Teacher's Mead, huh? You're a fucking liar and a killer. I'll see you hang for the Lieutenant. He wasn't nothing but a babe. Hardly even shaved."

"It wasn't Matthew," I said in a waste of breath. "He's ..."

The man's fist caught me on the jaw, sending me back to the floor. I heard him order the place burned through a ringing in my ears. I tried to protest, but he slugged me again. I was barely conscious when they bound my hands behind me and threw me aboard Arrow. I managed to stay in the saddle, but was only vaguely aware of another disturbance.

"What's going on here?" The voice was familiar. Andre. Andre Tiller. "Why are you torching the place? John, are you all right?"

"This murdering Injun killed my lieutenant. We're burning out this nest of red bellies. Who're you, anyway?"

"I'm his neighbor, Andre Tiller. And he didn't kill nobody. Get some buckets and put out that fire."

"Mind your own business. I'm in charge here," the sergeant bellowed.

Andre edged closer, and I collected my wits enough to caution him to see to the hidey-hole after the fire was out. That was where our gold and silver was hidden. As the sergeant moved his patrol out, I twisted in the saddle to see everything I'd worked for burning. My house, my barn, my foundry ... my fields. Everything gone. The pigeons! They'd burn to death in the cote. All Matthew's work in setting up a way to communicate ... for nothing. What about the mare? Was she burning up, too? Oh, God! They'd probably hang me before the day was out. Todoh! What would happen to Todoh?

My mind continued to clutch at bits and pieces of reality as we started the seven-mile ride to Fort Yanube. Finally, I was able to focus on one fact. Matthew was safe. Safe at Teacher's Mead with our family.

My feelings, my insides, my anguish returned in a rush. They'd be hunting him now, convinced he had murdered Sharp Eyes and the lieutenant. The messenger pigeon I'd asked Andre to send yesterday was probably drawing him right back here, and I couldn't even warn him.

The ride to town was the longest I'd ever known it to be. Time, itself, seemed to slow. The hawk circling overhead was nearly motionless, and would surely fall out of the sky at any moment. The blood in my veins ran sluggish, weighing me down.

My spirits lifted slightly as we passed the blacksmith shop. Both Crow and Timo stood in the doorway and watched us pass. I nodded to the Absaroka, hoping he understood I needed to get word to Pa. Timo, leaning heavily on a cane, took a tentative step forward as if to intercept the column, but Sgt. Nielsburg kept his eyes to the front and plodded onward.

As we entered the fort, I looked at every man we passed, hoping to catch sight of Gideon. Not that he would be able to help, but a friendly face would have been welcome. Would it still be friendly? Or would he accept what the sergeant believed. Matthew and I were killers.

They wasted no time with formalities, throwing me into the same guardhouse where Matthew had been confined when he was denounced as a renegade. I sank down on the narrow cot affixed to one wall and folded my hands in front of me. Fragments of the two cultures mixed within me rose to the surface in ragged tatters. My first silent plea was to *Wakhán Thánka*, the Great Spirit, to keep Matthew safe. My second, was to the Christian God to give me strength to endure this ignominy with the dignity becoming a man.

My prayers were interrupted by no less than the fort's commanding officer. Col. Irons entered the cell with an armed private as a bodyguard. He regarded me coolly for a long moment before demanding to know where Matthew was. With that simple question came another chilling thought. Would the whites use this to force my family off the Mead? I met his gaze straight-on like a white man and altered my story. "He went off on one of his trips. Maybe visiting his wife on the reservation."

"Likely story. Brandt's running for his life right now. But I got men on his trail. He made a big mistake killing Scout Sharp Eyes. That turned the rest of the scouts against him. They'll have him before the week is out."

Despite my resolve to keep silent, I asked if there was a trail to follow.

"He tried to use Turtle Crick as cover, but they picked up his trail when he came out of the water. Found where his big-footed horse headed for rocky ground. But they'll sniff him out, don't you worry. Then we'll have both of you killers. You've been snakes in our bosom for long enough, Strobaw. But pretty soon, we'll be reptile free."

As he took his departure, I had to bite my tongue to resist asking for Gideon. Yet doing so would benefit neither of us. I'd lay low and take my medicine as it came.

The medicine that arrived was not the dose I expected. The door to the guardhouse banged open the following morning and Gideon stalked in. The corporal on duty shot to his feet. Before I knew what was happening, my cell door opened and Gideon waved me out.

"What's going on?" I asked. He clasped my arm and ushered me toward the door as I warned him they were searching for Matthew. "They think he killed the lieutenant. They'll shoot him down."

"You're free," Gideon said. "And Matthew's outside waiting for you."

It took all the willpower I possessed to keep from drawing my Other Self to my breast as he greeted me. He clasped my arm, Indian style, and I read the love and concern in his eyes.

I turned to Gideon. "I'm free? How did you do that?"

"Crow met us on the road, and we rushed straight here and told the truth to the commandant and that damned sergeant. We were both at the Mead when Nielsburg claims Matthew shot the scout and the lieutenant. And since you were standing right in front of him at the time, he can't accuse you of doing it."

"It was Raven."

"How do you know?"

"Two days ago, he killed my dog."

"What?" Matthew asked.

"Sapa went for him, and Raven shot him around behind the barn. By the time I got there, the snake had disappeared." I quickly explained the rest.

"That doesn't prove he ambushed the patrol," Gideon said.

"No, but what your own colonel told me does. Irons said his trackers found where the shooter had come out of the crick on his big-footed horse. Raven's still riding Mr. Killpenny's paint mule. Are we free to go?"

"Yes, but Irons is on the prod. You'll have to be careful." Gideon paused. "I understand the farm's destroyed."

"They set fire to everything. I'm going to take a look and see if anything's left, but I doubt it."

"You can rebuild. I'll help," Gideon said.

"I'm not going to rebuild. Not right away. You can rebuild it if you want Rachel Ann and Ides to live there. She's not going to be comfortable at the fort after this. Andre will keep an eye on them."

#####

I rode out of Fort Yanube with my back ramrod straight and my eyes fixed on the road ahead lest they happen to fall on one of the good citizens of the town. In my present mood, I couldn't guarantee not to lose control. At Mathew's insistence, we stopped at Timo's forge to let Crow know what was going on. Even though Timo Bowers had been a steadfast friend to my family for better than forty years and had been the first man to bring me to ejaculation, I had trouble looking at him without seeing the white beneath his sunburned skin. Uncomfortable with his awkward expressions of concern, I put on my Indian face and remained as civil as I could. The fact his wounds were such that he still struggled to accomplish the simplest tasks in his own forge failed to move me. That likely meant he was the bigger man because warriors of my flesh tones were responsible for those wounds.

We had brought them up to date on events before I thought of something. "Matthew, did you get the pigeon message Andre sent?"

He shook his head. "No. If he sent one, someone probably found it after we left yesterday. We camped last night."

"That means Pa's on the road right now. Crow, I don't want him riding into town. Feelings are too high. Can I ask you to go on the road again? Intercept him and let him know he shouldn't come."

The burly man nodded. "Pleased to. You want any help with the Cheyenne?"

Matthew answered in a growl. "Don't need any, thanks. Sorry about Sharp Eyes."

"That Mandan was a good fella. I'll go see to how they're going to treat him and then be on my way to the Mead."

We took our leave and set out for the farm. The closer we drew, the colder my blood ran.

"What would have happened if you hadn't been at the Mead with Gideon?" I asked.

"They'd be hunting me down and hanging you."

"And it doesn't bother you? You seem so unaffected by it."

"I feel it as much as you, John. But I'm used to it. I've been an Indian all my life. You ... you're just one whenever the white man reminds you of it."

My blood rose until I realized the truth of his words. I spoke around whatever was obstructing my throat. "Well, I know it now."

"Of all of us, you're the one who lives among them. Your neighbor and best friend is a white man. You do business with the biggest merchant in the territory. The rest of us just stay away and let them come to us. Keep it to a minimum. You seek them out."

"That's over now." My voice caught, and I shut up as the broken silhouette of the ruined farm buildings came into sight. The bridge was the only thing built by Otter's hand or restored by me still standing. The destruction was so total it was unnatural. Then, as we dismounted and stood among the ruins, I understood. A peculiar smell lingered. The flames had been encouraged by liberal doses of my own kerosene.

Even the cellar had been fired and partially burnt, although someone had removed the contents. In my heart, I hoped Howling Wolf had come by and taken the beef. It would give his men strength to fight these savages.

I reconsidered. After all, I owed this tragedy to him. At least partially. His raids had raised fear in the hearts and minds of the townsfolk and the troopers. And Raven. He shot the Mandan and the lieutenant. And I was responsible because I'd failed to kill the Cheyenne even after I understood how dangerous he was. Matthew's voice brought me aware of the fact I was standing amid the ashes of the barn staring at nothing.

"The hidey-hole's empty. Looted."

I cleared my throat and willed my limbs to move. "Maybe not. I managed to tell Andre to check it. The cabin was burning too much for the troopers to have gotten to it. Let's let the Tillers know I've been released."

"You want to stay there tonight? He'll likely offer his barn."

I shuddered. "No! I just want to let him know and take what's ours."

"John, Andre didn't have anything to do with what happened. And Timo didn't either. You were as cold to him as that crick water over there."

"Didn't know it showed."

My reaction to Andre was little better than to Timo, but Libby's pretty innocence unbent me a little. After we told the Tillers what had happened once Nielsburg took me to the fort, Andre made me forget he was white by telling me he'd come to town later that day to protest to Col. Irons that Matthew and I weren't killers. He further softened my heart when he handed over the contents of our hidey-hole and let me know most of the beef from the cold room rested in his cellar now, some of it half-cooked by the flames.

I don't know why our gold and silver coins weren't melted, but for the most part, they were in good shape. Matthew and I split enough precious metals and paper money between our packs to have put almost anyone in Yanube City to shame. Except for Caleb, of course. And possibly the saloon owner.

Andre had also been able to save the mare from the burning bar. The pigeons, of course, were gone. When I looked around for Todoh, Libby understood my glance and put a small, work-hardened hand on my arm.

"Those soldiers shot him when he tried to come help you, Mr. John. We buried him near Sapa." A big tear leaked from her left eye.

I groped for something to say. "I hope he died quickly."

"He did," Andre said. "I saw it. I also saw some of them head out after the ambusher. Don't know if they got him or not."

"They didn't," Matthew said.

I rubbed my eyes and sighed. "Matthew and I are going to do that. I'll not rebuild right away, Andre. We'll search out Raven and then go to the Mead for a while. If we don't get back by spring, you're free to plant the fields and take the crop. Might be better to have some activity on the farm from time to time, anyway. I told Captain Haleworthy he could rebuild if he wanted Rachel Ann and the baby to live there for a while, but I don't know his intentions."

"So this is goodbye?"

"At least for a while."

"What about the beef in the cellar?"

"Use it if you need to. If Winter Bird comes around, he's welcome to any of it beyond your needs. Andre, keep a sharp eye out, but I don't think Raven will have any reason to harm you now. He knows he hurt me about all he can except for killing Matthew or me."

"He came back, you know," Libby said.

We all turned to look at her.

"What? How do you know?" Matthew asked.

Libby seemed intimidated by his sharp demand. "Because I was over there this morning. One of the pigeons managed to get out of the cote while it was burning the other day. It was hurt, and didn't fly far. Just to the cottonwoods, but I couldn't coax it down. So I went over to see if I could find it and make it well. But ... but when I got there, it was pinned to one of the barn's burnt timbers by an arrow."

I glanced at Matthew. "He still carries a bow and quiver?"

He nodded. "Always has, so far as I know. I figure he likes to kill silently now and then." Matthew looked chagrined. "Sorry, Libby."

"It's all right, Mr. Matthew. That's the world we live in."

"That changes things," I said. "By rights, Raven should have lit out for the reservation as soon as he shook the troopers off his trail. But the fact he's hanging around means he wants to know what's happening to me. He probably believes I'm still in the guardhouse and Matthew's running for his life."

A dark thought crossed my mind and made me flinch. I turned to face my neighbor. "Andre, Raven doesn't have any way to get news from town or the fort. So I think he'll wait until he sees you go to town and waylay you on the way back to press for information. You stay close and keep a weapon handy ... both of you. Libby, keep White with you everywhere you go until one of us comes back and tells you it's safe."

My mate strode briskly to his horse. "Let's go, John. We don't want to lose the light."

Raven's tracks weren't hard to spot ... or even to follow. They made straight for Trickling Water and the breaks. He'd likely sleep there tonight and then return tomorrow to see if he could catch Andre and squeeze some information out of him. The skin on my back crawled as we entered the breaks. Shortly thereafter, Raven's tracks disappeared. He'd walked back to cover them.

Matthew pulled up, but I rode around him, muttering in a low voice that I knew where the snake was. My mate didn't question my announcement, just fell in behind me as I kicked Arrow into a run. It would be harder to shoot us from the saddle at speed.

CHAPTER 21

Near the western exit to the badlands, I pulled up in a small draw. As soon as Matthew joined me, I spoke in a soft voice to tell him of another way out of the breaks country.

"And Raven knows of it because he trailed Firm Foot and Crow Hop's party after they escaped a firefight with some troopers." My voice took on a bitter tone. "If I had remembered this the day Raven killed Sapa, we wouldn't have lost the farm and Todoh."

"You don't know that. There was only one of you. You go in at the bottom of the canyon, and he comes out the top. But that's not the way it is now. Tell me where to find the exit, and I'll block it while you send him right to me."

I shook my head. "No. You're going to drive him right into the sights of my Henry. This is my spilt milk, and I need to clean it up. Besides, he probably still thinks I'm in the fort's guardhouse, so he won't be expecting me."

"Unless he saw us ride the length of the breaks. Or maybe he's already gone."

"Not likely. He took the time to erase his trail. He's deep in the gully getting some rest. And remember, he wants news of what's happening to us." I read Matthew's look. "Don't worry. I know what a killer he is. He'll get no quarter from me this time."

As unhappy as my mate was with my plan, he knew it made sense and finally agreed. I told him how to recognize the entrance to the draw where I was certain Raven was hiding. Then I rode out of the badlands and circled to the south rim. An hour later, I stationed myself near the head of the hidden trail leading up out of the canyon. I had asked for that hour, but Matthew likely gave me more because almost twice that time had elapsed before gunshots set my nerves jumping. Had Raven shot my Other Self from ambush?

I checked my Henry to make certain the sleeve was fully charged and a bullet rested in the chamber. I urged Arrow closer to the lip of the steep, scrub-lined drop down into the coulee. I could hover within five or six feet of the rim and remain unseen until Raven was almost at the top.

Another exchange of gunfire almost drew me down the trail, but I steeled my nerves. A third series of shots raised hair on my neck and sweat on my brow. My hands trembled from the need to go in aid of Matthew. Then the world went silent. Even the prairie creatures grew quiet. My own breathing was all I could hear.

Another hour passed before I heard what I was listening for. A stone dislodged and rolled down an incline somewhere below me. Loose gravel. A hoof fall. I stilled an urge to call out to Matthew. I desperately needed to know he was all right, but I clamped my lips firmly together and waited.

The sound of an animal making its way up a steep, rough incline came to me plainly now. Yet sound could be deceptive, and I couldn't be certain how close Raven was. I changed my mind and placed the Henry in its saddle holster, drawing and checking my Colt, instead. Then I clasped my hands on the saddle pommel so that the weapon was not obvious and waited.

The paint mule's long ears appeared above the horizon nearly taking me by surprise, but I hung onto my resolve as the animal labored up out of the canyon. Raven was looking over his shoulder as his mount climbed out onto level ground. When the beast came to a halt at the sight of Arrow blocking his way, the Cheyenne whirled around to face me. His physical comeliness came near to unhinging me. Surely someone so beautiful could not be evil.

He recovered quickly. He moved his right hand forward slightly. It held his rifle. A subtle kick brought the mule closer. He spoke in Lakota. "Eagle, I thought you were in the white man's guardhouse."

"I was. Thanks to you."

"No time to talk right now. I'm gonna ride past you."

"Not this time, Raven. Not this time."

He made as if to shrug, but I saw what was in his eyes. The barrel of the rifle swung around. I simply lifted my wrist and pulled the trigger. His eyes went wide at the impact of the bullet. A spray of red spattered his chest. He lifted the sagging barrel of his rifle and fired. The bullet went wide. I loosed a salvo of three shots. One projectile hit the mule in the head as it reared. The other two punched Raven from the saddle. He fought his way to his feet, still holding his rifle. He staggered around trying to locate me. I fired the last two bullets in my revolver as he fought to lift his weapon. The life-light went out of his eyes before he pitched over backwards and rolled down the hill.

I reloaded before dismounting and walking to the edge of the bluff. After a brief hesitation, I climbed down after him. I found his rifle first. Raven lay crumpled at the bole of a pine a dozen feet beyond the weapon. He was no longer beautiful. One bullet had caught him in the right cheek.

This man had made more than one effort to kill Matthew. He'd raped me and made it clear he intended to do it again. He'd ambushed a troop of cavalry at my farm, resulting in the total destruction of my life's work and the threat of hanging for me and Matthew. Even so, I felt a sense of remorse as I looked at his lifeless body. The evil that had resided in his spirit was gone. Something – sadness, I guess – rendered me weak in the limbs.

I don't know how long I stood over him before Matthew appeared on the trail below. When he reached my side, he must have seen something in my eyes because he took me in his arms and hugged me close.

"It had to be, John. It had to be."

We left Raven where he lay and headed straight for the Tiller farm. They deserved to know the danger was past. We simply told them Raven was no longer a problem, and they asked no questions. Then we set out for Teacher's Mead.

Pa took the news about the farm stoically, but Ma expressed shock and outrage. Then she commenced to fret over how Rachel Ann and Ides were faring in the bosom of the villains who had burned us out and threw me in jail. Later, in a private talk up on the hollow hill, we told my father and Alexander about the death of Raven Strongbow. While Pa grunted, Alex gave me a sharp look. Had my brother ever killed a man? He'd certainly shot at marauders when they were bold enough to attack the farm, but had he ever brought one down?

Although I knew in my heart we would not remain long at the Mead, we allowed ourselves to be put to work. Crow hadn't returned from helping Timo at the forge, so there was an urgent need for horseshoes and nails. One of the big draft horses belonging to the stagecoach had a limp that demanded Matthew's attention.

We worked hard for a fortnight and slept in Crow's rebuilt stone cabin. Dexter Appleton was doing man's work in his father's stead and sitting for school lessons from Ma, as well. He would make a good hand for the farm. Whenever he caught Matthew or me alone, he peppered us with questions about Libby Tiller.

I argued for wintering at the Mead while Matthew agitated to make straight for Pine Ridge. Taking care of the problem with Raven was not enough for him. His heart was with the tribesmen. Although he would give no voice to the idea, he wanted to be in the middle of things should widespread violence break out. He sought revenge for the destruction of our home. His frustration was building to the point it required physical release. Sadly, his nightly assault of my fundament only relieved another type of need.

Nonetheless, when the first blue norther roared down from Canada, we were still at the Mead, and I came to understand he had discerned my depression over the loss of our homestead and the subsequent wish to help with planting next spring at the Mead. That was likely the reason he deferred tackling the uncertainties of our new life. He understood I was grasping for some sense of normalcy.

Before the real winter set in, we received occasional news of the outside world from the stage drivers. Over in Germany, a man named Karl Benz had produced a motor wagon that was said to be capable of moving under its own power without horses or oxen attached to it. Then came news of another wholesale killing, but this time it wasn't tribesmen falling before the wrath of the whites.

The Rock Springs Massacre took place in Wyoming when a mob of white miners attacked their Chinese coworkers, killing more than two dozen and wounding many others. The indiscriminate nature of the Americans' bigotry was oddly comforting. At least, we weren't exclusive prey.

Closer to matters of interest to us was President Grover Cleveland's warning to "Boomers" to stay off Indian Territory lands in Oklahoma. Then as the year ended, word came of Luis Riel's execution in November by the Canadian government. Rael had led the Northwest Rebellion, which many tribesmen had hoped would catch fire and sweep away our own white oppressors.

I was incautious enough to repeat that thought to Gideon when he and Rachel Ann arrived one December day. No longer comfortable at the fort, especially since the weather would soon confine her to quarters, my sister had agitated to winter with her family. Gideon had agreed and brought her and Ides home.

As he prepared to return to Fort Yanube the following day, I repeated the invitation for his wife and son to stay at Turtle Crick Farm when the weather cleared next spring.

"You have no intent to rebuild and replant?" he asked.

"Not right away. You're free to build a small house and a shelter for horses, if you wish. Andre will probably farm the acreage. I've left funds with him to pay the taxes, so I'm not abandoning the farm."

Gideon studied his hands for a long moment before lifting his eyes to mine. "Do you intend to remain on the Mead?" His thoughts were reflected in his fetching blue eyes.

"Until planting's done."

He sighed and stretched his legs beneath the table where we sat. "You're going to the reservation, aren't you?"

"Perhaps sometime next year. I have some beef stored at Andre's farm. I figure the meat might come in handy after a hard winter."

He studied my face with his white man's stare. "You know I can't protect you there, don't you?"

Matthew, sitting at my left, grunted. Pa, opposite him, said nothing.

I dry washed my face. "Gideon, your heart is in the right place, and you've demonstrated your good will to your wife's family, but let me be honest. The Strobaw reputation and my family's straight dealing with the people in Yanube City and the fort is what's kept the vultures off our backs. Billy Strobaw – from the grave – has done more for us than you or me or anyone else. The Red Win-tay had strong medicine. He tied us so tightly to Teacher's Mead nobody's been able to pry us off it by fair means or foul. They've tried it using the law and by using a gun."

My brother-in-law colored slightly. "I only meant to say that in some situations, my speaking up could help turn the tide. Such as getting you out of the guardhouse the other day."

"It was truth that opened the jail door, Gideon. To your credit, you're an honest man, and that's a boon."

I decided to make things plain. "We understand the position you're in. If Matthew *had* been the one to shoot that lieutenant at my farm, it would have been uncomfortable for you, but you'd have done your duty. Any of us would. And having two kinsmen, at least by marriage, riding on the reservation could potentially put us on opposite sides. But that would be no different from what a lot of people experienced in your big war back in the '60s. You'll do your duty, and we'll do ours. Nothing else is expected of the other."

I had not intended my words to sound like a declaration of war, but that's the way they rang in my ears. I have no idea how he received them as he returned to the fort and to duty soon thereafter.

My frank words to Gideon seemed to hang like a pall over the big stone house, but the children's enthusiasm for the coming Christmas gradually changed the mood of the place. Matthew and Alex cut a six-foot fir and fetched it home. While the others decorated the *tannenbaum*, I set about forging gifts for the children.

CHAPTER 22

The winter of '85-'86 was miserable for me ... for us ... even though the family was all together for the first time in years. Save for Hannah, who was only four miles distant. Of course, that four miles might as well have been four hundred during the white-out. Nonetheless, the comforting embrace of family made it easier to reconcile our losses: home, farm, and two faithful four-legged friends. I slowly came to understand they could all be restored over time ... except Sapa and Todoh, of course. Still, I was not yet willing to make the effort required.

Raven joined the Reverend Jeremiah Berglund in my dreams. His beauty restored, the ghostly Cheyenne chided me for his death, dismissing his own deadly intent. I often woke in the dark of night, managing to sleep again only when Matthew wrapped me in his warm embrace. His understanding of my inner turmoil and my daily pleas to both the Great Spirit and the Christian God – were they truly one and the same? – helped save my sanity.

As snowmelt took hold of the land, Matthew and I donned snowshoes and made the still arduous trek to Killpenny Farm to find our little sister's family had wintered well. Annabel was a fat, pleasant baby, and Hannah had the look of an expectant mother again. Esau beamed in pride at both of them. Our sister had married well. We took the opportunity to tell Esau his father's killer had paid the ultimate price for his crime.

Even as I grew more comfortable, unease descended upon Matthew as the snow slowly receded. Before the melt was complete, Crow showed up with his family, bringing news Timo Bowers had recovered his health sufficiently to handle his forge again, although at a reduced pace. The Absaroka had headed west for the Standing Rock Agency to bring his wife and children back home while the snow was still crusted and the runoff was not yet high. Conditions on the reservation had been so bad he'd given the money earned at the blacksmith shop to his wife's family.

Once the stagecoach started running again during the muddy time, and after our dispossession from Crow's cabin, I recognized Matthew wouldn't last through spring planting, so I proposed we depart ... for wherever ... within the week.

We struck out shortly after Ma's Sunday devotional. She was always fretful when Matthew took off on his travels, but this time two of her sons were leaving to walk what she undoubtedly considered the Warrior Road. Perhaps it would turn out that way, although I did not conceive of as such when we took our leave.

Pa sent a mule packed with salted meat with us as we headed for Turtle Crick to retrieve the beef Andre was storing. Cross-country was shorter, but the deep mire of early runoff prompted us to stick to the road. The Yanube was running swift and full. A walk-across would be impossible now, so the white man's bridges were the only way to traverse the water. Therefore we opted for the rough, less traveled wagon trace north of the river. The going was slow and difficult on the horses, requiring two overnights to cover the fifty-odd mile trip. Matthew's presence made the chilly, muddy camps bearable. Once we were abed wrapped in blankets we shared our warmth and slept soundly.

We arrived at Turtle Crick without encountering anyone on the road. Walking the ruins of our home and eyeing the spot near the bank of the crick where our two faithful dogs lay beneath a blanket of earth filled my heart with so much lead that Matthew became concerned.

Instantly, he became a loving and consoling husband. He spoke of how we'd someday rebuild the place and make it better than ever. He talked of enlarging the house so when friends and relatives passed through, we'd have a sleeping room to accommodate them. Perhaps even a nearby cabin for those who wanted a protracted rest. We had ample money, he reminded me, most of it left behind in the hollow hill at the Mead. Some coins and ingots were stowed in our packs and others sewn into our clothing to guard against robbers.

When speaking of future plans failed to rouse me sufficiently, he cleared a corner of the ruined outhouse and built a fire in the peat-burning fireplace we'd used for the comfort of our animals. He prodded me into helping him rig canvas tarp scraps around the stove, making a shelter where he spread our blankets. We'd found our home for the night, apparently.

He did not wait for the sun to go down and darkness to fall. He pushed me down on the bed and removed my clothes, article by article. Yet, lethargy's grip did not loosen until he stood naked before me, making me realize the two most precious things in the world were still mine: Matthew and his love.

He spread himself atop me so that our rods lay alongside one another, each seeking the comforting touch of the other as if they were entities unto themselves. Then his eyes examined mine, mere inches apart.

"I love you, John." He switched to Yanube, a tongue no longer much used. We generally spoke English or Lakota. "I will protect you against the elements with my body. But mostly I will cloak you in my love. It may not turn aside a bullet or fend off attack by rabid animals, but it protects against a darker danger."

A smile tugged at the corner of my lips. "And what is worse than that?"

"Loneliness. Being alone. But because of moments such as these, you will hold some part of me with you even after I walk the Western Road. You'll hold memories of everything we've done together."

My heart stuttered in my chest. "Don't talk like that!"

He shook his head. "You have much to learn about a warrior's life. That possibility walks with us all, hour by hour."

He moved down to kiss my left nipple, to tease it with his tongue and teeth until it stood damp and proud. Then he stirred up the right one in like manner before exploring the whole of my torso with his lips. I pulled him up to kiss, to taste those full lips. He curled his tongue into a cone and thrust it into my mouth as if fucking it.

Unable to speak my pleasure, I moaned the message. He lifted his chest and stared at me a moment before kissing each of my eyes. Then he kneaded my belly with his chin, chuckling as he drew grunts from me. Finally, he kissed the tip of my rampant rod, opened his lips, and took me into his mouth. I threw my legs around his waist and played with his thick black hair as his head rose and fell over me. A hand on my stones made me jump, and he came up to laugh again. Then he returned to his task, seriously this time. I tried to relax and prolong the pleasure, but my muscles rebelled. They sought release. My stomach tightened. My testes drew up. My legs moved against him, almost in spasms. I drew in my breath and sang his name.

I erupted, filling that beautiful mouth with a surfeit of warm, living seed. He stayed with me rather than drawing away as he usually did when I ejaculated. This time he did not finish me with his hand, but with a moist throat and a warm tongue. The electrical charges wracking my body were so intense they were near to painful. But a pain such as I would gladly bear. When I could finally reason again, I understood this for what it had been: an orgasm unmatched in my experience, deliberately provoked and brought about by the skill and devotion of my manly husband, Shambling Bear. Yes, Shambling Bear. Matthew Brandt was gone, and I knew not when – or if – he would appear again.

Bear allowed me little time to recover before rolling me over. He parted my buns with his broad hands and teased my sphincter with busy thumbs. When I wiggled in lustful delight, he replaced his digits with that long, thick pole I loved so much. His glans was awash with clear excitement juice, so he entered me easily in one long, slow thrust. He filled me with himself, claimed me with his sword. Then he rendered me helpless with the application of it, fucking so enthusiastically and noisily the critters on the prairie must have taken refuge in their dens. Distant coyotes answered his howl as he came. Then, from the Tiller farm, a mile away, we heard the excited yap of Libby's dog. Bear collapsed atop me, laughing between gasps for air.

We took a ritual sweat bath in the *okinare*, the only structure left undamaged, and spoke our prayers early the next morning. I'll swear a chunk of ice struck my thigh when I jumped into Turtle Crick and immersed myself briefly before tearing up the bank and seeking the relative comfort of our peat-warmed enclosure. We rubbed away one another's goose-flesh and dressed quickly. It required more time beside the slow-burning flames before we ventured out into the brisk air again. Nonetheless, I felt cleansed and refreshed in both spirit and body.

Andre and Libby were happy to see us and insisted we come inside to share the breaking of their fast and give them news of Teacher's Mead. Eggs and fat flaky biscuits and thick slabs of bacon went down easy. Where Libby had learned to cook like that, I did not know, but she would make some man a good wife one day.

As that thought crossed my mind, she asked about that blond-headed boy. "You, know. Dexter."

Hiding a smile, Matthew and I took turns extoling the virtues of the fifteen-year-old beanpole. But in truth, we did little exaggeration. Dexter Appleton was a hard worker and would grow into a fine man. I nearly laughed aloud as I noticed she blushed when she spoke his name, just as he did when he called out hers. Mayhap there was a platform here upon which Ma could build her scheme.

It was plain that Andre's heart rested easier in his chest since Raven was gone. He told us a patrol had blundered on the dead paint mule on the south rim of the Trickling Water badlands, prompting the discovery of the Cheyenne's body. So far as Andre knew, the dead deserter had caused little or no flap among either the military or the Sheriff's Office. Apparently, they considered it the result of mayhem amongst tribesmen. In that, they were right, of course.

Andre expressed disappointment we'd not changed our minds about rebuilding the farm right away. He could not understand our reasons why, and I had only an infirm grasp on the concept myself. Nay, that's not true. My warrior husband felt the call of his blood, and now I was finally free to accompany him on whatever quest he undertook. Time enough to rebuild later. The difficult part of that, of course, was to keep squatters off the land.

To that end, I renewed the invitation for Andre to till my acreage at no cost to him. I planted the suggestion he might wish to take on a hired hand and build a shack where our house or barn had once stood to shelter a helper. Andre's reap should more than cover the cost of such an expense. I also reminded him to pay my taxes in a timely manner.

By the time we left at dawn the next morning, trailing both the mule and my black mare bearing full loads of salted beef and jerky, Andre had agreed to do all that I wished. I saw in Libby's dreamy eyes she hoped to influence her father to hire Dexter away from the Mead. In truth, Andre could do worse.

We were not yet halfway to Pine Ridge when I sensed trouble. A man wrapped in a coat of thick buffalo hide rode toward us on a big strawberry horse with long ears. I'm not sure what alerted me, but the hair on my neck bristled. "Bear ..."

"I know," he muttered quietly.

Arrow's ears whipped to the left. "I think there's another one in a ha-ha to the south."

"Aye, and a third on the other side of the road, likely."

As the man approached, I caught a glimpse of metal in his hand as the strawberry did a little dance sideways. He held his six-shooter low at his side.

"I see." Bear eased his hand gun out of its holster and rested it on the pommel just as I drew my own.

Understanding he no longer had the cloak of surprise, the man in the great coat gave a cry and spurred his horse forward. Bear slipped to the left, hooking his right leg over the pommel of his saddle to fire from beneath Wind's neck. After shooting at nothing but space, the man's eyes registered shock as he rocked back in the saddle, struck by Bear's bullet. He didn't lose his seat, but he dropped his pistol and pounded past both of us.

I turned to the left as a second robber rose up out of a ditch and made for us on foot. My first shot missed, but the second caught him squarely in the chest. He flopped over on his back with his boots sticking up out of the gully he'd been hiding in.

I whirled at a flurry of shots and saw the third man aboard a big gray blasting away with his revolver. Bear, completely hidden from the man's sight by his pony's flank, shot back, but Wind screamed and danced sideways, causing my mate to miss.

The man was almost alongside me now, and I fired the last two bullets in the chamber, nicking his arm. He loosed a shot at me, hitting the mule behind Arrow. With a squeal, the beast went over.

I grabbed my Henry and twisted in the saddle. Before I could get a line on the fleeing ruffian, Bear's rifle spoke, and the man collapsed over his saddle and rolled into the mud. The thug on the strawberry was far down the road. I threw a few shots after him, but to no avail. Swaying uncertainly in the saddle, he continued to beat a hasty retreat.

Bear and I examined one another for wounds and found nothing.

"What do we do now?" I asked. "I don't want to overburden the horses, but I hate to abandon all that beef in the mule's packs."

Bear dismounted and walked around to examine his mount.

"Is Wind all right?"

"Just a scratch on his neck. Didn't penetrate. Wait here." Bear walked toward where the desperado I'd faced had scrambled up out of the ditch. Moments later, he came back leading a roan. He dismounted and tied the horse's reins to Wind's pommel and started tugging the pack off the exposed side of the dead mule. "Come on. We have to hurry."

He asked for my lasso and looped the noose around the mule's neck. Then he handed the butt-end to me and told me to pull at an angle. With Matthew holding onto the pack as I dragged the dead animal off the road, we freed the salted beef. Then he took his knife and started carving on the dead animal's hip. I was puzzled until he held up a flap of skin bearing

149

the Mead's brand. He stabbed the flesh beneath the skinned place savagely to erase any deeper mark the hot brand may have left.

As we secured the pack to the dead robber's roan, Bear explained the situation. The wounded hooligan would make for the nearest settlement for treatment and report tribesmen had set upon him and his companions as they were bringing goods for trading. The law would find two dead men, one shot in the back as he fled. Then some sheriff and his posse would come after us, convinced of the justice of their pursuit.

"But ..."

"Eagle, stop acting like a white man. Who do you think they'll believe, us or him? It doesn't matter that there are two of us telling one story with no one to support his. He's a white man, and we aren't."

We collected the robbers' weapons before heading out, pushing the horses harder than we wanted. I fervently prayed the man on the strawberry died before he reached civilization. All the while, my back prickled with the thought there might be a posse riding our tail.

CHAPTER 23

We did not head straight for the Pine Ridge Agency. Instead, we deserted the roads and obscured our prints before taking a maze of gullies and ha·has until we were well within the reservation's boundaries. Indeed, we did not pause at the settlement around the Indian Agent's headquarters. Matthew led me to a camp a bit to the north called Rivers Bend, although the logic of the name escaped me. There was neither river nor bend in sight. A cluster of tipis and wooden shelters sat on high ground semi·surrounded by the stumps of a growth of trees long ago chopped down for firewood. In fact, the butts had been hacked away as the need became more desperate. The remains of the forest was likely an indication that a waterway of some sort had once passed this way, although not one of such depth and breadth as the mighty Missouri that lay a distance to the north of us.

Bear dismounted before a rude shack of warped, unpainted planks. Puzzlement turned to joy as a familiar figure emerged from the hut. Winter Bird unleashed a dazzling smile and bounded forward to grasp my mate's forearm in greeting. As I slid from my saddle, he turned his attention to me.

"Medicine Hair! It's about time you came for a visit." His grin died abruptly. "I heard what happened to your farm. I hope we didn't bring that down on you."

I took his arm in mine. "Nay, Raven Strongbow brought that disaster upon us."

"He'll not do any more such mischief," Bear said.

Bird shot him a look, but did not ask questions. Instead, he made us welcome and introduced us to his family. Stout Ox, his father, once undoubtedly worthy of the name, carried no extra flesh on a frame of over six English feet. Sweet Grass, Bird's spare, shrunken mother looked older than her likely years. They greeted Bear as a familiar, and me as a savior, making me understand how critical our trading with Caleb had been to these people. When we made known the beef we packed, Stout Ox quickly sent word to other families in the settlement and went about distributing the meat in an orderly manner. Within the hour, the food was gone.

After we explained how we came about the roan gelding, Ox sent one of the younger boys to take the horse to meld into the camp's herd. Then our host insisted on a medicine bath in the communal *okinare* while Sweet Grass prepared a meal. As we covered our nakedness with blankets and trooped to the lodge, the little settlement turned out to watch. My speckled head drew comments. My reputation – doubtless inflated by Winter Bird – had preceded me. I should have stomped on the medicine rumors as soon as they rose.

Once we were settled in the sweat bath, Bird and his father told of the loss of four kinsmen last winter. My young friend was of the opinion not all had actually starved to death, but they had been so weakened by hunger, other maladies had stolen in to take their lives. The more talk that went around, the more I realized many on the reservations were simply waiting for a sign or a call to action. If that were to happen, the entire territory would go up in smoke.

Later, as we sat in Stout Ox's small house, the hair on my neck rose when some of the younger men looked to me for that purpose. Little Moccasins, a nephew of Stout Ox, was a tall man about my age and his uncle's height. He pushed me on the matter.

"What say you?" His Lakota was clipped and harsh, yet he did not strike me as deceptive or brash.

"What is there for me to say?" I asked. "I have no standing among you. I have not lived and shared your hardships. My history was determined years ago by the Red Win-tay and my father, Dog Fox, and by River Otter."

Moccasins' bright brown eyes traveled to my hair. "I have heard of your medicine. None of those you mentioned gave that to you. That came from the Great Spirit."

"If you speak of my hair, my father gave me some of it and my mother the rest. What poor power I have comes from studying and learning the white man's way. And I see him as I see us. Some are good and some are bad."

"Please show me some of the good ones," Moccasins said with only a trace of irony.

"I agree with Medicine Hair," Bird said. "But it is the bad who have us under their thumb. And if we kill the bad, the good ones will believe we've taken the warpath, and they will come after us."

I nodded. "Just as we will go after the good if the bad become too oppressive."

"How many have to die before we see that time is now?" Moccasins stretched his legs as we sat in a circle on the floor, giving me an indication of how he came by his name. The platform upon which his lanky form stood was small for a man.

"I have some knowledge of the white man others might not have," I said. "Not about the business end of his guns, you have experienced that more than I. But I understand where he comes from and his nature better than some. This race came from across the great ocean over two hundred years ago and spilled across Turtle Island so fast none of the tribes recognized the danger until it was too late. Go outside and look up into the night sky. There are more of them than the stars you can number above your head. And those are countless."

I sighed and allowed my chin to drop. "The time for overthrowing them and reclaiming what is ours is past. We have no chance of that unless all the nations rise at once, and even then our long guns might not prevail against their cannon."

Moccasins made a clicking noise with his tongue. "So what is the answer? Sit and starve. Sit and watch our women and children die of disease and hunger?"

"No. The answer is to become as learned as the white man. Education is the key to everything. It is what has allowed my family and me to survive in their midst. That is what lets Shambling Bear move among them at will."

Bird rubbed his brow. "I believe you. But our people are starving *now*. By the time we become educated, no one will be left."

"What do your chieftains and your shamans say? Has Sitting Bull called for war?" I asked.

"No," Moccasins said, "but he thinks on it. One day, he may give the signal."

I paused before speaking the words that might alienate me from these people. "Perhaps his time has passed, as well."

Moccasins nodded gravely. "Some say that is true. That we must find younger leaders."

"Leaders like Howling Wolf?" Bear asked in a derisive tone.

"At least he acts on what he thinks."

I spoke up. "And others pay the price for it. He leads a score of men, gets half of them killed, and raises the white man's blood against everyone in the nations. Raven Strongbow may have fired the shots that cost us our home, but Howling Wolf and his raids prepared the ground."

I was impressed. Despite the harshness of my comments, the half dozen men sitting around the small room took my words seriously and seemed to give them consideration. Some leaned one way and others a different direction, but there was no hostility among them. Finally, Moccasins stared past me and asked a question.

"So you counsel peace?"

"I see no other course unless something changes. It seems to me our task is to find a way to help our people survive. We must organize. Some of us must get good at talking to the agent and to the army. Others must figure a better way of foraging. And some must teach our young people."

After a lengthy pause during which each man mulled over my words, a man of middle years who had been introduced as Lazy Eye, spoke for the first time.

"I know a place up north where you can find a little bit of the yellow rock the white man covets."

Bear raised his voice. "Stay away from it and don't ever tell anyone about it."

"If you do," I said in a more measured tone, "they will swarm over us like vultures on carrion."

#####

Winter Bird offered to share his tipi, which sat near his father's hut. As Bear and I lay wrapped in heavy buffalo robes that first night, I struggled to remember if I'd ever slept in a skin home before. Likely not. As Bear's hands began an assault of my body, turning my rod into a hot ingot, I was mindful of Winter Bird wrapped in his blankets on the other side of the tent and tried to shrug my lusty lover away. He would have none of it. When he brought his lips close to mine and sought a kiss, I hissed in a frantic whisper, "Bird."

"What about him?" Bear pressed his kiss upon me, almost drawing a moan. If I sought to be quiet, he didn't bother. He rose up and pulled my sleeping shift away. Despite my reluctance, he soon had my ankles on his shoulders. He rubbed my fundament until he worked up enough excitement juice, and then he entered me eagerly. Even in the near-abject darkness, his eyes glowed as he fucked me. Rough at first. Then gentle, with tender kisses and murmured expressions of love. Back to hard and harsh once more to finish the job.

He came with a physical explosion and a whoosh of air from his lungs. I grasped myself and followed him in an uncommon orgasm. Despite my desire to be quiet, I could not suppress a strangled moan. Finished now, Bear cleaned us with a rag and a bowl of water and then arranged his long, muscled body against my side. I dropped off to sleep wondering what Bird thought of our antics.

The next morning, our host said nothing about our rising naked from the bed. I who had never been shy about revealing my body to other men, felt somehow exposed as his eyes casually swept over me. He grinned and nodded, relieving my inner tension a tad.

Later, when I spoke to Bear about my discomfort at having intimacies while another was in the tipi, he laughed and asked if I thought everyone vacated the premises while couples created babies.

When I embarked on that journey with Shambling Bear, I had not realized how drastically my life would change. For one thing, I had not anticipated the lack of privacy. Bear and I erected our own tipi at a short remove from Stout Ox's small shack, yet the thin walls of a skin tent was little guard against others. Everyone was polite enough, calling out to request admittance, but more than once I am convinced some man or woman stood outside while Bear finished plowing my furrow.

As the months rolled onward, I became embroiled in following my own advice to Small Moccasins. He took my words seriously and prevailed upon me to accompany him and Winter Bird to the agency. His request firmly placed me on the horns of a dilemma. Given the air of danger, distrust, and unrest that swirled about me, I did not want it known that I was John Strobaw of Teacher's Mead and Turtle Crick Farm. In that persona, I could possibly play on the influence of my family name, the Red Win-tay's lingering shadow, Caleb Brown, and Captain Gideon

Haleworthy's kinship. Yet if things went sideways, my activities might expose my Teacher's Mead family to danger.

The people here knew me as Medicine Hair, but that might be traced back to Turtle Crick, so I devised a way to hide my speckled mane. On my first visit to the agency with Bird and Moccasins, I bound my hair in a bright red cloth in something approximating a turban and adopted yet another name. A name for the whites. Red Turban. An Indian is known by the tribe, clan, societies and kinsmen he claims, but I eschewed all of that, knowing full well it would stir curiosity among the agent and his staff. I adopted only the artifice of being Lakota by blood.

Bear, of course, was already known to the agency people. He was identified as a Brulé Teton, despite his Yanube mother. All of that, Major James Morrow had entered years ago into the records at Fort Yanube when he gave Matthew and his family the American name of Brandt. But Bear did not accompany Bird and Moccasins and me to see the agent. His task was to see what he could do about foraging.

My first sight of the settlement around the agency at Pine Ridge raised the hair on my neck and sent my stomach plunging into my nether regions. The place oozed tension ... danger. Even Sheriff Landreth's office – hardly a friendly environment – had never filled me with such foreboding. Bird, Moccasins, and I joined a line of other men waiting to see the agent. And there we stood for two hours shuffling from foot-to-foot or sitting on the edge of the planking. No one spoke, unnatural for a group of men this size. *Someone* should have been loquacious. Before we reached the door, a stocky Indian with walnut skin dressed in a uniform of some kind muscled his way through the throng of waiting men.

"Bottom Lip," Moccasins whispered in my ear. "Heads up the Indian police. Be careful of him."

"How does he come by his name?" I asked.

"Bottom lip sticks out so far he's always tripping over it. Bad medicine," Bird said.

A short time later, a pudgy man in a cotton-star shirt pushed his way inside.

"Hard Head," Bird offered. "He's the judge."

"They have an Indian judge here?"

"All the reservations got one. Mostly, anyway."

"Maybe we should go see him. If he's a judge, he ought to be educated."

Both of my companions chuckled. "Educated about alcohol, maybe. But that's all. Hard Head got appointed by the agent because he will do whatever the man tells him to do."

High noon arrived before we were ushered inside. The room was large and undecorated, containing a rude, homemade desk and three chairs. Apparently, petitioners were expected to stand as all seats were occupied, although two small benches stood against the exterior walls. The man named Calhoun sitting behind the desk was not the same Pine Ridge agent who'd traveled down to Fort Robinson when Bear and I were held captive there. Calhoun was flanked by the policeman and the judge. All three eyed my flamboyant turban, setting off an itching on my scalp.

"Winter Bird, Small Moccasins, who's this dandy you've brought me?" The agent's voice was deep and manly. This one would have no tolerance for win-tays, so I became a no-nonsense man.

"I am Red Turban from Rivers Bend."

"Ain't seen you before," Bottom Lip said in Lakota.

"Haven't been here long," I responded in English. "Been away at school, and when I returned, I stayed up on the Cheyenne River with my friends, Touch the Clouds and Buffalo Leg. But after my wife died, things got bad there, and I wanted to see how my kinsmen were faring."

When the Agent frowned, I read his thoughts clearly. *Who is this fellow who speaks English as well as I do?* I usually tried to hide my education, but now I wanted to make an impression. To be taken seriously.

"You been to school, then you got a civilized name. What is it?"

All I could come up with was Tom Smith, which he chose to ignore. What can I do for you, Red Turban?"

So I began a litany of petitions, all of which he'd heard before. Short rations. Poor seed for the farmers among us. Confinement to the reservation made earning a living difficult, if not impossible.

He dealt with me the way he did with every other Indian who showed up before him, I imagine. Claimed he was doing the best he could.

"Sir, the treaties signed by the government wherein we ceded our lands guarantee allotments to us. Crops have been poor these past few years, and the allotments don't come or are short. Our people are totally dependent upon you."

"I take my responsibilities seriously, young man. I plead your cause, but I can't conjure the allotments. If they don't come or if they're short, we just have to live with it."

"Yes, *we* do," I acknowledged. "But do you?" From his frown, I judged I'd crossed the line. Nonetheless, I continued. "At least, give us the freedom you and your people have to go pursue other opportunities."

"Don't talk to me about pursuing opportunities. When you people get off the agency, you take up the hatchet and go around robbing and killing. You've brought this upon yourselves. Now live with it. If that's all, you can leave."

"One more thing. The people at Rivers Bend want permission to hold a dance and invite other tents to join us."

Calhoun squinted. "Permission denied. It's too close to the Summer Solstice, and you'll try to make a Sun Dance out of it."

"That is not my intent, but now that you mention it, why not? It would mean a great deal to the people on the agency."

"Gets people all stirred up. Fills them with superstition."

"No, sir. It is a religious ritual. It has nothing to do with superstition. It's rooted in the People's spirituality. It seems to me a Sun Dance would go a long way toward lifting these people's spirits."

"Raising their blood you mean. You know the rules, no sun dances, no scalp dances, no war dances of any kind. And Congress has banned the practice of aboriginal religions."

Although I'd fully expected my request to be denied, I argued with the man. He tolerated it out of surprise, I think. We spoke of the advantages and disadvantages of depriving the People of the very thing that made them Lakota, the spirituality they had lived since birth. Although short, the exchange was useful. It was the first time I realized how thoroughly the whites wanted to eradicate Indian civilization. The tribes could become white or die, and it didn't matter to this man which choice they made.

As we left, having gained nothing except a little insight, Bottom Lip rose from his chair and followed us outside. A distance from the agency building, he halted us.

"Who are you?" he demanded. "I know people in Touch the Cloud's camp, and I ain't never heard of you. What's your other name?"

I answered in Lakota. "I have several. But as you can see for yourself, I'm one of you."

A big Indian, he squinted down at me from his greater height. "You didn't learn fancy American talk around here."

"No, I went away to school. That's likely why you don't know me."

"Where?"

I named the only Indian boarding school I knew, a place in Pennsylvania that took children from many different tribes and tried to change them into whites. "Carlisle."

Bottom Lip scowled. "Who's the man that run it?"

"The headmaster's name was Pratt."

I'd read enough about the place to know Henry Pratt founded the school in 1879, but I had no idea if he was still there. Yet, it was likely this policeman didn't know either.

"You watch your step around here, you hear? Don't need no firebrands with fancy ideas stirring up things."

"Haven't you heard? Carlisle made good white boys out of us."

We turned and walked to our horses, leaving the big man standing in the middle of the street, his face puckered like he was doing some hard thinking. On the ride back to Rivers Bend, Moccasins chortled that while we didn't get permission to dance, we'd at least made an impression.

"And that might bite either way," I noted.

CHAPTER 24

Bear and I went to work. I built a forge near Stout Ox's shack and located an old anvil, tongs, and a hammer in a nearby settlement. After I traded for those, Bird helped me fashion a bellows. The first thing I crafted was a plow blade from scrap iron littering the grounds near the agency. Bear set about instructing the reluctant young men of Rivers Bend in the finer points of agriculture, even though it was too late in the year to expect anything but a poor autumn crop.

Meanwhile I made a few shovels and a rude auger, which we used to dig two wells at opposite ends of the settlement. Water from the wells helped us make crude adobe-style bricks, even though the clay content of the soil was inferior. Utilizing these, we constructed two large shelters against the winter. During the worst of the snow, the settlement's residents could take refuge in them.

Rivers Bend had no shaman, so I sent the children of the settlement scurrying to find medicinal herbs to treat illnesses. I'd brought Otter's Pandora's box of curatives, but it needed refreshing.

The next project was to send Lazy Eye in the greatest secrecy to fetch some of the gold he claimed to know about. In between times, I started teaching the children what I could of reading and writing and figuring. A stick in the sand became our lettering boards. As Otter had learned when instructing Bear and me, I found practical problems framed in the students' own language to be the most effective tool. So inches became hand-spans and yards the length of a man's step.

After I fashioned some balanced pitching horseshoes, we set up iron pegs nineteen feet apart from one another and introduced the game of horseshoes to the camp. The younger people took to it instantly. So much so, that we set up several play areas around the little village. Happy the game provided a respite for the villagers, I was dismayed at the betting that took place around the games. I should not have been surprised. To an Indian, life, itself, was a gamble.

When Bear and I finally repaired to our own tipi at the end of long days, we agreed we'd never worked so hard, not even on the farm. The Lakota in general were loath to become farmers, and the people of this settlement were no different. A few of them would take to the life, but most would fall away as soon as we stopped prodding them. So Bear came up with the idea of teaching them to ranch. That, he reasoned, was more like man's work.

"Where would we get the cattle?" I asked.

"Mr. Roosevelt might sell us a few head."

"And they'd be slaughtered and eaten within the first hour."

"Maybe. But Stout Ox is a smart man. I think he'd see the value of building a herd. Winter Bird and Moccasins certainly would."

"If we bring cattle on this reservation, all the camps would come like horses to water and steal or trade for them," I said.

"Probably. But it's worth a try, isn't it?"

"What do we use to buy the cattle?"

Bear scratched his right ear. "We still have the gold and silver we brought with us. I'm willing to donate my share."

"So will I. All right. I'm eager to meet this white man you're so taken with."

A few days later, Lazy Eye returned from wherever he'd disappeared with a small rawhide bag half-filled with small yellow pebbles and dust. I knew nothing about gold except when minted into coins or small ingots and suspected this was the pyrite that some called fool's gold. Even so, it was better to take the material far from the reservation to test its mettle. So we added the bag to the small load of beaded moccasins and fetishes and other items we intended as gifts for Mr. Roosevelt.

Several in the village wanted to accompany us, but I argued a large party's intentions might be misconstrued. In the end, Bear and I went alone, trailing my black mare behind us bearing what we'd managed to scrape together for trading. The trip north was uneventful except for having to hide in ha-has whenever cavalry patrols appeared in the distance. We rode uneasily for several miles after these near-encounters, fearful outriders or scouts would find our tracks and investigate.

The shadows were lengthening when we reached the Elkhorn Ranch two days later. Bear had worried the owner might not be in residence, but he broke into a smile when a stocky man with a thick, reddish moustache and eyeglasses without frames walked out of what looked to be a blacksmith shop to greet us.

I instantly saw why Bear was drawn to the American. He was a human vortex, pulling everything and everyone to him. He spoke in a rush, as if each word – and there were many of them – might be his last. He greeted my mate by his Indian name and focused on me as I was introduced as Medicine Hair. The intensity of his attention seemed to put me under a human magnifying glass. He gave the impression I was all that mattered in his life for that brief instant.

We retired to the long porch – what he called a piazza – on one side of his rambling house to partake of coffee and tea. We had no chance to explain our intentions as we faced a fusillade of questions barked at us, as if by an interrogator. In minutes, he knew everything we knew about conditions on the reservations and the undercurrents of violence lapping the land.

"What a tragedy it will be if warfare breaks out. I know the yoke on the red man's neck is heavy, but taking up arms isn't the answer. I fear the tribes will be annihilated if they do so."

"Then what are we to do?" I asked.

"Negotiate. Educate your people. Education is the biggest gun in the arsenal." He paused and pursed his lips, making his moustache wiggle like a bushy worm. "I'm doing all I can with friends back east, but it's slow going. But to take up arms? Madness. The white man will never give up this territory."

I drew a breath and let it out slowly. "I understand that, sir. I see the inevitability of the thing, just not the rightness."

"Bully for you. That says it all. It is both inevitable and unjust. You're a bright young man who sees with clear eyes, so you'll understand the futility of standing against the tide of history."

"Standing against it isn't the issue, Mr. Roosevelt. It's how to get out of the way without being crushed."

# # # # #

We overnighted in a small shack near the barn and rose early to greet our host. After we ate with the rest of his crew, he took us outside to the piazza for a talk.

"What can I do for you men?" he asked as soon as he was settled in a rocker.

"We told you yesterday how bad thing were at Pine Ridge," Bear said. "We're trying to help out all we can. We'd like to buy some cattle and haze them back to the reservation so the people at Rivers Bend can start a herd and become at least partially self-sustaining. We have money. We can pay."

The bluff New Yorker fell silent and studied the flooring of his porch. Then he straightened in his chair. "Keep your money. At least until next year. It's too late to feed an animal and put any weight on him this year. Come back next spring and help with the calving. That'll earn you a few head, and you can buy some more."

His words made sense to me, but Bear stirred in his chair. "How about we buy some to take back for butchering right now."

Roosevelt repeated the words I'd spoken to Howling Wolf. "The calves don't carry enough weight yet. But I've got a few cows past their prime. They'd make decent beef. I'll sell you half a dozen. Probably throw in another two ... three, gratis."

"There's something else, sir." I pulled out the small buckskin pouch of yellow rock and dust. "For the last few years, foreign Indians have been coming through on their way east from California bringing little bits of this stuff. We collected all we could find from around the reservation."

After I handed over the sack, Roosevelt dipped his hand inside and rubbed some of the dust between his fingers before sending for his foreman and a pan and water. In a few minutes, the ranch hand swirled the contents of the bag around in a broad pan with sloping sides half full of water. He sloughed off the debris that floated to the top and filtered the rest through some cheesecloth. What was left was much less in volume but looked infinitely more promising.

After they put their heads together, Roosevelt nodded. "Gold. That's what you've got there. How long did it take to collect this?"

"Don't really know." I expounded upon my lie. "Found out about it accidentally, and then searched it out. I'd guess a couple of years."

"Not much profit for two years' work, but it's earned you the six head of cattle we discussed. And I'll throw in four more so your trip's worthwhile. We'll round them up this afternoon, so you boys can start off early tomorrow. You realize we'll have to be careful about this metal. Looks like placer stuff to me, and we don't want to start a rush."

I nodded. "Our feelings exactly, sir. Nobody'll learn of it from us."

"No use involving the reservation. We'll come up with some tale about miners from Alaska coming through. Delighted to do business with you men."

Before we left the next morning driving ten head of mature cows before us, Roosevelt gave us a proper bill of sale and a written invitation to return to do more business next spring. He wrote of his appreciation of the presents sent by the people of Rivers Bend and reciprocated with the most precious gift he could have imagined, a fat box packed with medicines and medical supplies.

Driving wayward cattle made it more difficult to be elusive on our return trip, and just inside what we figured was the boundary to the reservation, we were halted by a full platoon of troopers. The colors they carried stirred unease in my belly: Seventh Cavalry. The same outfit Crazy Horse had nearly wiped out at Little Big Horn. Or Greasy Grass, as Bear termed the battle he had participated in.

The officer, a silver-barred lieutenant, wasn't especially hostile, but neither was he friendly. He read Roosevelt's letter, examined the bill of sale, and demanded to see the medicine box noted in the missive. After an empty threat to arrest us for breaking out of the reservation, he gathered his men and rode away, leaving us to resume our journey.

Upon arriving at Rivers Bend, we held counsel with Stout Ox, Winter Bird, and Little Moccasins. We agreed to slaughter only one the cattle to feed the village and put the remainder to pasture near the horse herd under the watchful eye of boys and young men. The other animals would be taken down as needed, provided we could keep them from being stolen. After that, the four of us walked the modest field planted with potatoes and other vegetables we hoped would mature before winter set in.

Despite the Indian agent in Pine Ridge, we decided on a dance that night. We did not plan to invite other tents, so we didn't figure we needed anyone's permission. I, the grandson of Cut Hand, the last chieftain of the Yanube, was so alienated from my people that I'd never attended a powwow. Nor had I owned regalia, except for the outfit Otter had made for me in an attempt to bind me to my roots when I was but a half-grown youngster.

That night, I learned the power of such ceremonials. The villagers brought out drums and rattles and whistles and flutes and gave them full-throated voice. There were no more than fifty people in Rivers Bend, including elders and children, but when I came to my senses after the heady, infectious excitement of the dance, there were twice that number dancing around the flames of a bonfire and standing or sitting in a circle around the dancers. Without knowing the proper steps of a single dance, I pranced and cavorted around the flames dressed in my white man's clothing and sporting three hawk feathers some women had affixed to my black and gold hair.

Near to dawn, Bear fucked me in our tipi with all the vigor of a man attacking a troop of cavalry, eliciting cries of joy and ecstasy that must have been audible to all the village.

The next day, a platoon of cavalry showed up at the village demanding to know if we'd held a forbidden dance. Stout Ox, with no sign of guile in his watery eyes assured the captain in charge we knew nothing of such heathen doings. As he spoke the words, a big haunch of beef cooked on a spit in the dance fire of the evening before. Earlier in the morning, the women of the settlement had swept away thousands of footprints ringing the flames.

#####

The year rushed toward its inevitable end. We took a very modest reap from the field. Nonetheless, we stored a few tubers and green vegetables in the large cellar we'd built as a cool room as well as a shelter against the black, twisting winds called tornadoes that occasionally stalked the broad, undulating grasslands.

One thing I did not like about my new life was that we received news slowly. Word seeped in of something called the Haymarket Riot with bomb blasts and gunfire at a general strike in Chicago. Little Moccasins was convinced this and Seattle mobs rioting and destroying parts of the city were the beginning of a great uprising of whites against whites like the big civil war of two decades ago. I pointed out the Washington riot had been a rampage against Chinese workers and that there was no sign the army had pulled out to go fight a war in Chicago.

Then news came that put an end to Moccasin's hopes. In September, the great Apache warrior called Geronimo had surrendered to General Miles in a place called Skeleton Canyon down in Arizona.

#####

One evening after little winter had set in – cold and snowy but not yet sharpened by the bitter Canadian blizzards – I realized it was December 31. The white man's year of 1886 ended that very night. I lay snug against a sleeping Bear and relived other Christmas and New Year's celebrations. This was a festive time at Teacher's Mead. Had they missed us? Of course they had. Bear and I were family.

CHAPTER 25

The winter that began in '86 and saw its end in '87 blew in, driving towering, icy clouds before it. Like the last freezing season, this one proved to be hard and harsh. But the work we'd done the previous summer and autumn made the long, cold time easier on Rivers Bend than on many other settlements. More than once the populace – grown to better than sixty now – sought refuge in the two common houses to conserve firewood and to share resources. The remaining cattle, all butchered and stored in the cold room, helped us survive.

Snowmelt in the spring brought news that on the previous February 8, the American Congress had dealt the tribes a blow more dire and drastic than any previous policy. What was labeled the Dawes Severalty Act or the General Allotment Act, sought to do away with the communal system of the tribes and impose private land ownership such as practiced by the whites. Individual tribal members were declared eligible to receive land allotments of up to 160 acres along with full citizenship rights.

The goal was total, abject, and unforgiving assimilation ... nay, call it what it was, utter subjugation. For centuries, who and what the Indian was, had been focused around the structure of clan life. This law would render the tribes asunder and leave families rudderless in a foreign and hostile world. Ironic that I, a man who came from a family with a landholding of some 600 acres at Teacher's Mead and who, himself, owned 340 acres at Turtle Crick should see things so clearly. Why not? Had I – indeed, had *we* – not been deprived of the value and benefits of a tribal culture? Was I not simply a white man who was not white?

Still, if living apart had been good for the Strobaws, then why not for the rest of the red men? Because my family had had the strong, steady hand of our patriarch, Billy Strobaw, the careful wisdom of Otter, and the stubborn persistence of my mother, Mary Jacobsen, to guide us through the transition. Would others have such guidance? Besides, had it truly worked for me? Had I been a white American by birth, no army troops would have dared burn down my home. My story was what faced the rest of my people. And they *were* my people now, not some indistinct habitués of a hellhole of tragic discontent hovering off to the west of my farm.

Only through the goodwill of lifelong friends had I been able to hold onto my land at Turtle Crick. At least, I hoped I would be able to do so. Absent such friends, how many of my people would be able to cling to the land. And it did not strain the mind excessively to understand that thousands of individuals on their own would be even less successful at protecting the land than the tribes collectively. These nations had already lost millions of acres even while standing together.

Simple arithmetic showed that if every Lakota on Pine Ridge accepted his allotment, the excess lands given over in forfeit would have shrunk our horizons drastically. And there was little doubt the whites would use the new law to seize this "excess." I saw the doom of my people and my culture in this pernicious act of the American Congress.

Reality of another sort set in when representatives of Rivers Bend were summoned to Pine Ridge for an explanation of this act. The message was not sent to Stout Ox, but to Red Turban. The older man's quiet acceptance of this snub effectively passed the power of leadership to me, a man less than half his age. Then I remembered something Otter had told me countless times. A man was free to move from fire to fire any time he determined the leadership of a community was lacking. Now I understood why the village was growing. Word of the settlement's prosperity – at least when measured against others – drew people to us.

Unwilling to run around in a red turban, I allowed the women to dye my mop so that the spots of golden hair were no longer visible to the eye. That allowed me to knot the red cloth around my neck like a kerchief. The first time I did so, I experienced a strong kinship with Billy, who had worn articles of red in homage to his pseudonym of the Red Win-tay.

In this manner, I presented myself – along with Bear, Stout Ox, Bird, and Moccasins – to the council in Pine Ridge late in *istawicayazan wi*, the Moon When Wives Crack Bones for Marrow Fat. That was the month the white men called March. After representatives of the settlements gathered on a cold, soggy field around the formal council seated on thick buffalo robes shared with the Indian agent and an army general, a fat white man with long bristly sideburns gave a long-winded explanation of the General Allotment Act. Following this, the tribe's leaders stood one by one and spoke on the matter. Most of the talk was cautious. Finally, I could be silent no longer. I stepped to the edge of the buffalo robe and cleared my throat for attention, a brash act since I was no round-belly and unknown to most of the people there.

"Identify yourself," the Agent ordered.

Stout Ox had moved to my side. "This is Red Turban, headman of the people at Rivers Bend."

"Well, speak up," the man with long sideburns said.

"First, I would like to ask for a copy of this act."

"Would you be able to read it?" asked the nameless man, who was said to have come all the way from Washington to explain things to his "children."

"I assure you, sir, I will be able to read every word of it. But even without having that opportunity, I have some thoughts on it." I turned from him to the leaders of the tribe seated in council. Noticing what I took to be interpreters at their ears, I continued in English.

"We must ask ourselves if we want to become white men who are not white men because that is what the law intends. If we look at land in the same manner the whites look at land, we will lose our culture, our language, and our tribal membership."

"Enough of that!" Washington Man sputtered.

166

A dark Sioux with a commanding voice called from the council to let me speak.

I raised my voice. "Think on it. What does the white man covet most? Land. Our land. And if he gives each head of household land of his own, that will make us like him. Men who hold onto our few acres and deny access to others. How long will it be before the tribes, the culture no longer matter? And this, too, I know. Once the allotments have been made, all the excess acreage beyond that will be forfeit. Seized so whites can move in and take our homelands."

I shut my mouth and moved back into place. But others took up the cry. These men and their forefathers – my forefathers – had fought and many had died to hold onto what land we had left. My reasoning had struck their hearts. The outcry grew louder.

The first thing I knew, a rough hand gripped my arm and pulled me around to face the policeman, Bottom Lip. "Come with me, troublemaker."

Bear tore the man's hand from me, and Bird shoved him away. Stout Ox stepped between us and raised his voice, claiming the police lackeys were trying to take me away for speaking my mind. It took the intervention of Agent Calhoun to settle things and order me released. Shortly thereafter, Bear insisted we leave and return to the fragile safety of Rivers Bend.

It proved an illusion. The next morning, Bottom Lip and four of his police came and took me away to Judge Hard Head to face a charge of inciting a riot. Virtually the entire population of Rivers Bend followed along in protest.

I was not dumped into the jail house. Instead, I was taken directly to a small room with a table and one chair adjacent to the cells. Hard Head's expression changed from dour to alarm when a host of Indians flowed inside with Bottom Lip and me. Before he had time to recover, there was a stir at the door as Red Cloud and virtually the entire council crowded into the courtroom.

I had seen little of the Lakota chieftain since I'd been here, except when he spoke up for me from the council robe yesterday. He was an impressive man with a hawk's visage. He spoke little but well. He had led the Oglala and other tribes in what was called Red Cloud's War, which ended with the Treaty of Fort Laramie of 1868. That treaty forced the army to abandon its forts in the Powder River country and pledge to vacate Lakota lands. Since that time, he had been a steadfast peace chief.

At his appearance, Hard Head's speech went nearly unintelligible. It took only my denying any incendiary words at the council yesterday for the old judge to release me. As I left the courtroom with a host of friends at my back, Red Cloud barred my way.

After staring at my right earlobe for a long moment, he spoke in Lakota. "Medicine Hair, I knew your grandfather and his father. They were good men. I also knew your spiritual grandfathers, the Red Win-tay and River Otter. They were wise men. I was pleased with your words yesterday. You will be good for us, I think."

With that, he departed, leaving the way open for us. I walked with two strong thoughts. My true identity was known, at least among the natives ... and I had just met a man who was to me what Theodore Roosevelt was to Shambling Bear.

Speaking up at council had put me in Agent Calhoun's line of sight. The army took more interest in Rivers Bend, as did the People. Our lodges numbered better than thirty within a few weeks, which meant something like 100 men women and children had turned themselves over to my care. A burdensome responsibility I had not courted but would not shirk.

I became so busy planting new fields and organizing the village that by the time early May came, Bear and two other young men made the trip north to the Elkhorn Ranch. Armed with our own gold and another small pouch of yellow dust from Lazy Eye, they left to provide labor for Mr. Roosevelt until calving time was over. Then they would bring what cattle they could back with them.

I'd also prompted Bear to ask Mr. Roosevelt to replenish our supply of medicines. They'd seen liberal use over the winter. My fumbling efforts at keeping the people of the camp healthy spurred the growth of my reputation as a medicine man. When Winter Bird showed an affinity for this type of work, I began sending patients to him. My friendship and affection for the handsome Lakota prospered, although I never even thought of betraying Shambling Bear.

Although I did not believe it would ever happen, I eventually got my hands on a copy of the GAA, as the Americans were calling the Dawes Act. To me, reducing the General Allotment Act to three letters of the alphabet perfectly displayed their laziness with the language. Upon the reading of it, I was even more alarmed. The promised "full citizenship" came only after a man agreed to live separate and apart from his tribe. Male heads of households would receive 160 acres, while single males over eighteen-years-of-age would be given 80 acres. Single males under eighteen were eligible for forty acres. Women, the traditional caretakers of our land, received nothing unless they were married to a man. The allotments, which most likely would be selected by the government, remained in trust for twenty-five years.

This document would cause more devastation among the tribes than all the armies and all the battles ever fought. In fact, it might well provoke more such bloody battles. The Lakota leadership at Pine Ridge spoke out loudly against this unjust law. I do not know whether or not that was the reason, but we saw no effort to impose land allotments on us. That was little consolation because the government was free to enforce the Act whenever it saw fit.

My beloved and his two drovers returned from the Elkhorn a moon later, driving an unruly herd of calves and five or six mature cows. It took a day and a half to settle the animals down to the point they recognized this was their new home. Until that was done, I saw little of Bear. When we finally were able to take a proper medicine bath, he told me Mr. Roosevelt had asked about me and commented on my strange hair, which reminded me the golden spots were beginning to show again. I needed to ask the women to apply more coloring before the yellow became too revealing.

As we had no running stream to wash off the sweat, we stood naked beside the *okinare* while children gleefully threw buckets of cold well water over us. Fortunately, our erections had died before leaving the small shelter.

That night, I once again came to appreciate the richness of married life. I do not mean just the fantastic, exhilarating experience of orgasm, but also the loving comfort of strong arms around me, the company of like minds, and simply his presence. It was even more than that. This beautiful man was an extension of me, yet apart from me. While our minds and hearts reflected an amazing singularity, our bodies were distinct and capable of exciting physical stimuli. One concept was as sensual as the other.

I woke before morning light to find him entering me again, amazing after the athletic fucking of earlier in the night. For long moments, he did not move after he was sheathed in my fundament. And I was content with that. Feeling him throbbing inside me while motionless was a rare treat, one I savored.

"I don't know what I would do without you," he whispered in my ear in that deep voice that almost went bass when the serious side of him was ascendant.

"You won't have to. Unless you bring another mate home. Then ..."

"Never! In all the time we've been together, I've never touched another human ... man or boy, woman or girl. I've never wanted anyone else. Not like I want you. I won't say my cock doesn't get hard sometimes, but then I think of you and the temptation is gone."

"You are my only love, as well." I swallowed around a swell of pride clogging my throat. "It is a miracle that we found one another."

"Not a miracle. Destiny. The Great Spirit saw to that when he took my mother and brother and caused Otter to deliver me to Teacher's Mead."

He fell silent and began to move his hips. His long, slow strokes whetted my appetite, and I soon urged him to more urgent measures. He ignored me. Lying on his side behind me, his strong thighs rubbed against me each time he thrust. He forced my knees up so that he had better access and penetrated me deeper. His flat, hard belly playing against my fundament drove me to action. I arched my back and met his thrusts.

Instead of the excitement I expected, a pleasant sensation of timelessness overcame me. This could go on forever. Hold the world at bay. Cement our union … the union of the moment and of our lifetimes.

It wasn't timeless, of course. His breath started to come in gasps. His efforts more forceful. I knew an instant before he reached orgasm that it had been as profound for him as it had been for me. He groaned and sighed his love into my ear as he finished his ejaculation.

Then, remaining inside me, he reached around to touch me. I straightened my legs, giving him full access. Instead of grasping me as expected, he held me loosely in his fist and stroked the underside of my glans with his thumb. It took no more than that. I exploded and shoved my butt hard against him as my seed shot out of me. I whimpered heart-felt endearments while shuddering through a sweet climax.

In a way, that was the most pleasant summer and fall I'd experienced since the burning of our home. We'd had no excess hunger because of the cattle, even though I put a strict limit on the slaughter of the animals. We butchered only the old barren cows and the steers, carrying over the heifers. I wanted to find a bull and begin to mate them to produce more calves. In my mind's eye I saw Rivers Bend becoming self-sufficient so that when the agency withheld all or part of the stores promised under treaty to the People, we would survive.

If the cattle were prospering, our efforts to raise a crop were not. Rainfall came sparingly, and some sort of malaise overtook our fields. I knew from talk that others were experiencing the same problems, even the whites outside the reservation. Nonetheless, we coaxed enough greenery from the ground to put away a few vegetables for the winter.

A great cloak of suspicion lay over the land. The tribesmen were fearful of whites, especially of their military, and the Americans were terrified of Indians. People like Howling Wolf and even Firm Foot leading breakouts off the reservation to raid and pillage farms along the Missouri only intensified the mistrust. Wouldn't it have been better to devote all that energy to finding ways to improve the lot of the People? Few, it seemed, shared that conviction.

CHAPTER 26

For the most part, I was successful in keeping my people from raiding. But shortly before the winter set in, something happened to incite the inhabitants of Rivers Bend to near rebellion. I had sent Little Moccasins and two of his contemporaries north to seek out the trader who had sold me peat for a number of years. The fuel would serves us well this winter. We had no local source, but Canada had large fields. While it did not burn as hot as wood, it lasted longer and its usage helped conserve what few plants survived in this largely treeless territory.

The party left late in October with one man driving a wagon I'd traded for only a week before. I urged my friend to hurry on his mission as I feared an early and hard winter. For a period of years, each of the cold seasons had vied to be harsher than the one before. There was little reason to believe this one would be different.

A *senight* later, I began to fret over the party's absence. Another two suns passed before a man from another settlement rode in to say Moccasins was in trouble. Matthew and I, together with half a dozen young men from Rivers Bend, mounted and followed the stranger north. We rode hard, and within ten miles halted at the crest of a hill to look down upon a scene of horror. The wagon lay overturned, its load of peat spilt and its trace horse dead. A mounted squad of nine troopers and a lieutenant hovered around a body on the ground. One of Moccasin's party sat trussed up astride his pony, the reins held by one of the soldiers. When the troopers noticed us, the squad leveled weapons as if it were a single organism. The officer put his soldiers in a skirmish line facing us.

With a heavy heart barely beating in my chest, I raised my hand in the open-handed salute and told the others to remain where they were. All obeyed except for Bear, who rode down the hill with me to face the soldiers.

The detail's lieutenant, a man well advanced in years, should have had double bars adorning his tunic, indicating he was perhaps not a good leader of men. He waited, his sidearm at the ready as we approached. I noted the man lying in the dirt was not Moccasins. Nor was the captive.

I halted in front of the lieutenant. "I am Red Turban, headman of the Rivers Bend people."

"I know who you are, and I know this one, too." He nodded at Bear. "What do you want?"

"I want to know what happened. These are men from our settlement returning from purchasing peat. Where is the third man?"

The officer nodded over his shoulder. "Back there where we come across these renegades. When he pulled his rifle on us, we shot him. Then these two started running."

171

"Not an unreasonable response, given the circumstances," I noted in a dry tone. "But Little Moccasins wouldn't fire on you."

"Didn't give him the chance. These men are renegades. Most likely, they murdered the peat trader and stole his wagon."

"That is my wagon, and I have a paper noting the transaction. These men took trade goods to buy the peat. They are not renegades."

"That's your story."

Those three words said it all. Before responding, I looked into the eyes of all nine troopers. To a man, they were anxious, edgy, and evasive. Speaking around an ache in my core, I asked the officer to release his prisoner to me, promising to vouch for his good behavior.

"He has done nothing wrong," I added.

"Him and these others broke out of the reservation."

"And have paid dearly for it. Release him and save yourself some paperwork. You have enough for your report without him."

Releasing the captive, a young man barely out of his teens called Budding Oak, made no practical sense, but I had read the army man for what he was, a shirker who took the easy way out. He nodded to the trooper who held Oak's reins and motioned his squad forward. Bear and I sat without stirring as the troopers rode out of the gully, taking a route that went wide of the restless Indians on the hill.

As soon as the squad passed out of sight, Bear cut Oak free while the rest of my men rode down to meet us. We set them to up-righting the wagon and reloading the peat while Oak led Bear and me back down the trail to our fallen friend. Rage replaced lethargy when I saw the once-handsome young warrior shot to pieces by at least four bullets. His horse lay nearby.

#

I made two trips to Pine Ridge to see the Indian Agent and another to lay my protest over the deaths of my two men before the tribal council. This activity earned me nothing but the growing enmity of Calhoun and his minions. However, in the end, I was able to deliver an extra month's partial rations and some blankets to the families of Moccasins and his fallen comrade. Such was the value of the life of a red man.

We held our own council at Rivers Bend during which some of the younger braves demanded retribution rather than restitution. I steadfastly spoke for peace. As a result, a few lodges left for other fires.

Before the first blue norther fell upon us, an entire company of troopers rode into the village. Warned by lookouts of the approach of the column, I settled my remaining firebrands down and met the captain in command with a stolid but not hostile greeting. His message set my heart to soaring and yet burdened it with apprehension. Someone had ambushed the lieutenant who'd led the squad that had killed Moccasins and his companion. After threats and bluster, the army departed.

They had not asked after Budding Oak, indeed, had likely not known his name, so I was spared having to tell them his was one of the lodges that had deserted Rivers Bend for another fire.

The winter struck ... hard. On what I calculated to be after the turn of the year 1888, a blizzard heavy with snow struck with such ferocity we were unable to stagger the few hundred yards to tend the heifers we'd held over to build our herd. Indeed, the People struggled to reach one of the two communal houses in the village heated with the remaining stores of peat.

This past year, I'd had the walls around the two large community houses packed with solid earth so that they resembled the cones of volcanoes I'd seen in Otter's books. Decidedly unattractive, the structures nonetheless helped us survive the bitter cold. January 12 of that winter became known as the day of the Schoolhouse Blizzard. Many children in the outside world had perished coming home from school.

When we were finally able to fight our way outside, I found what I had feared. Most of the hundred or so calves in our budding herd had frozen to death. I ordered the carcasses butchered and the meat crammed into our cool room. We lost horses, as well, but the equines seemed hardier than the bovines and were generally sheltered closer to the people's tipis. Both Arrow Wind and Wind Rider survived.

The cruel winter of '87-'88 was only the start of a disastrous year. Stout Ox and his wife had faith in the small shed-like home that had sheltered them for years and both died of the cold. The Lakota would likely miss a whole generation. Many of the babies born during the cold time did not survive.

While our village did not starve because of our beef, other maladies took their toll. Oft times, when Bear and I made love, our troubled hearts drained some of the ecstasy from our coupling. Each felt the suffering of his people heavily. Sometimes in the midst of the act, Bear would pause, and I knew he was thinking of Moccasins or some other friend and neighbor we'd lost. Occasionally, we did not reach orgasm because of these burdens. Even at those times, I praised the fates for the blessing of Bear's company.

A late spring brought new hope, but even that was dashed. Our crops failed utterly at the end of the following growing season. I was given to understand the failure was so widespread that the whites were suffering as well. I knew what that portended. Our allotments would be stolen and sold to the outside world with no accounting to us.

As the year progressed, things developed as expected, and the mood on the reservations darkened. Our attempt at building a herd hovered on the brink of failure. Even though Bear and I had spent virtually all of our gold and silver and Lazy Eye produced little of the yellow dust, we took our meager funds on a trek to the Elkhorn. The trip had become risky because the army clearly knew the mood of the tribes and worked hard to keep everyone on the agency.

We finally arrived to find that six out of every ten animals in Roosevelt's herd had been lost to blizzards. Hundreds of thousands of cattle carcasses littered the Great Plains, victims of what he called "The Great Die-up." We returned home with only a dozen new calves.

In October of that year, Bear and Bird and I stood alongside other Sioux to witness the most extraordinary speech I'd ever heard from a white man. General George Crook, whom I had never labeled a friend of the Indians, honestly compared the white men to birds hatching out of their eggs every year, overcrowding the east and coming west to flood the country.

"They will not stop until everything is overrun," he said. "There is no way to prevent it. Not the President in Washington nor the Congress nor the Army could stand in their way. And when they arrive out here, they see the Indians have a big body of land they aren't using. And they want it."

Not nearly as prepared as for this winter as the previous one, we slaughtered the rest of our calves and hunkered down for the snows. There were once again near to 100 souls taking refuge in Rivers Bend. The Lakota might not countenance my peace talk, but they appreciated the fact Rivers Bend survived the cold months better than most villages. The winter did not disappoint our anticipation of another long and difficult white-out.

Once again facing a late spring, I was hard-pressed to find enough men to labor in the fields. I could not blame them. To the Sioux, dirt scratching was not man's work. Hunting and protecting their families were. Working cattle or a horse herd satisfied their manhood, but our calves were gone, and we had nothing with which to buy new animals. Bird and a cousin disappeared one day and returned two suns later driving half a dozen cattle into the village. I did not ask where they came from, merely inquired if he had put the village at risk. I accepted his assurance when he said no and made sure the unbranded cattle were quickly burned with the Rivers Bend mark.

We began to hear big talk that the President in Washington, a man named Benjamin Harrison, would permit white settlers to take over the Oklahoma Indian Territory. This president was the grandson of another, William Henry Harrison, who had fought the Indians at Tippecanoe and killed the Shawnee visionary, Tecumseh, at the Battle of the Thames.

General Crook's words were proving themselves in other ways, as well. White encroachments on the Lakota reservation became almost routine. When warriors met the interlopers and attempted to force them off our land, these "hostile acts" brought the army running, even though most of the time, the Sioux engaged in remarkably little violence.

174

#

Around midyear, news spread of a Paiute holy man teaching his tribe the Ghost Dance, a ritual bent on restoring the earth to the way it was before the whites came. His message of hope spread to other tribes, stirring a spiritual revival that raised fear among the whites.

"You must go to this Paiute," Bear said to me one day as we returned from Pine Ridge where we'd been summoned for a tongue lashing from the frightened agent.

"Why?" I asked.

"Because it is your Spirit Dream coming to life. Remember, a time of joyous dancing."

"Aye," I answered. "Followed by the death of a great man and a terrible slaughter."

He reined Wind to a halt. "Maybe you're that great man."

I laughed aloud. "Me, a great man? I don't think so."

"It's not how you see yourself with your own eyes," he said. "It's how others see you. Have you noticed people have stopped calling you Red Turban? You're being recognized as Medicine Hair everywhere."

"So long as the agent doesn't figure out who that is, I don't see the harm in it."

"Don't fill your eyes with sand. Bottom Lip knows what's going on."

When we arrived back at the village, a pleasant surprise greeted us. Crow Johnson grasped my forearm in his massive grip and laughed at our amazement. His wife had pestered him to visit relatives in Pine Ridge, so Pa gave him an even dozen head of cattle for him and his step-sons to bring us, a drive that slowed his progress considerably. Nonetheless, the animals were welcome.

He settled on a robe in front of our tipi and brought us up to date with news from the Mead. Alexander had managed to bring in a crop, albeit a relatively meager one, and Pa'd been able to save most of his cattle. Hanna had another daughter, and Rachel Ann had given four-year-old Ides a brother. She lived at the Mead more than she kept residence at the fort nowadays, but her union with Gideon seemed strong enough. Ma and Pa hadn't changed much, the Absaroka declared. They worried about their absent sons, but hid it well from everyone. Ma's scheme to get Dexter Appleton together with Libby Tiller progressed slowly. What else could you expect? There were fifty miles between those two.

Before he and his two sons started for Pine Ridge, Crow slipped a heavy money belt from around his waist and handed it to me.

"Cuthan thought you might be running short of funds." He gave a short laugh as he mounted. "Said you'd most likely spent what you had on a bunch of Indians."

CHAPTER 27

The year the white man called 1889 saw heightened tensions as the powers ruling this land feverishly prepared for statehood. Anticipating admission to the nation as an official state, new settlers arrived daily to cast covetous eyes upon reservation lands. Continual incursions at the borders incited acts of reprisal from tribesmen. Defending our own land brought the military increasingly into the fray. In the background, the Ghost Dance craze swept of the land.

I made a point of talking to anyone who had visited other reservations where the dances were taking place and slowly came to understand that Wovoka, the Paiute medicine man, claimed to have awakened from a trance on the first day of the year when the sun died. He said he'd gone up to Heaven and talked to God and all the people who had walked the Western Road.

There had been an eclipse that day, which probably accounted for the reference to the death of the sun. Wovoka had been raised from his teens by a white family named Wilson, who renamed him Jack, so he likely had been exposed to Christianity. Was the reference to God the Christian God or the Great Spirit?

Whatever the case, Wovoka began to preach the message he'd been told to bring the People: They had to be good and love one another, and not fight, steal, or lie. He claimed he'd been instructed to give a dance to his people and urge them to dance, dance, dance. This would bring back the dead and restore things to the way they were before.

What leapt to my mind upon hearing these words was the Book of Revelations from the Christian Bible. Of all the chapters in that holy tome, this was the one I found most puzzling and mysterious ... just as I found Wovoka's message enigmatic. With my own Spirit Dream teasing my consciousness, Wovoka's preaching engendered fear in my breast, not hope.

Still, as I learned more, the Paiute's message seemed one of promise, not danger. He spoke of peace and good character. There was no call to war. Dance, and the world would be like it was. Our dead would return to share the restored landscape. He spoke of peace and acceptance of the white man.

I recalled a conversation I'd had with Otter years ago following my vision quest. He'd told me about another Northern Paiute prophet named Wodziwob who, twenty years earlier, had called for a Ghost Dance to bring back our dead and clear the land of whites. Wadziwob's preaching came to nothing, so it was likely Wovoka's would amount to no more than a flea on a dog's rump, as well.

Although he called upon the Indians only to dance – something already deeply ingrained in them by their ancient culture – the rub might come from the Indian Agency's prohibition against such celebrations.

As the days passed one after the other, Bear and I were caught up in helping Rivers Bend recover from the disastrous crop failure of the year before. With our funds restored, we once again bought calves from the Elkhorn and brought them back to the village, which by now boasted around 120 inhabitants.

The army's presence was felt everywhere. No doubt, this was intended to keep things calm, yet the effect was to agitate our young men into a state of constant anger. When a white soldier stole a young woman from the village, I nearly faced open rebellion. Even after it was learned she went willingly and was loath to return home, hostility rode the air. It got even worse because the community shunned the girl, causing conflict with her family.

"They are like cattle," I complained to Bear. "One starts off in one direction, and all the rest follow."

"It only seems that way," he said. "These are the most independent-minded people I know when it comes to some things, but conventions must be met and respected or else the herd instinct is aroused. The girl violated them."

"And caused disharmony throughout the town."

We were settled in our blankets a mere hour after I'd broken up an argument between the errant girl's family and that of the young man who had courted her before she ran away with the white trooper. Bear pulled me atop him and stroked my face with his long, slender fingers.

"You are a strange win-tay. I think at times you are more man than I am."

"Nay. You're the warrior of this couple. And I am content with that."

I started to move down him, but he held me in place and wrapped his legs around mine. I began to move against the flesh of his belly and nether regions. His silky bush excited my cock. Soon, I was fucking his stomach with such abandon I could not control my reactions. I came, spurting semen between us. I writhed against him seeking to meld our flesh together, to morph into this strong, handsome man, this lover of mine, this Other Heart.

He smiled through the half-light of a dying fire and flipped us over to wash his throbbing cock in my sperm. Then he lifted my legs and entered me. He paused to gaze at me fondly before fucking me with all the vigor of a Lakota warrior in the prime of life.

Despite everything I could do; despite all the agricultural lore I'd gained over the years, we were in the midst of the third crop failure in a row. Next year, I'd be hard pressed to find anyone willing to labor beside me in the fields. Everything was wrong. The weather wouldn't cooperate.

There was no rain. Temperatures were erratic. The plant seed was poor, probably diseased.

On the other hand, the cattle we'd purchased in the spring were doing well. We'd brought a young, uncut bull back from the Elkhorn to begin raising our own calf crop next year.

In the midst of all this, the agent sent Bottom Lip to fetch me. To a meeting, he claimed. Bear feared it was an arrest and insisted on accompanying me to Pine Ridge. He was a sour companion for the trip, muttering dire predictions for the Indian policeman's future if this was a trick.

Calhoun insisted on meeting me alone. By that I mean, *I* was alone. He had an army colonel and a preacher with him. He offered me a seat at a table in the corner of the room where they were all seated.

"You're a mystery, Red Turban. You're a seemly young fellow. Educated. But don't anybody seem to know you." He paused and drew on a long cheroot. "All you fellows have more than one name. What's yours? Medicine Hair, maybe?"

I adopted what Otter had termed my "Indian face," and stared back at him like a white man. "I have been called that."

His eyes scanned my forelock. We skirmished a bit about where I came from, but it was obvious this was not foremost on his mind.

"What do you think of this Wovoka and his Ghost Dance superstition?"

"It seems to me he has provided you with an opportunity," I said.

The three men straightened in their chairs. "What do you mean by that?" the agent asked.

I nodded to the colonel seated to my right. "I'm sure it's clear to you tension is building among the people."

"If you mean war fever is rising, you're right," he answered in a gruff voice.

"It's not war fever. No one – other than a few hotheads – is looking to dig up the hatchet. But when you withhold what has been promised by treaty, discontent is bound to surface."

Agent Calhoun went red-faced. "Hell, man, things are hard all over. Crops failing left and right. People leaving and heading back east."

"Looking for a place to make a better living, I imagine," I said.

"Damned right! Sorry, Preacher. Looking for better horizons."

"But you deny my people the right to do the same. You hold us here. Yet, even as you say people are leaving, others flock to the territory. And when they cross onto our land and set up homesteads, you call in the army any time we try to protect what you claim is ours."

Calhoun stirred in his chair. "We're getting off the railroad track here. You said something about an opportunity."

"So far as I can tell, Wovoka isn't preaching an uprising. In fact, he seems to be saying the opposite. By being peaceful, we'll eventually be restored. All he tells us to do is dance. And that's in our nature. If I threw

179

my hat on the ground, some Indian would start dancing around it. You should allow it. Encourage it, even."

"No!" The army man pounded the table. "That'll just give voice to the hotheads. The fever will rise, and we'll have an uprising for sure. This Ghost Dance business will lead to disaster, mark my words." The colonel tugged on a sideburn. "Go on, Calhoun. Get about what you was gonna do."

The Indian agent fixed me with a beetle-browed stare. "You talk against the Ghost Dance. You tell 'em how foolish it is, how dangerous, and I'll come up with another month's rations for you."

I didn't hesitate. "Two months' full rations. No half measures."

"Done!" Calhoun said with a satisfied smile.

I went outside and joined Bear while the agent sent to the warehouse for my bribe. My mate watched carefully as one of Calhoun's men brought around a spindly mare loaded with a pack. I examined the contents, taking my time until I was satisfied the agent had cheated me only a little. That was all right, I planned on cheating him a lot.

"I'm throwing in the pony," Calhoun called from the porch when I mounted and prepared to leave.

As we rode toward Rivers Bend, I explained to my mate what had gone on inside the agency. "So when anyone asks, tell them Medicine Hair doesn't support the Ghost Dance."

"Hell, I oughta go back and make a deal with them."

I examined my conscience and found nothing lacking. In truth, no amount of dancing was going to bring back the world that had left us behind, and I seriously doubted any dead Indians would be restored to us, although it would be nice to see Otter and meet Cut Hand, my blood grandfather. The fact the Ghost Dance frightened the Indian Service and the army so much rendered it dangerous by that measure alone.

I decided to tweak Pine Ridge's nose by holding a dance. In that mysterious way – some call it the moccasin telegraph – word of the celebration got around, and before I knew it there were more than three hundred people gathered in our little town. That was far too many for Bottom Lip and his Indian Police to deal with, but there was always the possibility the army might show up. No one did, although I could have used Bottom Lip's help with a few hot bloods who got tighted up on homemade whiskey.

As expected, my summons to the agent's office arrived the next morning. Bear climbed aboard Wind with some difficulty. He'd been one of the hot heads over-indulging last evening. Nonetheless, he insisted on accompanying me.

The same three individuals awaited my arrival at the agency. I'd figured out the colonel's name was Price, but the preacher remained nameless. Agent Calhoun started things off.

"What was you thinking, holding a dance after what we talked about? You made a deal with us."

"And I kept the deal. Our dance wasn't a Ghost Dance. Holding a celebration was the best way I could figure to get a crowd together, so I could say I didn't approve of the Ghost Dance. I even used the extra provisions you gave me for the dancers. So you could say you helped organize the thing."

The three exchanged dubious glances before Col. Price addressed me. "You kept our deal? You said the Ghost Dance was a bad thing?"

"Of course. Several times I said this wasn't a Ghost Dance and never would be."

"That's it? That's all you said?"

"You should have said it's superstitious nonsense," the no-name preacher said.

"I'm sorry, sir. I don't know who you are."

"I'm the Reverend Richard Holcumb of the Native Evangelical Assembly."

A shiver whipped through me. Another reverend flashed through my mind. Jeremiah Berglund still haunted me, refusing to acknowledge his crimes whenever he appeared in my dreams.

"Sir." I refused to address him by title. "I believe I know my people. The message was delivered."

If the whites could bribe me, I could lie to them. And in truth, it wasn't an outright lie, merely shaded truth. The more sober people would take away that message; others would merely think I was putting one over on the whites since I had freely admitted their attempt to buy me.

No one was happy except me by the time I went outside to find Bear asleep on the porch. I woke him, and we were soon on the way home. He asked no questions, so I suspected he dozed in the saddle. I had no time for that. Thoughts clogged my head. The crops were on the verge of another failure. Our cattle enterprise was going reasonably well, but people from other villages had begun stealing steers. I'd posted guards, and they'd scared off a robber or two, but our herd continued to shrink.

But most of all, my mind was occupied with the Ghost Dance the Indian Service and the Army were so concerned over. I must find out more about this thing that was spreading a new religious fever among some of the tribes.

In the Moon of Falling Leaves – on November 2, in fact – Dakota Territory was admitted to the United States; not as one state, but as two. Our part of the territory was specified as belonging to South Dakota, whereas Mr. Roosevelt's Elkhorn Ranch was in North Dakota. Among the whites, this was accompanied by great celebrations involving a lot of gunfire and copious amounts of liquor. What changes would this bring to the tribesmen? Whatever came would not likely improve our prospects a whit.

CHAPTER 28

The Ghost Dance did not arrive on the Lakota Reservations until the summer of 1890, mostly because Sitting Bull was reluctant to permit it. Apparently, he had the same sort of questions as I about this dance. My gold-flecked black eyes could clearly see what Wovoka preached was nothing but superstition. This was an ill wind sweeping Indian country. No amount of dancing would put us on a par with the white man, bring back our dead, and as now claimed, restore the buffalo to the land.

Sitting Bull had bowed to pressure and sent two emissaries named Kicking Bear and Short Bull to the Paiute reservation to speak to the prophet and see the dance for themselves. When they returned, they brought a perverted form of Wovoka's dream. From all I had heard, the prophet preached peaceful existence alongside the white man.

Sitting Bull's two representatives claimed the Paiute's vision was one of throwing the white man off the land. Kicking Bear even introduced something called the Ghost Shirt, a garment that when properly blessed would turn aside the white man's bullets and protect the wearer from harm. He even added the myth of an Indian Messiah, who was to appear sometime next year.

It was as if the prairie burned from horizon to horizon with a religious fervor I'd not witnessed before. Even Shambling Bear, as educated as he was, was tempted by its lofty promises.

"Miracles happen, Eagle," he said to me one night in the privacy of our blankets. "The Bible tells of a bunch of them. Maybe it's a matter of believing hard enough. What harm can come from giving it a try?"

"Do you remember my Spirit Dream?"

"Of course. It tells of tragedy, but first it speaks of great joy. This is it. Why shouldn't we partake of it?"

"It is already having consequences, Bear. The whole village ... damnation ... the whole reservation's gone crazy. I can't keep people in the fields, and it looks like this year might be a decent harvest. When we assign people to look after the cattle, someone shouts 'dance,' and they're off to join the crowd. What's going to keep us alive next winter?"

"*Tatanka*," he said. "He's coming back, haven't you heard? Then we won't need to tend cattle."

"That's a joke. I've seen neither hide nor hair of a buffalo, and you haven't either. If we don't try to keep things going, we'll starve when the snows come."

The situation deteriorated as autumn arrived. The entire reservation came to a halt. Nothing was getting done except for dancing. The agent objected, but the police were helpless to put a stop to it. The army made threats, but didn't move, except for sporadic forays to intimidate the dancers. Between virtually single-handedly harvesting what crops I could and checking on our rapidly diminishing herd, I attended some of the dances with Bear.

Colonel Price appeared at one event with an entire company of mounted troopers and announced the dance had to end. When he was ignored, he had the drums seized and destroyed, thereby showing his ignorance. Some of the instruments had been family treasures, handed down from one generation to another. I held my breath as I waited for the sound of gunfire. Fortunately, it never came.

As fervor for the Ghost Dance increased, the Sioux started a dance that was to last for five straight days without interruption. Newspapers daily decried the threat of the Ghost Dance religion gripping the tribes. Wild tales of depredations spurred the demand that the authorities put an end to such dangerous practices. We lived in a world of fear and suspicion and hate. Then in November, the army forbade the dances on all of the reservations. The People continued to dance despite the prohibition, and tension mounted. Because the People danced rather than worked, we entered the winter poorly prepared for the coming snows.

One day near the middle of December, some familiar faces I'd not seen for a time turned up at Rivers Bend. Firm Foot and Crow Hop wore smiles as they gazed down on Bear and me from horseback. Howling wolf scowled, but I took that to be his usual mien. Perhaps it was a bit deeper because we had been at odds a few times in the past. Two others rode with them, although they were strangers to me.

As Bear and I made them welcome, Winter Bird rushed over to join us. Because the group would overfill our lodge, we led our guests to the smaller of the two communal structures. As we settled ourselves, women made spare offers of food and drink to everyone.

The small fire in the circle of stones centered beneath the building's smoke hole relieved the gloom only faintly. The flickering flames animated the stern visage of Howling Wolf. The fervor in the shaman's eyes was frightening ... at least to me. He spoke in Lakota.

"The signs are clear. The time has come. Our time has come. We have danced the dance and worn the shirt. The prophet has spoken. We are invincible. We must rise."

Silence greeted his words. Excitement lighting some of the younger men's expressions worried me. Bear pursed his lips a moment before asking what Sitting Bull said.

Howling Wolf shook his head, and the dead eyes of the wolf-skin headdress he wore seemed to sweep over us. "He says nothing. He doesn't say to rise, and he doesn't say to keep the peace. That has always been his way. Remain aloof and apart. Lend encouragement, but don't lend aid. Ever since coming back from Cody's Wild West Show, at any rate."

Firm Foot waved a hand. "He made money working with Buffalo Bill. And he used it to help his people. He's the greatest medicine man of our time."

"Until he made a fool of himself posturing for the white man and his audiences," Howling Wolf said. "He's just a frightened old man."

Firm Foot seemed angered by the Brulé's words, but it was Crow Hop who responded. "Sitting Bull has been a rock for us. For years he stayed clear of the white man and gave sanctuary to those who fled the blue coats. His vision foretold the great victory at Greasy Grass."

Buffalo Leg's son paused for breath. "And when he went to that white man's Wild West Show, he tricked them. He cursed the onlookers in our tongue, and they didn't know the difference."

I had heard that rumor, as well, although I tended to discount it. There were plenty of Indian fighters around who would have understood enough to raise a cry if that had happened.

Crow Hop turned to me. "What say you, Medicine Hair?"

Howling Wolf flicked dirt toward the fire. "What do you expect him to say? He's more white than red. He's a farmer, not a warrior." He looked me straight in the eye, a gesture of rudeness. "I see they burned down your farm without any provocation from me."

Matthew growled low in his throat. "This is a farmer who killed an army sergeant bent on murdering us. A farmer who avenged the hanging of his grandfather. If only we had more farmers like this man."

Crow Hop spoke. "He has white blood in him, so he can think like a white man as well as a tribesman. This is good. And besides, he has medicine."

"Enough *about* him," Wolf said. "I want to hear from him."

As all eyes turned to me, I glanced around the group. From the talk, I gathered Firm Foot had been chosen as leader of what was growing into a *tiospaye*, a band. Crow Hop sat at his right. Howling Wolf served as their shaman. These three and the two seasoned warriors with them named Dog Face and Spotted Pony made up its council.

Years back when Firm Foot had named me Medicine Hair, I'd considered the name of no consequence. What was the harm if he thought me possessed of something I didn't have? Now I clearly saw the echo of that decision. I was caught in a bramble bush. Nonetheless, I held true to my habit of speaking my mind.

"Winter is here. A hard time even when the army's not hounding us. But it is not just the army." I looked at the Brulé medicine man sitting across from me. "Howling Wolf and others like him have raided and burned and killed so much that the whites are frightened. So they support the army.

"I have seen some of their newspapers. The press, they call it. The press is howling for our blood. The people who write stories for those papers sit in the sutler's store around a warm stove and dream up the day's news. They report on Wolf's raids and call them rape and murder.

Then they make up other atrocities so they can sell their papers to frightened people all across Turtle Island."

Howling Wolf's sour expression had not changed. I continued. "There are soldiers from the Seventh Cavalry in the area, and they're thirsting for revenge over Crazy Horse's victory at Greasy Grass. So here is what I believe. If we do not cease dancing and return to our homes to prepare for the winter, there will be a great slaughter before the snows blow away. When spring comes, there will be no one left to greet the Moon of Red Grass Appearing."

"Is that your medicine speaking or your quaking heart?" Howling Wolf's voice held a sneer. His hands twitched nervously. The harshness of his words revealed he considered me a threat to his position.

Matthew came to his feet. "Hold your tongue, man, or we'll have an accounting."

"I forgot you were the man in your tipi."

I felt my ears flame. "I'm man enough to face you, Wolf. I'll hide behind no one."

Firm Foot rose. "Enough. This is not the time to squabble among ourselves. This is why the white man rules us. We must stand together."

"That is the only reason this man is not dead." Matthew turned his back on Wolf and sat down again.

Crow Hop had watched the exchange with interest. Now he spoke up. "I remember when War Eagle came to Fort Robinson in search of his brother, Shambling Bear. This was before Firm Foot gave Eagle his name of Medicine Hair. He spoke of his *hemblecha*, and I heard the telling of it with my own ears. It was made of three parts. Great joy and dancing. The death of a great man. And a mountain of corpses. The People's corpses. Our corpses."

Crow Hop drew a breath that seemed filled with sadness and foreboding. "We have seen the first of these prophesies come to pass. The Paiute shaman Wovoka's preaching gave us the Ghost Dance. That brought hope, and hope brought joy and dancing. Now the war clouds are gathering to wipe out the dancing. I fear the other two events are close upon us."

I picked up on Crow Hop's comments. "It is all this joy and dancing that has frightened the Americans. They see us as a defeated people living in poverty and captivity. To their minds, we should cower in submission. But when subjected nations dance and laugh, it sends fear running through the blood of the conquerors."

I rubbed my eyes as I drew a breath. "What the white men do not understand is that the Prophet preaches non-violence. The land was to be reclaimed from the white man without war. But when Sitting Bull sent Kicking Bear and Short Bull to learn about the dance and the Paiute's vision, Kicking Bear added the idea of an Indian Messiah who will appear in the spring of next year. Then he claimed the ghost shirts would turn away the white man's bullets. It was then that the dance turned from one thing into another. It gave the white man a real reason to fear us. Thus, it should give us fear, as well."

Howling Wolf spoke, his lips spraying spittle. "You dare speak like that of Kicking Bear. He's a great man. A bigger medicine man than you will ever be."

"Even great men make mistakes, Wolf. And when they do, the consequences are greater. And small men must listen with their own ears and minds and try to discern these mistakes. I have ears, and it is my duty to use my mind to consider what they hear. Were it in my power, I would stop the dancing and have everyone return to his home."

"Then leave," Wolf said. A serpent's hiss hid in his voice. "Crawl away and go hide yourself at Teacher's Mead while your brothers fight for you."

"Nay. My heart may lie elsewhere, but my right arm is here to lend aid. My advice is on the ground between us, but I am pledged. Where Shambling Bear goes, there I will be."

Winter Bird cleared his throat. "I have witnessed Medicine Hair's power. I've benefitted from it more than once. As I lay wounded, he made me invisible to the army officer who came and looked on me. The blue coat left without killing me or arresting me. Then Medicine Hair healed me. And another time he came and opened the door to the army's jailhouse so that I walked free. So I give his words great weight. My counsel is to listen to this man."

An argument raged for the better part of an hour as each man present spoke his mind. Some rallied around Howling Wolf who spoke words to raise a young man's blood. Others sided with Winter Bird, Bear, and me. I watched Firm Foot carefully. It was his choice to make, but if he did not listen to others and made the wrong decision, the group gathering around him would disintegrate.

He sought to appear firm and forceful, but I saw indecision in his black eyes. There was silver among the black hair of his head, and I judged him a man of not yet forty snows as he stood and looked down on us.

"We will go to Standing Rock. I want to speak with Sitting Bull myself. I want to know his thinking. But I will not throw salt in your eyes. I see what Medicine Hair sees. A war is coming. I do not know if events will end as he dreamt them, but if our people stand to fight the army, I will be there to stand with them. We leave tomorrow morning."

I rose and moved to his side. "I will come with you."

"As will I," Bear said.

CHAPTER 29

The weather was cold. Yet heavy winter had not yet settled in as we started the trek to the Standing Rock Agency where Sitting Bull and his Hunkpapa lived. Too big a group might catch the attention of the army, so we limited it to six: Firm Foot, Crow Hop, Howling Wolf, Winter Bird, Bear, and me.

We made our way safely to Sitting Bull's village on the Grand River about forty miles north of Fort Yates in North Dakota. We did not approach the old man's wooden cabin so late in the day, but found shelter in a bachelor's tipi some distance away.

Winter Bird and Crow Hop, excited over the prospect of meeting the Lakota's principal medicine man, talked far into the night. I looked forward to the meeting as well, but would have sooner rested for the occasion. Bear, Firm Foot, and Howling Wolf had all seen the man before, so they settled into their blankets quickly. I lay for a time listening to Bird and Crow Hop murmur before sleep claimed me.

Something woke me before darkness broke. Excited shouts pulled us tumbling from the tipi to find the entire village rushing around in confusion.

"Sitting Bull's house!" someone shouted. "The police are taking him away."

We followed the general rush toward a house partially illuminated by torches. Arriving at the scene along with what I judged to be at least a hundred others, we saw a group of Indian police surrounding the house. A dignified old man who had clearly been roused from sleep argued with a tall man in a blue uniform bearing lieutenant's bars. Although we were not close enough to hear the conversation, the police lieutenant seemed to be urging the chieftain to mount the horse Buffalo Bill had given him. Sitting Bull resisted the instructions.

Everything happened so quickly, it was uncertain what set off the events. The Lieutenant, Henry Bullhead by name, ordered his men to force the chief aboard the pony. When they moved to comply, a gunshot rang out, striking Bullhead. The Lieutenant fired his pistol directly into Sitting Bull's chest. Another officer, who I later learned was Red Tomahawk, shot the chief in the head. Then a battle raged. Several of the policemen went down, but some of the villagers fell, as well. I did not raise my rifle, but Bear and the others did.

After the shock of battle passed, the tribesmen hurried to gather their families and flee the village. We paused long enough to see that while Sitting Bull was not yet dead, he was dying and beyond the help of such medicine as I was able to provide. We recovered our horses and melted into the weakening darkness along with the others. The people were apparently heading for the Badlands before the army arrived. As we followed along behind, my mind focused on one thing. We had seen the joy of dancing and witnessed the probable death of a great man. I knew what was to follow.

While we lay hidden in one of the canyons of a badlands much larger than the breaks along Trickling Water, I agitated to return to Rivers Bend. We knew not if the entire Sioux confederation had arisen after the murder of the most respected man among the tribes. The people of my *tiospaye* needed me.

We made several efforts to return to the village that day, which I calculated to be December 15, a mere ten days before the Americans swarming our land would turn holy and celebrate the birth of the Prince of Peace. Would they at least stop killing Indians for that one day? Our efforts came to naught. We turned back each time when army troops were spotted in the distance. For four days we attempted to get past the patrols without success. Even under the cover of darkness we made little progress.

One night, we were discussing breaking up and making the trip alone or in pairs when a Miniconjou named Talking Man joined us as we gathered around a small fire, trying to ignore the cold and our empty bellies.

"They say all the People are fleeing into the badlands. There won't be anybody left at your camp," the young brave told us.

"And where are they going?" Firm Foot asked.

"To join Spotted Elk at Cheyenne River. They say he's taking his people south to Pine Ridge to seek the protection of Red Cloud."

"That will take us home," Bird said. "We can join them, and they'll take us right home."

"Only problem is, Big Foot's sick," the Miniconjou said, referring to Spotted Elk by his other name. "So the going might be slow."

"What's wrong with him?"

The brave lifted his broad shoulders in a shrug. "Sick."

"Sounds like a safer way than going on our own," Firm Foot said.

"It'll be quicker if we split up and go alone," I argued.

Bear spoke the obvious. "Hasn't been so far. We wasted a *senight* trying to make a run for it."

My Other Self's words made me aware Christmas had come and gone. The year 1990 was rushing toward its end.

An air of despair hung over us. One of the Hunkpapa we'd met this afternoon had told us Sitting Bull had clung to life until high sun the day he was shot. His son had died along with him.

Bird looked at me. "Your medicine is strong. Everything happened just as you said."

"To my sorrow. By killing Sitting Bull, it's as if the Americans have cut out our tongue. He spoke for us."

Winter Bird wouldn't let it go. "And what comes next in your Spirit Dream? A big battle where we all get slaughtered."

"Enough!" Crow Hop said. "Not everything from a *hemblecha* comes to pass."

"So far it has. And we'd be fools not to consider it," Bird said.

Crow Hop flushed. "What is there to consider? If it happens, then that is what the Great Spirit intended. Do you think you can walk away from your fate?"

Bird's back stiffened. "No, but if I walk a wiser road because of that knowledge, perhaps things will turn out different."

"You can all do as you like," I said. "But I want to get back to my village. If Big Foot is leading his band near there, then I will join him."

"So be it," Bear said.

We settled in our blankets, but sleep would not come. Sadness and anxiety and fear pressed down upon us so heavily the acrid fumes of the dying campfire wafted sideways to clog our nostrils instead of rising into the cold night air.

#####

Avoiding heavy cavalry patrols delayed our progress, and we did not catch up with Big Foot and his band of some 300 Miniconjou and Hunkpapa Indians until they were a short distance from Porcupine Butte. The procession straggled for miles, but from what I could see, it was mostly women and children. If Big Foot could count much over a hundred warriors, it would surprise me. We heard enough to know the chief was truly ailing, but we did not get close enough to determine the nature of it. Perhaps the coughing sickness that sometimes comes in the winter.

There was little food, and the slow-moving throng seemed to subsist on rumors. Sitting Bull wasn't dead. He'd risen and was the Native Messiah. No, he was stone cold and already buried at Fort Yates where the Standing Rock Agency was located. There was an order of arrest out for Big Foot, as well as all the other principal chieftains of the tribes.

That night, a friend of Firm Foot's invited us to share his lodge. There was no food, but he was full of gossip. Big Foot intended to join Red Cloud, and the two of them would call all the nations to rise. No, Big Foot was too sick, and Red Cloud preached peace. The Seventh Cavalry was nearby and plotting revenge for Custer's killing at Greasy Grass. When we settled down, I heard drums in the distance. People without food, without strength, without hope still danced to regain that strength and hope. I shook my head. Foolishness.

The migration began again the next morning, only to come to a halt when a strong troop of cavalry intercepted us soon thereafter. My heart dropped into my stomach when I saw a battle flag and realized this was part of the Seventh. Those rumors, at least, were true.

A major came down the hill to confer with Big Foot. Shortly thereafter, we turned west for about five miles before setting up camp along a stream called Wounded Knee Creek. The soldiers took up the high ground around us and passed down a smattering of rations so that most of us had a modest meal.

"I do not like this," Bear said to our group as we shivered around a campfire.

"Nor do I," I said.

Crow Hop nodded up the hill. "Those are Custer's men."

"They are of his outfit,' Firm Foot said. "Although most of them are too young to have known him."

"Tradition is sometimes stronger than truth," Wolf said. As usual, he growled the words in his throat.

"We need to leave tonight." Bear tossed a handful of grass on the fire.

"Tomorrow, when the column starts moving again, we'll slip away," Firm Foot said. "We aren't familiar with the territory, which makes it dangerous. Besides, the soldiers surround this entire valley. But there aren't enough of them to keep an eye on everyone when we start moving."

The consensus was to rest tonight and make our move on the morrow, so I acquiesced and wrapped myself in blankets to rest. Even then, I heard drums. Someone danced under the very eyes of the army.

#####

The next morning, we realized what a mistake we'd made. During the night more of the Seventh Cavalry had arrived to strengthen those already there. We were ringed by a field of blue. Even so, we might be able to slip away one by one when the column started moving.

But it did not move. Some officers rode down into the camp to speak with Big Foot. Shortly thereafter, more soldiers came down the hill and word went around that the army was disarming everyone.

The six of us immediately headed for the horse herd to recover our mounts. When shouts rose behind us, I turned and saw an older warrior wrestling with two troopers trying to take his gun away. A shot was fired. I wasn't sure if it was the old man's rifle that discharged accidentally or if the report came from elsewhere.

It made no matter. At the sound of that one shot, the soldiers on the hill opened up, and the final stage of my Spirit Dream became truth. The hills surrounding us reverberated with not only rifle fire, but also a sound that frightened me to my very core. Heavier and faster and more concentrated. A cannon. Something Gideon had called a rapid firing Hotchkiss cannon.

In the distance, I saw the ground ripped apart. Tipis collapsed and burned. Everything in the field of fire of those lethal guns fell: men, women, children. Indians and white soldiers alike. Panic reigned. Many of the warriors had already surrendered their weapons, but others took out hidden rifles and fought back.

Our guns had not yet been taken away from us, but rather than shoot futilely up a hill, I urged the others to the horses. There was no escape without them. Before we got to the panicked animals, one of the big guns opened up on them. Many were blown to pieces, others fell from shrapnel. Yet others limped in circles with horrible wounds.

Amongst the thinning horde, I saw Arrow galloping toward me. A shell crashed into the ground beside him and bloodied his beautiful coat. The animal screamed and limped forward another half dozen steps before his legs collapsed, dropping him on his nose. He lay still.

Crow Hop, running alongside me grunted and fell. Bear called the rest of us into a gully where we found a number of frightened women and children. With some difficulty, we got them up and moving south down the long ditch where stunted brush gave some cover. We managed to go about a mile before we heard the thud of horses. Bear urged the women and children to lie down and make no sound.

The troop, it sounded larger than a squad of nine men, passed us by. Shortly thereafter gunshots and screams came from farther down the ditch.

Bear appeared at my side. "Get ready. They've found others in the gully ahead of us. They'll work their way back toward us."

"These are women and children. Surely, they'll not ..."

"Do you think those are men screaming?" he struggled to contain a shout. "They're killing everyone."

The sound of more horses came from behind us, slowing as they reached our position. When they halted, I knew what was coming next. They were forming a skirmish line. Bear cocked his rifle.

"I love you, Eagle," he said as he drew the stock to his cheek and waited.

"Oh, God, Bear. This can't be the end. It can't!"

I saw him tense and whirled to see three troopers urge their mounts over the side of the gully. Bear pulled his trigger, and one pitched headlong from the saddle. The other two managed to discharge their carbines before I shot one of them in the head. The other one clutched his shoulder and fled down the gully, running roughshod over women and children. After recovering my senses, I discovered Bird standing unharmed at my side.

When I turned to Bear, my world collapsed. He swayed in the floor of the ditch, one hand clutching his chest while a sea of red spread across his shirt. His rifle fell from his hand as I reached him. It took both Bird and me to get him into some scruffy bushes hard against the embankment closest to the soldiers.

More troopers appeared at the top and began firing down into the midst of the fleeing women and children. They were more intent on killing humans they could see than looking for ones they couldn't. I kept my hand over Bear's mouth to muffle his agonized groans, but the sound that really terrified me was a terrible rattle in his chest.

As the battle faded into the distance, Bird helped me get my mate to his feet before going to see if he could be of assistance to any of the others.

We had not gone a hundred yards before he appeared above us on the embankment to lead Wind Rider down into the gully. Bird had found the animal wandering and unhurt.

It took both of us to get Bear aboard the gray. Then Bird took off in search of other mounts. I warned him not to take any army horses. After collecting weapons from the two dead cavalrymen, I walked down the gully in the general direction of Pine Ridge, leading Wind by the reins. Bear slumped over the saddle horn, his forehead resting on the pony's long neck.

Half an hour later, Bird rode up behind me, riding one pony and leading Howling Wolf's palomino. I barely heard him say the Brulé was dead as I vaulted into the saddle and picked up the pace a bit. Bird followed along behind in case Bear couldn't keep his seat.

Except for the bodies of murdered women and children, and the occasional old man, we had the gully to ourselves. The survivors, probably in a state of shock, had crawled out into the open. When the ditch became too deep, we struggled up onto the prairie. Bear managed to remain in the saddle, but the ordeal was hard on him.

Seeing no soldiers on the horizon, my confidence grew, and we made better time. I had no idea where we were headed, but we followed along with others who seemed to have some destination in mind.

CHAPTER 30

Bear grew so weak he could no longer sit a saddle, so I climbed aboard Wind behind him and held him in place. Slipping my hand beneath the blanket we'd taken from a dead woman, I pressed a wadded piece of cloth hard against his torso. The rattle in his chest abated somewhat but was still worrisome.

Bird's pony trotted at my side as he led the palomino I'd abandoned. "There's a place called the Drexel Mission on White Clay Creek about fifteen miles north of Pine Ridge. Let's shelter there tonight. He shivered. The temperature was dropping fast.

Incapable of speech, I nodded. Bird moved ahead of me and headed slightly west. My lover wrapped in my arms, I followed. The journey seemed endless, but it was still light when we arrived. Bear had no control over his limbs, indeed he seemed lifeless except for his eyes. We carried him into the Catholic mission and found others had arrived before us. Banners proclaiming the joy of Christmas hung around the old church as what must have been fifty Indians, many of them gravely wounded, crowded inside.

We found an unoccupied spot in a corner of the apse and spread blankets for Bear. While we made him as comfortable as possible, Winter Bird whispered that Rivers Bend wasn't far. He was determined on trying to reach there and summon help. He promised to be back before nightfall. As distracted as I was by my concern over my mate, I was loath to let him go. To lose another companion would be unbearable. Nonetheless, he was his own man and departed soon after.

Bear was beyond speech except for a few grunts, but I anticipated his wants as best I could. I managed to bring a little water from the creek, but he was unable to drink despite his raging thirst. Infection had already set in. He froze one moment, and then fought his blankets in a fever the next. The ragged hole in the right side of his torso was as ugly as anything I had ever seen. It marred the beauty of his red-brown flesh … nay, destroyed it.

A peculiar lethargy overtook me, and it was all I could do to hold my lover close and murmur encouraging words. Except for moans of the injured and whispers of comfort from loved ones, a strained silence settled over the little building.

Darkness had fallen before Bird reappeared. After asking about Bear, he told me everything was gone. Rivers Bend had been attacked, and the town destroyed. No one was there. The cold room had been looted, but he'd found a few pieces of smoked and jerked meat. We took enough for ourselves before he distributed the remainder to others. Bear was peaceful, so I did not try to force food on him.

As if the white army was not trouble enough, the weather deteriorated. Temperatures dropped so low, I am certain they fell below zero on the thermometer ... had I had one. I wrapped myself around Bear from behind, and Bird spooned himself against his front to lend him what body heat we could. As the night deepened, the room fell silent. All I heard was the weak, inconsistent rale of Bear's pierced lung. Sometime before dawn, he startled me with a word.

"John?"

I hadn't been called that in a very long time. I clutched him closer and whispered in his ear. "I'm here, Matthew."

"You ... know where ...?"

I nodded. "Yes. I know."

Wrapped in misery, I don't know when the sucking sound in his chest ceased. But when I realized it was gone, my blood froze. I pushed my lips against the back of his head to stifle a cry of pain. I willed my heart to stop, but it betrayed me and thudded on. My tears washed his beautiful black hair, now tattered and matted from battle and a hard journey. Winter Bird stirred and laid a hand over mine briefly. I barely caught his words of sympathy. I was alone in the midst of dozens of others dealing with personal tragedies.

# # # # #

I had been around enough dead people in my time to know that bodies are sometimes messy. But Bear had had so little to eat and drink that he merely looked to be asleep the next morning. With limbs that weighed like iron and a heart cast of lead, I rolled him in a blanket and made ready to leave despite the sudden blizzard forewarned by last night's plunging temperatures. As Bird and I started for the horses, a few warriors under a Brulé chief called Two Strike arrived at the mission. They had attacked the Ninth Cavalry's supply train earlier that morning and now warned that soldiers were coming.

Bird and I, together with every other able-bodied man rallied to Two Strike's side. Before long, a group of us fought our way through driven snow toward where the soldiers had been spotted. When we came to a valley, we saw the blue coats on the floor below us. I don't know if the officer leading this element of the Seventh was sheltering from the weather, but for whatever reason, we had the high ground this time. Two Strike sent warriors on either side of the draw, and we opened fire on the troopers.

We battled the day through. We fought the weather and we fought the Americans. I don't know how much we hurt them, but we kept them pinned down until more soldiers appeared on the high ground with us. These were black troops, the Buffalo Soldiers I'd heard of but never seen before. They unlimbered a Hotchkiss gun, and under the pressure of superior firepower, we retreated.

Together with Winter Bird, I made my way back to the mission where we loaded the blanked shrouded body of Shambling Bear ... of Matthew Brandt ... onto Wind Rider. All was lost. The tribes were broken. We were at the mercy of the white man more than ever now. Our leaders gone, our warriors dead, our families rent apart, we were now what he'd always wanted us to be, a defeated, subjugated people.

With an empty heart and a hollow body, I fought my way through a three-day blizzard, Winter Bird dogging my footsteps. Not south to the abandoned Rivers Bend or to Red Cloud at Pine Ridge, but eastward. To Turtle Crick to keep a final promise to Matthew. Then I could die for all I cared.

EPILOGUE

The blizzard had ended and the skies were a clear, cold blue as we passed north of the Tiller place. I angled toward Turtle Crick. The coming task of breaking through the frozen earth required more than Bird's war hatchet. Maybe there was something left at the farm to serve. If not, I'd have to go to Andre.

The snow on the north side of the hill that had sheltered my cabin was too deep to mount, so we skirted the hillock. Although they were covered by a blanket of white, I could tell the fields had been tilled this past season. When we rode into the farmyard, I pulled up.

My jaw fell open as I scanned the scene. My outhouse had been restored alongside a rebuilt forge. And in the stead of the burnt-out cabin, a proper stone house stood in its exact spot. I recognized rock from the quarry near Teacher's Mead. How many hundred-mile round trips had Pa and Alex and the others made to create this fine structure?

Neither Bird nor I had uttered a sound when a noise drew our attention behind us. A tall young man clutching a rifle emerged from a more modest stone cabin on high ground near my irrigation well. A young woman followed as he strode toward us. I recognized neither of them until the woman let out a shout and ran forward.

"Mr. John!"

Libby! And the youth was the Dexter Appleton I'd last seen plus four years. For the first since the slaughter, a smile touched my lips. Gold on her left ring finger glinted in the sunlight as she reached up to me. So Ma's plans had born fruit.

Then she turned to my companion. Breath caught in her throat. Her gaze slid to the bundle across the Wind's back, and a sob escaped her.

I summoned the strength to speak. "Dexter, I'll need a spade."

"Yes, sir. And a pick, too, I expect." He paused before moving to the barn. "The horses probably need feed and water."

I nodded and slid shakily from the saddle. "It's been awhile since they ate."

Libby, her eyes brimming with tears, clutched my arm. "You, too, I'm guessing. Come inside."

Bird took the palomino's reins. "I'll help with the horses. Be back soon."

I trailed Libby into the cabin and shrugged out of my coat and the blankets covering my shoulders before sagging into a chair at the table. Libby rushed around throwing a meal together. She had grown into a fine-looking woman, her beauty only marginally diminished by the hard life she led as a farmer's wife. Her hair had darkened into the rich chestnut tones I vaguely recalled on her mother.

"Pa'll be so glad to see you." She studied the pan she held in her hands. "But he'll be so ... sad to hear about ..."

I spoke around a sizeable lump in my throat. "Yes, he was fond of Matthew."

"I have pigeons, Mr. John. I'll send a message that you're safe. And about Mr. Matthew."

"Thank you. That would ease my mind. They're all right then? You know, at the Mead."

"Yes. They managed to escape the troubles. And they all came, every member of the family – including that Army captain – to rebuild the place."

As soon as the other two men came through the door, Bird and I ate ravenously. Dexter and Libby joined us at the table. The boy – man – made an effort to talk but soon gave up.

When we finished eating, I rose and realized this was the first time I'd been warm ... actually warm ... in days. That made it harder to go outside again. Nonetheless, Bird and I pulled on coats.

Dexter stepped to my side. He was taller than I was now. "I'll go with you, John. I can help."

I shook my head. "Stay with your wife. But thank you."

"Come back when you're finished," he said. "I'll build a fire in the house. It's been waiting for you."

With a solemn, silent Bird leading Wind, I skirted the hill and turned the palomino's nose toward the glade a mile distant. To the place where I'd had my *hemblecha*.

To the spot where Standing Rock and Dew Drop and Otter awaited their kinsman.

THE END

ABOUT THE AUTHOR

Born and raised in a small Oklahoma town, Mark Wildyr has had a lifelong interest in history, as well as mythology. After earning an undergraduate degree in history, Mr. Wildyr served in the United States Army and then pursued a career as a businessman. He presently resides in New Mexico, the setting of many of his stories, which explore developing sexual awareness and intercultural relationships.

Wildyr's Website is www.markwildyr.com, and he encourages contact from his readers.

earing any underwear. "Excuse me," I said, having a hard time lool

linded by that bulge in his crotch, "but don't I know you?" "Maybe

ind of t   bout

with Ray   God,

t loser?   in?" h

aid. "Lik   s stror

ce body   e on C

illy, he l   s I eve

u up to t   any id

istaking   he san

n, I coul   ery lo

ood raci   ne sw

ing with   e in s

we go   behir

ill see u   in pu

ed?" he   vent t

privacy.   grabb

-hard. I

ck, traci   t, so f

ed it, ha

with m   bing

bbing, I   n coc

he sound of unzipping filled the small space. I don't know who's h

, but before I knew it, I had his rod in my hand, and mine was in hi

nt to do?" he asked, his tone challenging. I knew exactly, and sank